CALLING EARTH II

MOVING THROUGH TIME AND SPACE

Shirley Battie

ISBN: 978-1-9995949-2-3

First published in 2019

OTHER BOOKS
BY SHIRLEY BATTIE

Calling Earth   volume one

Channelling

Being Human

Spirit Speaks

Beyond the Stairs

www.littleowlonline.co.uk

DEDICATION

To all those who work towards a bright future for our beloved planet and whose selfless endeavour is bringing this about. I also dedicate my books to my children, my grandchildren and great grandchildren who will inherit a loving world in which everything is as it should be.

ACKNOWLEDGMENT

I thank all those who have read the first volume of *Calling Earth* and for their comments and reviews. This has given me encouragement to continue. I thank Nene and Verna Green for their proof reading, without which I would have many mistakes. I thank my friends and family who have supported me, even though they may think I am crackers.

PREVIOUSLY in CALLING EARTH 1

SUPERPOWERS FIGHT FOR DOMINION OVER EARTH

In a quiet Dorset garden, twenty-five-year-old Kate hears a disembodied voice. The voice is of time and space traveller Sechem from The Pleiades, part of a cosmic team with impish Jamére and powerful Master M from Space Command. They are engaged to prepare Kate to discover her true origins and abilities. Kate and her hybrid father Jacob are thrown into intrigue and danger, involving mind travel into space, government restricted areas and a shadow government. The Space Command Council tells them of an alien force infiltrating Earth's secret government operating outside the control of elected leaders.

She learns that dark self-serving races from other star systems wish to take over Earth while other extra-terrestrial races support the continuation of human existence on Earth. The outcome will either be survival for humanity with a spiritual upgrade, or absolute control by an evil alien force. The future on Earth depends on the spiritual awakening of the human race.

The secret government uses mind controlled boss Helga Mortensen to keep Kate under surveillance. A powerful alien creature, Gork working within the secret government is intent on destroying Kate and brings in hit men Silas and Marco to frighten and warn Kate off.

Space Command Council asks handsome Colonel Adam Fenshawe, who is himself a time traveller inserted undercover into the Shadow Government, to protect Kate who falls in love with him. Kate and her father have to escape with the help of Adam and his space friends and are later relocated to another part of England.

Government psychic spies detect Kate's activities. The Galactic Council, Space Command and Lords of the Universe finally acknowledge that humans on Earth may be worth saving. In spite of destroying a mind control satellite, Kate and her friends know that their work isn't finished and that they'll continue to work together for a positive future for planet Earth. However Master M and the time travelling Space team are concerned that Gork is not finished with his objective to destroy Kate.

CONTENTS

CALLING EARTH II

MOVING THROUGH TIME AND SPACE

CHAPTER ONE

JOURNEYS INTO THE FUTURE

It was a cold and quiet night. On the little street in Berkshire where Kate and her father Jacob lived, people were unaware that a time traveller was visiting their world as they slept.

"It is time." The voice had been prodding the sleeping fair haired girl awake night after night and would not leave her alone. "It's time to take things a step further. It is not enough just to talk. It's time to teach."

Kate, half asleep stirred, and mumbled into her pillow. "Time for what?"

"It's time to take things a step further. It is time to come out of the Space closet." The voice came again, stronger now. It would not be denied. Kate sat bolt upright at this last statement pulling the warm duvet up to her chin. She recognised the melodious voice of Sechem, the time traveller. Moments ticked by in silence. Kate decided it was her imagination after all and lay back down. She snuggled into the warm covers and tried to go back to sleep. But the voice came again, this time almost as a whisper close to her ear.

"It's time to take things a step further. This is urgent. Are you listening to me?"

"Oh, it *is* you. What is it *this* time?" Kate asked, still drowsy and not a little annoyed. She didn't want the cheeky, cosmic explorer disturbing her sleep. She wouldn't have minded if it had been Adam, her handsome love, but he was no longer with her. As a serving colonel he had to be away somewhere else, as usual. She sighed and pulled the duvet over her head and tried to ignore her strange and colourful friend. She burrowed even deeper into the bedclothes to blot out the voice and soon she slept once more.

***

Almost immediately she fell into a dream and found she was dressed in a long, white flowing gown standing at the foot of golden stairs. As she climbed the wide steps she lifted her skirts to avoid tripping up. Kate looked down and saw that the staircase wasn't supported by anything at all. These were just steps and there was nothing more. There would be nothing to hold onto if she fell. It was quite steep, but she felt upright, stately and at ease. She continued upwards until she reached tall double doors of burnished bronze. Using both hands she pushed them open. The scene changed as soon as she walked through. A lot of trees, bushes and abundant flower beds surrounded a large, well-kept lawn. It reminded her of a great country estate with manicured hedges and tended flower beds. On hearing laughter close by she turned her head and saw it was coming from a cluster of happy, giggling children. They noticed her hesitating by the doors and came rushing towards her. They began to pull at her clothes urging her to go with them. She felt very tall amongst these children. They tugged and tugged, pulling her along, till she had no choice but to follow.

They came to what appeared to be the edge of a cliff. Together they looked over and saw the world far below. Even though it was far away they could clearly see much activity and what was going on down on Earth. A lot of smoke and dust rose from the surface. Kate had difficulty in seeing through a grey contaminated haze covering the land and the cities. The sudden sound of gunfire startled her and made her jump. It was war. There was war with fighting and violence going on below. They all watched in horror as women on the ground held on to their screaming, frightened children, and were running as fast as they could, trying to escape.

The unborn watchers drew back from the edge in alarm when they heard the whoosh of rockets and felt the shudder of earth below as grenades and bombs exploded. Although they were far removed from it in their safe position above, they could see and feel it was a hell, as if they were down there. This was a nightmare they wanted no part of. It was clear to Kate that the children didn't want to go down to Earth.

They looked at Kate, pleading with her. "Can you change this before we have to go? We don't want to go when it's like that. We're not looking forward to going into *that*." The clamour of their voices got louder.

Kate put her hands to her ears. "Shush my darlings. I can understand your viewpoint," Kate said, "but I don't know what I can do."

One of the children piped up: "We have free choice. We don't have to go into that. We could wait until it improves, couldn't we?"

Another glowing child with long blond curls piped up, "Well, if we all stay here there'll be no more children, and there won't be a generation to follow us. We'll have to go sooner or later."

Several of them joined in, clamouring to get their point of view over. "Well, we're not going until it's better. We're not getting mixed up in that awful stuff."

Kate looked at the stricken faces of the children. "It's not all war you know. There are many lovely places down on Earth. It's not all bad. There are some beautiful calm and happy places on the planet. And good people too," she added.

A tall lanky boy from the far edge of the group shouted: "You show me then, because I haven't seen any."

At that Kate put her hands over her eyes and mentally asked her spirit friends to find a spot that was happy and calm. As soon as she asked, the scene below rolled away to one side. They now saw the tops of hills, such as you'd get in Wales, with rounded hill tops. It was peaceful there. Sheep were grazing, heads down. It was so peaceful, so peaceful.

A tiny child dressed in yellow with sharp eyes and a thin, anxious voice asked, "Where are the people, and where are the houses?" She frowned. "There don't appear to be any. While it's peaceful there are no people. What's the good of that?"

A burly kid with a red energy field roughly pushed her to one side. "Don't you know it's the people who've created the disorder and the war?" He scowled at her. "Where there are no people it's naturally peaceful. It's the people who've created the disorder, it's not the planet, and it's not the gods. It's the people themselves."

Kate felt a tug on her arm. A teeny boy in green rubbed his ears whined. "How can I go down if there are no people. I can't be born where there are no parents." He started to cry. Kate gathered him to her.

"It's a problem, isn't it?" Kate told them all: "Why don't you ask for people to begin going to the peaceful places? Ask for peaceful people to go to the hills. Speak your mind only to those people." The boy looked doubtful.

"I don't believe you," he said with a whimper.

Kate hugged him tight and planted a kiss on his head. "Your thoughts will reach them my darling and you'll find that people will travel to the peaceful areas to escape war. Then you'll have a family to go to."

"I'll give it a go," he said in a small quiet voice, and wiped his nose with the back of his hand. Somehow Kate knew it was a habit he'd kept from a previous life. "I'll give it a go," he repeated.

One after the other the children piped up, afraid to be left out. "I want to go to the peaceful places too. I don't want to go to the towns and cities, or where there's fighting. I only want to go to the peaceful places too."

"You can't all go there." Kate told them.

The fat child who said he wasn't going, stamped his foot. "Well, I'm going to wait. I'm not going now. I'm going to wait, so there."

Kate looked around her. She knew these were not only young children but represented young and inexperienced souls. There must be some mature souls, some evolved souls here, she thought. They too might re-incarnate. She looked around her in the hope of seeing the wise ones. Then she noticed, far over to one side, quite a large gathering of mature souls, bright and evolved souls. They shone in such a bright light that it lit up the whole area where they stood. They were all talking together, discussing and debating and seemed to be talking of mighty matters. Should she interfere? Kate decided she could and pulling her long white gown close around her she left the children and went over to them across the fresh grass.

She stood on the fringe of their group gathering courage, and timidly tapped a pink robed soul on the shoulder. At her touch he turned around to face her.

"Excuse me, how about you? Are you going to re-incarnate, and are you only going to choose the happy and peaceful areas?"

The tallest one there, wearing a blue robe and with eyes full of compassion heard her question. He too turned and looked at her. He said in such a sad voice that Kate almost cried:

"No, we've allotted to go into the war-torn areas. We've agreed to go into the darkest places on your planet and see what we can do to change the situation."

Even in this dream state Kate thought of Adam, who'd bravely gone into the den of those who wished to take over the world. She sighed and blinked back a tear as she listened to the words of the beautiful soul.

"We've chosen to be the pioneers, to go down and see how we can transform matters," he said.

A golden one patted Kate on the arm. "Those young ones may then have more space in which to reincarnate. They'll have more non-violent areas to be born into than there are at present."

The other souls nodded in agreement. "We have a difficult job to do," they said, "but we've decided that there's no alternative to this. Somebody must go, and so we're going. We know it's not going to be easy, and we know that very few of us will survive a full life span. We may have to come back before we are ready. But it doesn't matter, for we know that when we return we'll have done as much as we could."

"Are you going to be born as new babies, or are you going to go in as Avatars, wise men, or become Walk-ins and take another body?" Kate asked.

The golden one raised his eyebrows, surprised at her question. He looked around at the others before replying. "Avatars are few on the ground. We have but few who can make a claim to be such a one. There's to be a mix of us, and a spread over time. Most of us will be born as babes and will be the specially gifted children, known as Indigo children and super psychics. Others of us will become Walk-ins. We must arrange things so that we can go when and where there's a need. We won't all go together or at the same time."

Kate became aware of flickering flames, of lights. She turned to look and saw it was reflecting on where the children were still looking down on Earth. They were looking at fires alight on the planet, fire in the troubled places.

The tall beautiful soul in blue said, "This too has a beneficial effect, for it's a cleansing fire. Where there's fire there can be rebuilding. Maybe there's hope after all, even in these places." The others nodded in agreement.

Kate turned and waved goodbye to the children. After watching them for a while she again gave her attention to the evolved souls. She put her arms around their shoulders, gave each a hug and wished them well. It was time for her to go back through the bronze double doors. She walked slowly until she reached the staircase, reluctant to leave. She too had to return down to the Earth below, down to the troubled sphere.

Sechem had not finished with Kate yet and was making sure her dreams were emphasising what she needed to see. She dreamed of spring, which came as it always did at the same time each year. Or did it? Something had changed, and Kate couldn't work out what it was. She looked around hoping to see the usual signs, like buds opening and birds singing, establishing their territory. Instead what she saw was a whole city laid out, a vast metropolis. But it was silent, nothing was happening there. At first she thought she was looking at the past. Only this was not the past that she was seeing. It was so quiet, no smoke anywhere, nothing, nothing, it was dead. No sound of traffic, no lights, no general hum that one gets with a city. Nothing! Why, why, was there no sign of life?

"This is a possible future that you are seeing." A voice in her thoughts told her. "This is a possible future that you are seeing," it repeated, as if she hadn't got it the first time.

"Where have the people gone?"

"Some are still around, but not where you're looking. They've vacated themselves elsewhere. Some were too late, for they didn't believe." Kate tried to take it in. There was heaviness in the air and dread swept over her. Then she woke up.

With those dreams still filling her head, Kate got out of bed and thrust her feet into slippers. She headed along the landing to the bathroom. As she looked into the mirror above the basin she fell back in shock and alarm. Staring back at her was a sweet little old lady with snow white hair. Recovering her senses, Kate put her hand to her cheek. The little old lady did the same. She stuck out her tongue and the reflection did the same. What was happening? A ripple ran over the mirror. It all changed back. It and life were normal once more.

Whenever anything happened that Kate didn't understand she meditated and asked her spirit friends to explain, and she usually got an answer of sorts. She said a prayer for protection and asked to only get information that was for the highest good. She used her preferred method of self-hypnosis, counting herself down stairs and entering a new world. The stairs method made sure she bypassed the conscious rational mind and anything that was given came from a deep and pure place. Once she was in deep she wasted no time in asking for time traveller Sechem to join her. She reckoned it was better than having her sleep disturbed by him again. At least this way she could stand face to face with him and observe his reaction to her questions.

Once in she found they were both standing in a meadow. Sechem was paying close attention to a group of cows grazing nearby. Kate cleared her throat loudly to get his attention.

He half turned to her. "It occurs to me that the land needs cows as much as cows need land," he said. "When animals graze, they nibble on grasses which exposes their growth to sunlight and stimulates further growth. Their trampling breaks any crusted earth, aerating it."

Kate coughed again, more loudly. Sechem ignored her but the cows looked up.

"Trampling presses the seeds in, giving them a chance to germinate, so you have a greater diversity of plants. Grazing cows press down dying and decaying grasses too, so that they can be acted upon by microorganisms in the soil. It keeps the decaying process going. Their waste fertilizes the soil."

"That is all very interesting, Sechem," Kate said impatiently. "but I have a question for you and it's not about cows."

"I hate factory farming, don't you?" he said. He turned away from looking at the cows and said, "Now let's sit down and you can tell me all about it."

They both sat on the grass and Sechem lay on his back and looked at the blue sky. Kate thought no one would ever believe that they were in another reality, another world.

"Why did you bring me to this field?" she asked.

"You did ask for a more peaceful scene with no warfare, didn't you? In your dream, remember?"

Kate looked at him in astonishment. "You know about my dreams?"

"Of course. Who do you think gives them to you? We try to give you messages in your dream state. Don't you know that?"

"I suppose I do. Is it only you that gives messages through my dreams?"

"No, not just me. Remember all is connected and we certainly are, aren't we?" He laughed gently. "What you think and feel, you bring into form. Where your thought is there you are, for you are your consciousness, and what you meditate upon becomes your world. However, remember that thoughts alone can never become things until they are clothed in feeling."

Kate sighed. She had to agree with that.

To her surprise he suddenly flipped the scene and Kate was immediately back with the children waiting to be born, but they were now sitting at desks waiting for the answers she was to give them.

"How do you do that, Sechem? And what about my question?" Kate looked at the children who appeared to be frozen in time.

"Think about this. What scene do you focus on when I give you one?"

"Well the one I am in."

"That's your answer. Work with the scene you are fully conscious of. It doesn't matter which one it is, as long as it's the one that helps you the most. It's not that difficult. Use your mind. The mind is all, the mind is everything." He looked at her to see if she fully understood before continuing. Kate nodded, pleased to see she was back in her normal state.

"It's your own subconscious mind that provides what you ask for and what you focus on," Sechem said. "Now, about your question."

Kate took a deep breath. "Sechem, what when asking to see what the future held for me I'd moved forward into my own future? What if we could travel back and forth in time? What sort of a world would that create? I mean, if *everybody* could do that."

Sechem turned on his side, raised himself on his elbow and winked at her. The colours that always surrounded his body danced up and down and made her feel giddy. Kate was sure he did that on purpose.

"Stop that Sechem. Stop fooling around."

He grinned mischievously. "You create within the life you are conscious of," he said. "That doesn't mean that there are no other lives you've also created; of which you are unaware."

"So which life should I focus on?"

"The one you are conscious of. When you deliberately time travel you consciously move into that time. However, remember to state that you wish to maintain your own form and age. If you don't, you might find you have aged, or died, or reincarnated to the time you chose. You mustn't simply say, 'I wish to go twenty years ahead, else you will be twenty years older, or might have passed on.' Say instead, 'I wish to *view* twenty years ahead with today's body and mind.'"

Kate scratched her head. She had to take this in. "But I didn't decide to see myself as an old woman in the mirror," she said.

"We showed that to you to give you this lesson. It worked, didn't it?" Kate nodded.

"The soul is free. Do you hear that Kate? Haven't you realised it yet? There are no limitations. It's only your belief system that says it isn't possible."

"How do I experience this freedom for myself?"

"Well I could tell you, and you would jump feet first without thinking it through. That wouldn't be good for you."

"What do you mean?"

"You're experiencing freedom right now, aren't you?"

"I suppose I am, but it doesn't last."

"It's your Oversoul that decides what you can and cannot experience. It alone has the wisdom to know what you can take. Think of it as a parent who looks after your wellbeing."

"The Oversoul?"

"The Oversoul itself doesn't enter into physical embodiment. It remains within the higher realms so that it can oversee and guide your collective experience. The realm in which the Oversoul resides is outside the time-space domain. There are various definitions of the Oversoul. For the time being, think of it as personal to your current life. The main core of your original soul sends out many threads, different soul aspects of the group soul. Each aspect starts its journey with a specific interest. It seeks to learn and experience in that chosen field. Over its lifetimes it chooses to stay in environments where it can learn bit by bit and develop a skill more and more fully until it is mastered. That way it learns through incarnation with that goal in mind. It may choose parents where genetic influence will help or even present a challenge. An appropriate astrological sign may enhance its chosen characteristic. It's a combination of things. Each aspect considers its need to experience different things, and different places. You're currently a human with the specific intention of teaching the connection between other off world intelligences, and spiritual development of the races on Earth.

"You once said there are no limitations and now you're backtracking," Kate said.

"I also said your belief system can stop you." Sechem wagged his finger at her.

"What if I said I do believe?"

"Just saying it isn't enough."

"Do you mean I have the option of going backwards or forwards in time?"

"Yes, but if you wish to return and maintain your current form and mind, you *must* state this condition before you time journey. Be very careful." He placed a long bony finger on her forehead and tapped it. Kate gave a shudder.

"Can I do this travel for the benefit of others, and not make it personal to me?

"Yes." Sechem smiled a sweet smile. "I know what's ahead of you. You've already time travelled. You simply have no memory of it. Other Time Travellers have come back to restart or re-direct the human race. I'm one of them. The difference is that I remember what I've been and who I was."

"You're lucky then, Sechem." Kate frowned.

"Not so lucky, for there were times I would prefer to forget who I'd been." Kate looked at his thoughtful face and wondered who he might have been. Then he brightened.

"You're too serious, Kate. Remember that the key to knowing about any changes your life may encounter is to reach your subconscious state through meditation. Perhaps you're one of the many who sense that the inhabitants of the planet Earth are destined to experience a miraculous change in the not-too-distant future."

CHAPTER TWO

GALACTIC COUNCIL

The Galactic Command Council called mischievous Jamére and Sechem to attend a special meeting on the state of planet Earth. They were the two most colourful space travellers in its team. Coloured lights flickered around the walls of the circular chamber and soft music played in the background. It was a small gathering, seated at an oval table so each representative could see all the others. Not all were quite human in appearance, but those present had the same objective, that of ensuring a positive time line of development for the human race.

The magnificent robed golden chairman of the council spoke first. A glimmer of a smile crossed his bird like face as he looked at Jamére and Sechem and tried to look serious.

"We've been watching you both and it seems to us that things in your area have been too quiet for far too long. You've rested on your laurels after your past success with Kate and her father Jacob. It's time to get things moving again. We need their services. We will not tolerate what's happening on Earth much longer. There is far too much aggression and cruelty, which is spreading like a virus across the globe. We need to push the spiritual movement of the human population before they slip back again. Their future depends on it, more than they can ever realise. Have you given Kate a preview of what can happen if humans do not continue their movement to a more positive timeline?"

"I've tried," said Sechem looking glum, "but she woke up too soon."

Master M, the birdman spoke up. "It's time you explained Timelines to her."

"She's at the right stage to activate the implant now. It's been dormant since she was born," said the Great Lord from Sirius sitting opposite him. His cobalt blue eyes flashed with passion. "We've gone to a lot of trouble and effort to get her in place and now we need to see the results."

"I'm not sure she's ready yet." Sechem said with a frown on his face.

The Lord rose from his seat, showing his great height. "Once you've explained it all to her she will accept the responsibility. She's one of us, after all."

A sudden rustle of movement and fidgeting drew all eyes in the direction of Master M, the Galactic Command's chief representative. He banged his fist down hard on the table before him.

"Why won't they listen on Earth?"

"Aren't you supposed to be beyond getting agitated?" Sechem leant across the table and grinned. "Get a grip on yourself," he added and couldn't help but smile at the idea and image it brought up.

Master M wasn't amused. "I agree with the chairman, it's right that we put Kate to work again. After all, she's had plenty of time to get over her transfer of residence and the work she did for us before. She'd make others listen." Master M pushed his chair back and stood up and stretched to his full height. He was an impressive figure in blue robes reaching down to his feet. He looked around at the collection of spiritual lords, gathered together as requested. His magnificence and stature made it easy to see who had asked the Galactic Command Council for the meeting. "She's getting restless and is beginning to have her mind journeys again, but they are without *any* direction from us. This will not do." He sat down again.

A ripple of colour ran through the gathering. They knew the Great One from Sirius, Master M never called for a meeting unless it was important. Bright and bubbly Sechem from the Pleiades felt he had to speak up and defend Kate, his charge. "You of all souls should know that as a Sirius human hybrid she'll always be seeking to discover more. She can't help herself. You yourself opened her up, didn't you? But I do agree the time has now come for her to come out of the space closet.

Master M grunted and nodded, acknowledging the part he'd played. "It's time we put her to work once more."

"Don't forget Jacob, her father." Sechem reminded him. "After his meeting with his Sirius mate Joslene, he only agreed to go back to Earth to be with Kate and to support her in her work. That was his commitment and sacrifice. So work she must."

Jamére stood up. All heads turned in his direction. He wasn't one to be ignored. His colourful attire and good looks made sure he would be noticed. Jamére was known for his tricks and ability to change and become anything or anyone that suited his purpose. He liked to have fun, but everyone present could see he was deadly serious now about his role in waking up the world.

"You're also forgetting the man she fell in love with, Colonel Adam

Fenshawe. He's still in your service, isn't he? You, all of you, have to consider their combined happiness, not just the work you have in mind for them." Jamére sat down, having said his piece.

"Yes, yes, point taken," Master M said. "Now get down to planning what has to be done."

The golden robed chairman tapped the table with a golden rod. "It seems we are agreed.

The meeting is over. The matter is closed." Master M bowed his head. Jamére and Sechem hastened out of the chamber, muttering as they went.

"What about Adam?" they both said at the same time. "Will he understand?"

"Well he too is one of us, so he should."

"But he hasn't had that implant, has he? He can't possibly understand what it's like. Even Kate won't understand until it happens. It will be a shock. Do you think she'll cope?"

"She has no choice. We'd better get her prepared."

***

Two figures moved silently around the darkened room. Sechem bent over the sleeping man and whispered in his ear. "Jacob, Jacob, wake up!" Jacob stirred but did not wake. The two time travellers resisted the urge to shake him.

Sechem groaned. "What are we going to do with him Jamére? He's lost in a world of dreams. Are we right to disturb him?" Sechem was getting impatient. He stared at the inert figure. "He used to be so alert and open to us, but he seems to have become one of the sleepers on the planet. He doesn't even meditate anymore and hasn't attended any spiritual or psychic development circles since he left Dorset."

"Jamére nodded in agreement. "We're going to have to do something. Time's fast running out and the Galactic Council is again becoming dissatisfied with the way humans are running the planet. It's opening the way for the dark forces in space. We need him if Kate is to be used again. If we're not careful she too will become so idle in her connection with us that she won't work as well as before. She'll be tempted to give up. I've seen it happen to so many others before her. The enthusiasm and excitement they had at the beginning wanes and they settle back into everyday boredom."

Sechem looked at his colourful companion and his eyes brightened. "If anyone can do something it's you," he said. "Why don't you play one of your tricks?"

"You tried that the other day and all it did was to give her a fright. It resulted in a bad dream and I know you tried to take her mind off it. But at least she's now contemplating travelling in time."

"Well, that can't be bad, can it? At last she's thinking outside the box. Isn't that what we want? We need to let her view the future, and how it could be if matters don't change in the present. We need to tell her about Time Lines." Sechem did a little dance in joyful anticipation. Kaleidoscopic colours trailed behind him as he moved around the room. He loved to take people into the future.

They both looked again at the sleeping Jacob. "Dreaming of Joslene I suppose." Jamére shook his head and sighed. "We have to do something, and soon. Perhaps we should get Adam to shake them both up. You know he's in love with Kate, don't you?"

"Yes, but his job in Washington DC keeps him away from her. He can only go to see her if the Galactic Command Council orders it."

"Well, they're the ones who want us to do something. So let's do something."

***

Kate sat at the dining room table, running her hands through her fair hair as she mulled over the last few months. She gave a big sigh. Such a lot had happened and now here she was playing with her breakfast and wondering what the next few years would bring. It was quiet, too quiet. She and her father had settled comfortably in their new house in Pinks Lane near Aldermaston and the Atomic Weapons Establishment. Kate wondered, not for the first time, why the Galactic Command had relocated them so near to such an important nuclear base. Their little house was in a quiet lane, with a few side roads leading to dead ends, with a mixture of detached and semi-detached houses, each having more or less well-kept front lawns. They were in a small lane branching off the main road in a two-bedroom semi with a short driveway. All should be well with her world, but it wasn't, and the recent dreams had unsettled her. She heard her father moving about in his bedroom. She knew he too was getting pretty restless and bored. He was losing weight and that bothered her. But his appetite hadn't diminished, and he still loved his tea and biscuits. So why was he losing weight? She wondered if he too could have had a similar experience to hers in the mirror. Kate chewed her lip in concern.

Jacob clattered down the stairs and entered the kitchen. Kate looked up and noticed he'd hardly combed his hair and hadn't yet shaved. "Any toast?" he asked. His voice was dull and listless. Kate didn't know whether to be relieved or upset at his tone. It was clear he'd had no event with a mirror.

"Dad, I was wondering . . ." She tailed off and put a plate of toast on the table. She passed the marmalade over to him and poured his tea and decided to say nothing.

"You are always wondering," he said and planted a kiss on her head as he sat.

"No dad, I'm serious." Kate took a deep breath and told him about her fright with the mirror and the dream that had left her with foreboding. "What if we could travel back and forward in time? What would that mean?"

"You're not serious, are you?" Jacob frowned as he searched his darling daughter's face. "Aren't you happy with your life sweetheart? Do you want to scoot ahead to avoid being in the here and now?"

Kate waved off the question, embarrassed by it. She wasn't happy but didn't want her father to know it. But then he didn't seem happy either.

"No, no dad. It isn't like that. I'm just curious, that's all. I mean our life isn't exactly buzzing after all the excitement we've had, is it?" Kate twisted her fair hair around her fingers. She didn't want her father to be worried about her. He'd done enough of that in the past. Jacob reached for the sugar and put spoonful after spoonful into the cup. He stirred his tea. Kate noticed he hadn't cut down on the amount of sugar he used and was pleased. She really didn't like him losing weight, in spite of her constant nagging to do so before all that had happened to them both. She liked him to be his normal cuddly self.

Before! That wasn't so long ago, but it felt like a lifetime away. She wondered what her elegant, social climbing mother Francine was doing these days. Her friend Poppy would also be wondering where they were, despite the explanatory note left by Adam when they'd fled. That was another thing. Adam was so often absent from their lives. There'd been little or no contact since he left to go back to DC after she'd successfully destroyed the satellite capable of targeting and bending people's minds. Surely if Adam truly loved her he'd have found a way for them to be together. She began to wonder if she'd been used just for her abilities to get into secret places by using her mind. She hadn't done any of that lately. Was this how life was to be for her now that her tasks had apparently been completed?

"Penny for them," Jacob watched his daughter as she pushed toast around her plate in silence.

Kate turned to her father. "Dad, do you fancy a mind journey?"

He looked up, surprised. "What brought that on?" A deep furrow appeared in his brow. "I thought we'd left that all behind."

"Yes, I thought so too. But I get the feeling that *they* are trying to get in touch with us again." Kate hadn't forgotten the recent conversation she'd had with Sechem. We had such fun and excitement before, when I went deep into myself and told you what was happening to me. We did do some good, didn't we, Dad?

Jacob rubbed his chin and brushed a crumb off his lip. "You know what that scamp Sechem is like. If he'd wanted to get in touch he would have done so. He doesn't need you to call him in. He probably has other things on his mind. Let's have a fresh pot of tea. This one is cold." Jacob picked up the teapot and handed it to Kate who carried it to the kitchen.

"You know, don't you, that once you start opening yourself up again it can lead you into a whole new world. Are you ready for that?" he called out.

Kate grunted and ignored his question. She busied herself getting more tea. Should she tell him? Finally, she sat down in front of him and looked him straight in the eye.

"Sechem has already been in touch, Dad. He went on and on about time travel."

Jacob's eyes brightened. "Time travel eh! That's more like it. Alright my darling girl, how about tomorrow evening?" He slammed his fist on the table, excited now.

CHAPTER THREE

SECRET GOVERNMENT

In the form of man, they amongst us,
but only to sight were they as men.
Serpent-headed when the glamour was lifted
but appearing to man as men among men.
Crept they into the Councils,
taking forms that were like unto men.
Slaying by their arts the chiefs of the kingdoms,
taking their form and ruling o'er man.
Only by magic could they be discovered.
Only by sound could their faces be seen.
Sought they from the Kingdom of shadows
to destroy man and rule in his place.
from The Emerald Tablets of Thoth

The tall, narrow, brick building in the back streets of North London gave no indication of the meeting taking place in a darkened room several floors up. There were no signs or numbers on the brick wall facing the street, and the matt, black painted door was blank. There was nothing to show what might be happening inside. Anyone passing wouldn't even notice the door was there and would walk straight by, but if they were to look up they might see and wonder at the array of security cameras mounted high up on the wall.

In contrast to the building's outside appearance the meeting room down the green carpeted corridor was almost opulent with soft, padded black leather chairs placed around a rich oval walnut table. Expensive cut glass tumblers and water carafes were set out in perfect order alongside heavy folders. Blinds were drawn across the large windows.

A giant, dark suited man who was speaking was almost invisible in the gloom of the room. "You mucked that up, you fools," he shouted.

Nobody had ever fully seen his face. For that they should be grateful. Word was he wasn't human. They said his name was Gork, but very few wished to call his name in fear of having him appear to them. Judging by rumours circulating and reports of his actions this could be believed, and nobody was willing to chance it. Silas, one of three summoned to the meeting was standing closest to the dark figure. In spite of himself, a shiver of fear ran through him.

Silas himself scared most people with his cold, black calculating eyes and tall sticklike figure, but even he was intimidated by the dark form that blotted out any possible view through the window blinds. He was more used to doing the reprimanding than being on the receiving end. He ran one shoe up against the back of his trouser leg to shake off any possible lingering dust, not that Silas was ever anything other than immaculate. The huge, dark figure maintained his position with his back to the three waiting figures.

"They had help or they wouldn't have got away," Silas spluttered. He smoothed down his dark, sleek hair with nervous fingers. In spite of the tense situation he couldn't resist a look at himself in the black reflection of a dead monitor screen.

"Enough!" They all jumped. The voice had a force to it that rattled the glasses set out on the table. "No excuses. I demand an explanation."

"We did our best," stammered Silas in a weak voice. He shifted uncomfortably on his feet.

"Your best? *That* was your best?"

Silas looked down. The figure didn't turn around to face him, and for that Silas was grateful. He'd met those eyes once before and had almost fainted with shock. The eyes were frightening and had seemed to him that they were definitely not human eyes. He'd felt he was looking at reptilian eyes. The vertical slits had opened and shut rapidly. It had been like a camera shutter taking shots of him. Click, click, click. He was glad the creature hadn't yet turned around. Well over seven-foot tall it had a bulk that would put a prize fighter to flight. To any who saw it, at first glance they would think he was just a large, well-dressed man, until they saw the eyes. Finally, the creature slowly turned to face the occupants of the room. Silas nearly passed out with relief. Dark glasses covered those dreadful eyes.

"Well?" it thundered.

"They got away. Someone helped them. I'm sure of it." Silas spluttered.

"Don't you even know who that might be? With all the information we've given you? You're useless." An uneasy silence filled the room. Everybody held their breath and waited for the onslaught. What was coming next from this terrible man? Would they be banished to some deserted outpost? To Silas that would be worse than death. He loved his creature comforts and access to a good tailor was an essential part of his existence. He knew that one of the three there, the bulky, but not very bright Marco would do whatever he was told, wherever it might be. Marco was a bully boy, but like all bullies he was also a coward. The third one present was Helga, who enjoyed a good, and in her eyes, important position in her firm. Some would say a little power crazy, and a social climber for sure. She enjoyed her connections with influential people and a social life. She at least had the good sense to keep quiet. She sneered at Silas's discomfort.

The dark figure continued to stare at them in silence, as if thinking. It was a cold, blank stare. The thought crossed Silas's mind that he/it was receiving or even giving instruction.

"We'll give you one more chance to get rid of both the girl and her father. Or at the very least find out where their help is coming from." He shifted his attention to Helga, the only female in the room.

"You Helga. You had her right close by your side. You had every opportunity to stop her." He snarled and seemed more animal than human. He moved towards her. Helga hurriedly took two steps back, stumbling as she went.

Silas watched in amusement as she opened and shut her mouth several times before she could speak. He couldn't resist a smirk.

"I tried everything I knew," she said in defence. "I zapped her with psychic attack, invaded her thoughts and installed bugs in her house. She managed to block me at every turn."

Helga wasn't used to being intimidated. Tall and skeleton thin; she was still a formidable figure. It was clear to Silas that to cross her would be a huge mistake. She stuck her chin in the air. "It's not my fault she gave her notice in."

The dark figure snorted. He glared at her behind his glasses. Silas sniggered, enjoying seeing Helga quake. Marco started to pick his nose and edged away.

"I'll arrange another meeting with those who'll know what to do. Better than anything you've tried," he said with a growl. "It'll take place at your home." There was no 'May we…?' or 'Would that be alright?' It was a command from Gork, who would not be disobeyed.

Silas spotted Marco quietly retreating as far away from *it* as he could. He realised Marco hoped not to be noticed. He was almost at the door when Gork called out.

"Marco, come back here. What excuse do *you* have?" Marco moved a few tiny hesitant steps closer. Just like a nervous dog afraid to go near its master, Silas thought. Marco kept his eyes down and mumbled something incoherent.

"Speak up man. *If* you are a man." Marco flinched at the ferocity and scorn in the voice. The dark one scrutinised heavyweight Marco and noted his physical strength and bulk. "Surely *you* were able to stop her?" he looked Marco up and down and sneered.

Silas couldn't resist a snort of derision as Marco mumbled something. Whatever he said, it would bring more wrath upon his head.

"I tried," he snivelled. Silas remembered Marco's brief flirtation with power when he had attempted to rape Kate and failed. Then Marco unwisely threw all caution to the winds with his next sentence. "You had the C.I.A. and your own agents bugging the phones and kidnapping her. You failed too, didn't you? Didn't you?" Silas gasped, horrified.

Gork exploded in rage. "Get out, all of you. We haven't finished with you yet. This conversation is closed."

They trooped out with heads down and shaking legs. Silas still managed to cast a sly look at his reflection in the glass as he passed into the corridor.

But before they had gone far Silas heard Gork pick up the phone.

"Where are they now?" he heard him shout into the mouthpiece. "Have you found them yet? Yes, both of them, the father and the daughter." He listened for a moment. "Yes, I know they've gone quiet and are not active, you fool. Do you really think that it will stay that way?" They heard him slam the phone down hard.

***

The traffic worked its way through downtown DC and its hum could be heard inside the room because somebody had wanted a window opened, regardless of triple glazed windows deliberately put in to stop outside noise. Several floors up there was no chance of being overlooked. Colonel Adam Fenshawe repeatedly tapped his Parker pen on the table, impatient for the secret meeting to be over. He hated the position he was in. He'd had to listen to all the careful plans proposed for takeover of the masses. Many well-known public figures of governmental and business concerns were seated around the table talking among themselves in muted tones. Adam studied their serious faces. If only the people outside this room knew what was really going on under their noses.

He had wondered many times why the Galactic Command Council had chosen him for this appointment. He'd been on Sirius when the call came. His sense of duty had overcome any reluctance to engage with the dark forces on Earth. Some of these were present at the table, some in their ET form, and others in a human skin. Yet also listening intently were good, well intentioned public figures with scientific clout and knowledge, completely unaware that they were being used. He knew they sincerely thought that what they did was for the good of the people.

Adam's top-level security clearance enabled him to miss many of these meetings with no questions asked. He needed this clearance if he was to succeed in protecting and monitoring Kate and her father Jacob. Without it he had no chance. He thanked The Spiritual Council for the Walk-In arrangement, where for any number of reasons a soul wanting to opt out of life, but who didn't want to commit suicide, could exchange with a soul, whose purpose of service to others was paramount. There had to be complete agreement by both parties, the incoming Walk-in and the outgoing soul. The implications arising from the exchange meant it wasn't an easy route for the incoming soul.

As a Walk-in he'd retained the outgoing soul's cellular memory of all that had taken place at these meetings over the years. The original soul known as Col Adam Fenshawe had opted to leave and be replaced. What was being planned by the Shadow Government had all been too much for his conscience to bear. Adam heard that at the latest count, over the last two years, seventy-four leading medical and NASA scientists had died. What's more their numbers were growing as discoveries were made concerning absolute cures for diseases such as cancer. Almost all deaths were officially labelled suicide or had suffered an accident. Why was that, and were they all suicides, or something even more sinister? Did they know too much and couldn't handle the implications of what they knew, rather like the former Colonel Fenshawe? Or had they threatened to spill the beans?

Adam shook his head as he remembered Glenn Thomas, a World Health Organisation spokesperson. He was just one of the more recent cases of a prominent key scientist's suspicious death. Reportedly an expert on Ebola and AIDS, he was aboard Malaysia Airlines flight MH17 when it was shot down with approximately one hundred other researchers. If these people did pay the ultimate sacrifice for what they knew and had knowledge of, then he'd try to find out the truth.

Adam was fortunate in that the body he'd taken on was young and good looking. But being tall, blonde and handsome could be a mixed blessing. Right now the only lady attending the meeting was the same one who months before had helped him leave early. Adam saw her trying to catch his eye, quite determined to engage with him. He knew the trick she'd used before to help him escape from a previous meeting wouldn't work twice. He'd have to sit through this one. It wouldn't be good to start a relationship with her either, for it had no future. Mind you, he mused, it would be fun for sure. He quickly dismissed the errant thought from his mind. He'd a job to do, and then there was Kate to think about.

He was learning a lot by being here and the Galactic Command Council expected him to pass the information on. According to the Spiritual and Galactic agreement there was to be no direct interference by them. If change on the planet was to come about it had to happen through the actions of citizens of Earth. This, he knew, was why many well-meaning ET races, having the best interests of the human race at heart, had chosen to either incarnate as humans or shape-shift into human form, or as he had done, arrange a Walk-in with someone who wanted to leave planet Earth. It was a successful method often used to circumvent the galactic law of non-interference. This was why he'd been given the opportunity to serve in this way.

As a human citizen, he could do much as a Trojan Horse within the underworld establishment. It was a perfect set up. In this position, there were few questions asked. He also knew he'd have to play it safe, for if they ever found out . . . he shuddered at the idea. They had their psychic spies.

The meeting stretched on interminably. A round faced general sitting opposite Adam was getting redder and redder in the face. Unhealthy blotchy patches appeared on his cheeks. His bristly white moustache bristled even more. Adam wondered if he was going to have to call the medics to him if those gathered together couldn't come to an agreement soon. They were trying to decide who to send through the Jump Room to Mars, or into the future. The problem was that not one person there could trust any of the others. Adam knew that each had a personal agenda and personal preference as to who and what they could most benefit from.

The chairman was addressing the gathering.

"You may be aware that someone, not under our control, I repeat, not under our control, has managed to travel through time and space, without the use of a Jump Room or a device of any kind. Who knows where this may lead. Our security will be breached. The defence of our country is at risk. We must at all costs put a stop to this. My clear information is that a young woman in England has direct contact with certain species not of our Earth but are travelling in our Earth space."

A long silence followed this surprising announcement while they all took in the implications. Then all hell broke loose with everybody talking at once.

An ageing five-star general with white hair raised his hand for attention. Adam knew this old soldier would never be invited to go through a Jump

Room. It was for the young ones who had the requisite strength and stamina. But the general had a much loved teenage grandson with ambition, and it was usually the youngsters who were put into training, some were started even as young as nine.

The general kept his hand raised for several minutes until he had the nod from the chairman to proceed. "We already know of those who've experienced the Jump Room and more importantly have been trained to go through. Are they safe? What is more important, what about the repercussions if it were to be known we have this technology? Can they be trusted to keep it from the public and other countries?"

Adam groaned aloud. Were they going to run over the same ground? Some of the older ones wanted disclosure now, but he was sure it was never going to happen in this room. The discussion on this could take forever and they'd never come to agreement. They had come a long way since the Montauk chair. If they only realised that some in powerful positions had also come a long way from Jump Rooms. The people present in the room didn't know that yet, and that was a blessing.

The Galactic Command Council had told him that without doubt that Kate was capable of jumping time and space without a Montauk chair or a jump room. Only she didn't know it yet either. Was she the one they referred to earlier? Thinking of Kate brought an aching desire to see her again and he groaned. He could only go to her if the Galactic Command instructed him to do so. There had to be a valid reason. The fact that he was in love with her didn't count with them. The need to glean intelligence and obstruct the workings of the Shadow Government mattered more.

His groan was loud enough to bring a sharp piercing look in his direction from the chair of the meeting. Adam sensed the chairman was not human and worked for the Dark Agenda in space. He'd have to be careful to avoid drawing unwanted attention to himself in future.

The elderly general was getting into his stride. "We know that some previous jumpers are coming forward and disclosing what's going on. There are five of them to date, and if people believe them, more disclosures may follow. These five went to Mars and came back. Others, many others, did not come back."

"Who didn't return?" asked a bright spark, eager to make an impression. His ginger hair and fresh complexion looked out of place among the more senior participants. What also offended them was that he hadn't raised his hand for permission to speak from the Chairman, and it wasn't the right question to ask. A long awkward silence followed broken only by fits of embarrassed coughing and muttering.

"You're not privy to that information," a short, overweight government man in a dark tailored suit replied. Adam recognised he was veering from the embarrassing question and had changed the subject.

He raised his hand and got the nod. "Those who are not keeping their mouths shut are Andrew D. Basiago, Michael C. Relfe, Arthur Neumann, William B. Stillings, Bernard Mendez, and a Mars colony recruit Laura M. Eisenhower," he said.

"*Colony* recruit? There's a colony? How many are over there now?" The young eager bright spark asked. He wasn't going to let the matter drop. Adam wondered if he would become another prospective whistle-blower?

Adam was well aware that there were indeed others who'd made the jump to Mars and who had been clearly identified by the whistle-blowers mentioned. They weren't likely to ever come forward themselves because of their current positions. Yet many in the know *had* identified them. He knew the public who seriously wished to search for the facts could find them. It wasn't as much of a secret as they thought and hoped it was. Whistle-blowers give enough clues for searchers to investigate for themselves. He looked down at the folder before him.

Adam knew quite well that the list of whistle-blowers was impressive. He held the papers inside the folder and in spite of himself his hand shook. He opened the file and began to read quietly. The Mars program made for extraordinary reading.

First on the list was Andrew D. Basiago, a lawyer in Washington State, who served in DARPA's (Defence Advanced Research Projects Agency) time travel program Project Pegasus in the 1970's.

Listed for his technical genius was fellow chrononaut William B. Stillings. Adam's eyebrows shot up as he read that they'd both openly confirmed in public the enrolment of Obama in their Mars training class in 1980. They wrote that they'd encountered Obama during visits to U.S. facilities on Mars from 1981 to 1983. According to Basiago and Stillings in 1980 they attended a three-week seminar about Mars, to prepare them for trips to Mars via teleportation.

They discovered that there is breathable atmosphere on Mars, despite NASA's claim that atmospheric pressure is too low to breathe and that walking on the surface doesn't require a suit, although a suit may be preferable as the surface air pressure is undoubtedly lower than that of Earth and is akin to mountain peak breathing conditions.

Remote viewing pioneer Major Ed Dames taught them this while serving as a scientific and technical intelligence officer for the U.S. Army. The course venue was The College of the Siskiyous, near Mt. Shasta in California.

They stated that ten teenagers had enrolled in the Mars training program. They identified two other teenagers in Major Dames' class as Barack Obama, using the name "Barry Soetoro," and Regina Dugan, who Mr. Obama appointed the 19th and first female director of the Defence Advanced Research Projects Agency (DARPA) in 2009.

Seven parents of the ten students, all with ties to the CIA, audited the class. They included Raymond F. Basiago, who was the chief technical liaison between Parsons and the CIA on Tesla-based teleportation; Thomas Stillings, an operations analyst for the Lockheed Corporation, who'd served with the Office of Naval Intelligence; and Mr. Obama's mother, Stanley Ann Dunham, who carried out assignments for the CIA in Kenya and Indonesia.

Adam looked up from his reading as a hubbub in the room caught his attention. The young firebrand was openly disagreeing with the old general on some moot point. Adam had missed that thread and said nothing. He knew each person there had the same file he was reading, since it related to teleportation. Had they read it all through? He returned his attention to the file before him.

He read on: From 1981 to 1983, young attendees teleported to Mars via a 'jump room' in a Hughes Aircraft building in El Segundo, California, adjacent to the Los Angeles International Airport (LAX).

Stillings wrote: "I confirm that Andrew D. Basiago and Barack Obama (using the name "Barry Soetoro") were in my Mars training course in Summer 1980 and during 1981 to 1983, I encountered Andy, Courtney M. Hunt of the CIA, and other Americans on the surface of Mars, after reaching Mars via the "jump room". Stillings said the primitive conditions on Mars involved a high level of danger.

In light of these risks, Mr. Hunt, a career CIA officer, showed Basiago how to operate a respiration device and provided him with a weapon for protection on Mars. He took him to the Lockheed facility in Burbank, California for training in avoiding predators on the Martian surface. When they then first teleported to Mars in 1981 one of their principal concerns was to avoid being devoured on the Martian surface. Some they could evade and some were impossible to evade if encountered.

Ed Dames had stated, "Simply put, your task is to be seen and not eaten."

Basiago and Stillings were told sending civilians was key to establishing a legal basis for the U.S. and assert a claim of territorial sovereignty over Mars. The expectation was that human beings from Earth would begin visiting Mars in greater numbers. Their mission was to acclimatise Martian humanoids and animals to their presence.

"Colonel Fenshawe!" Adam looked up as his name was called. Everyone in the room was looking at him. They waited for his answer. "Colonel Fenshawe, are you with us on this? What do you say?" There was an expectant silence in the room.

Adam realised with horror that he'd been so engrossed in his file that he hadn't a clue as to what was being asked. "Well, it all depends," he said, and hoped more would be forthcoming to assist him.

"Depends on what?" the chairman asked. "We either continue with the Mars teleportation program, or we don't." He banged the table hard with his fist.

Adam breathed a sigh of relief and tried to look thoughtful. "It depends on whether you're willing to risk more lives in trying to establish sovereignty on another planet. As you are aware, if you have read this file through as I have, that participants Mr. Basiago and Mr. Stillings agreed with Major Ed Dames, who said during their training class at The College of the Siskiyous in 1980: and I quote, 'Of the 97,000 individuals that we have thus far sent to Mars, only 7,000 have survived there after five years.' It's all in this report." Adam indicated the file before him.

His comment brought a gasp and a flood of comments from those sitting around the table. It was obvious to him that they had not read the file through. The chairman repeatedly tapped the side of his glass with his pen to get silence.

"We only take volunteers. They don't have to go if they don't want to."

Adam got to his feet and objected. "You know that's not true. The youngest of teenagers are entered into the programme by their parents. What choice did they have?"

The red faced general sitting opposite him waved him to sit down.

"Well you did ask what I thought," Adam called out.

The chairman brought his fist down hard on the desk. "Let us have a vote on it. All those in favour of continuing raise their hands." Almost all the hands went up. Adam saw that he was getting nowhere and went back to reading his file.

The next statement read: This first-hand, eyewitness testimony of Mr. Basiago and Mr. Stillings of the existence of a secret U.S. presence on Mars, is made possible by revolutionary "jump room" technology. This is concealed from the public, and is congruent with similar accounts given by three other Mars whistle blowers:

(1) Former U.S. serviceman Michael Relfe, spent 20 years as a member of

permanent security staff of a U.S. facility on Mars;

(2) Former Department of Defense (DoD) scientist Arthur Neumann, testified publicly that he teleported to a U.S. facility on Mars for DOD project meetings.

(3) Laura Magdalene Eisenhower, great-granddaughter of U.S. President Dwight D. Eisenhower, in 2007, refused a covert attempt to recruit her into a secret U.S. colony on Mars.

Mars researchers, including physicist David Wilcock, estimated that as a result of the 'jump room' technology, that Relfe, Basiago, Neumann, and Stillings had described, the U.S. colony on Mars might number 500,000 individuals.

Adam was really getting into the files when a further commotion interrupted his reading once more.

"Why wasn't I told?" The young man with red hair, who earlier had asked uncomfortable questions, raised his voice. "Why wasn't I privy to any of these facts?" Adam wondered, not for the first time why this seemingly inexperienced youth was present at this meeting. He couldn't see a folder similar to his own before him.

A heavily decorated veteran waved his arm for attention and got it. With a glare he quickly silenced the young man who sat down.

"Whatever we do, we don't want to get into a repeat ever again of what happened with the Montauk Chair. They should never have allowed it to happen."

Adam knew what the old man was talking about. The Galactic Council had briefed him before his entry into the body of Col Fenshawe on the history of the Montauk Chair. It was no wonder that the soul of the original Fenshawe wanted out. The Chair's development from early 1969 went through several changes and advancements. It was later re-named Phoenix11 so that funding could continue.

Adam's mind went back to the Galactic Command Council's meeting with him before he agreed to step into Colonel Fenshawe's body. It was Master M who'd given him the picture. He imparted, "Because of the terrible things that happened with the Chair the military closed the project and had the base sealed off with concrete on August 12th 1983. They emptied the base of people, equipment and had all extraneous personnel brainwashed into forgetting everything that had happened there. Almost a year later, in May or June of 1984, a unit of 'Black Berets' entered the base with orders to shoot anything and everything that moved. They purged the base for a second time, which removed any equipment deemed too sensitive to abandon."

"They must have been really scared to do that," Adam replied.

"Yes indeed, but it still wasn't enough. After that, they sealed off the underground chambers. According to reports, one of the rooms cleared out contained hundreds of human skeletons. You understand that this has not been verified.

"Finally, at the end of 1984 they poured cement into many of the elevator shafts and underground areas of Montauk Base. This sealed off all of the areas used for the most extreme of the space-time experiments. Afterwards, the gates to Montauk AFB were locked and the base was abandoned for a second and final time."

Adam looked shocked and stared at Master M's face to see if he was serious. "And you want me to go down into that sort of thing? No wonder the poor guy I've replaced wanted out."

"You must understand, Adam, the chair was an interface with consciousness. When in this chair, you focussed your mind on a particular place you wanted to visit. I am simplifying the procedure, but by doing this in the chair and using your mind it opened up a wormhole in front of the wall. You flew through the wormhole, and you ended up going where you wanted to go. The Montauk chair was reverse engineering of a seat from one of our ships. Human beings were trained to run the chair with their mind, open up a vortex, and send people through. The trouble was that the human mind decided to do other things with it, such as mind control and allowed mind manifestation of undesirable things. It had unleashed the devil."

Adam's attention was suddenly brought back to the meeting room.

The red-haired young man was shouting now. "I need to know more about this."

Adam thought to himself, *You are not long for this world, if you carry on like that, young man.*

The chairman waved his hand in a calming manner, but Adam saw him make a note of the outburst.

"No of course we cannot allow that to happen ever again. But this is why we must maintain absolute secrecy about Jump Rooms. In the wrong hands this would be disastrous to our defence."

Adam had to agree with this and prayed fervently it would never get into the wrong hands. He prayed that some of those present at the meeting were not already the wrong hands. He suspected that the technology was in operation in other countries and hoped that they had more common sense in its use.

He knew that in place of the chair, they had discovered another means, an elevator for teleportation. This was what they were discussing now, and the introduction of more jump rooms, and who they would choose to use them. Adam read from the reports that space/time teleportation devices, alleged to have been created under Project Pegasus, were not advertised in DARPA's official or public presentation. It was a hush-hush science program. He'd discovered that they took several small teams of covertly prepped individuals to planet Mars and back as regularly as three times a day.

The meeting abruptly ended without any resolution and they all filed out of the hall. Adam threaded his way through the people and made his way to the exit. The young man who had asked difficult questions waylaid him in the corridor.

"Excuse me Sir. What do you really think about all this?"

Adam thought carefully before answering. "Haven't you read the file? I heard that the main function for sending Beagle to Mars was to set up the elevator of a Jump Room. This would act as a receiving end catcher for any object or human to be transported there. Nowadays they need to have another Jump Room available at the other end in order to go from place to place. I don't know how true any of this is. Like you, they don't tell me everything."

"You seemed to know a lot about it," said the young man, not about to be put off.

"I was studying it from the folder they gave me," Adam explained, trying to be patient. "I'm more interested in travel through time, rather than just place to place. They say that we live in a multiverse of a multitude of time lines, that are both highly similar and yet highly dissimilar to the one we're on. We are always on one time line or another. They say that sometimes we move back and forth between this time line and alternate adjacent ones."

"Very interesting," said the young man, looking bored. Adam saw his only attraction was to Jump Rooms. They shook hands and went their different ways.

Back in his room Adam telepathically passed all the information from the meeting back to the Galactic Command as usual. He hoped that the knowledge gained would be put to good use and prevent those in power from using it as a weapon by irresponsible people on Earth. What was uppermost in his mind was his aching need to be with Kate, and that didn't look like being resolved any time soon.

CHAPTER FOUR

TIME LINES

Along the way, you will come across many things, some will be beautiful, some difficult, some uplifting and some disturbing. You may observe and pass by or decide to stay awhile before moving on. You have the choice whether to transform something ugly into something beautiful, to ease the difficulties you see, to bring others with you along your way, or to let things stay as they are. The choice is always yours. To move on unnoticed or to leave the footprints of your soul so that others may know you have passed their way.

From spirit

It was late at night when Kate wearily climbed into bed after a hectic day at the office. To her surprise a clear message entered her head.

"You must take mind journeys if you are to hear us. You know that."

Kate tried to ignore it, but her thoughts wouldn't shut off. She reflected she had her work at the Estate Agency to go to and that kept her busy enough. But it wasn't as exciting as the challenges she'd met while working at the satellite firm. At least at her current office she wasn't hounded by Helga or Marco, or worst of all Silas. He was highly intelligent, and capable of cruelty that would be calculated and set at the highest level of pain. Of this she was sure. His dark eyes were as cold as steel. She doubted there was any warmth in him at all. He gave her the creeps and her flesh crawled whenever he was around. She knew he could be intentionally cruel. She'd hated the way he would silently appear wherever she was. His cold dark eyes had frightened her. One good thing about moving and leaving her home in Dorset was that she would never have to see his face again. Kate turned over and tried to sleep.

***

CALLING EARTH – II

It was a cloudy day in Tadley when she went to work next morning. The forecast said it was going to clear up and the sun would shine. The hours passed quickly so she finished work early and tidied up her desk. Perhaps she could grab some of that late sunshine. She said goodbye to her unfortunate colleagues doing overtime. She'd had no need to use the car and enjoyed the walk home, taking short cuts through alleyways lined with trees and bushes. It was still light, but the birds had already started their evening song. She hummed a little tune as she walked. No threats to her safety here, as there'd been before in Dorset when a car had deliberately tried to run her down. She arrived home in no time at all. It was all going to happen tonight, or so she hoped.

Jacob was waiting for her with tea already laid out on the table. Just like old times Kate thought and was happy. They took their time over refreshments and didn't talk much, feeling rather anxious that perhaps nothing would happen at all that night.

Jacob got up and closed the curtains. Just like old times he disconnected the phones. Kate remembered when he'd once forgotten to do that. It had hurt her a lot when the phone's strident ringing painfully jolted her back to consciousness. They were not about to make the same mistake twice. At least he didn't have to go all over the house searching for hidden bugs. They'd be safe here in their new home.

Kate settled herself down, excited and nervous at the same time. What would the unseen voices tell her, and who would make the connection with her? Would she still be able to speak aloud what was happening? Would her father stay calm, whatever occurred? He'd previously freaked out when he'd seen her change into someone else the first time it happened.

She went down quickly using the self-hypnosis stair method she knew so well. It was all going as expected. As before, Jacob monitored the journey.

Kate coughed a bit as she went into deep trance and told him, "I've entered a classroom. I'm standing in front of a class of teenagers, ranging from thirteen to nineteen years. They're all eager to hear what they're going to learn from me. Clearly, I'm here to teach." She paused. "You know, Dad I need a little time to gather myself together because for me it was a very rapid trip to get here."

Ask them what period this is in, Jacob urged.

"What is this time frame?" Kate asked in her mind.

As before if Kate asked a question she usually got a response. If she didn't ask, then she wouldn't be told.

Her spirit friends responded using the telepathic link. "You are currently tapping in to the deep unconscious of many alive right now and those to come. We're also looking forward into 2020, and the time beyond. Those are the years when these young ones will become fully active. They first need to know what they're to do. You are here to teach them, to show them the various ways, not just one, in which they may use their minds to time travel. Tell them if they don't like where they've travelled to they can and should mentally change it. They can change the scenario that their minds have given them into something that's more appealing."

Kate turned to the youngsters and said, "When you mind travel avoid timelines you don't wish to enter. Avoid even touching one of these timelines where all the bad things happen. If one appears in the mind without warning, veer away sharply from the image. Never allow the mind to stay with it, even if you are intrigued. You may well be intrigued, in spite of my warnings. Stick to your own timeline, which includes everything that you had wished for. That's all you need do to avoid negative situations. Remember you can't change those who are reluctant and unwilling to change. Don't waste your energies there. You can be an example, in the way Jesus was an example, by being the best he could be. This is what you can do also. You don't need to get involved with the negative ones. Keep away from them."

The voice telepathically told Kate, "Stress to them that there must *always* be a spiritual aspect to this and not just act for selfish material gains. They must, all of them, always be thinking of the collective spiritual advancement. Any change isn't just for them. It will affect all. They can also be thinking of how best to benefit the planet, which is their home. This will continue to be their home, providing they do their work well."

The children listened hard as Kate passed his message on.

"If you find that your mind journey takes you into areas that you really don't like, you must change it using your mind. Much may be formed from what is currently going on in your mind and your thinking. If you don't like what you see is ahead of you then *this* is the opportunity for you to change it. Don't hesitate when that previewed moment occurs, but change it while it's in your headspace, and while you are viewing the scenes that are being presented to you. That is the time to convert and change things. That, in effect, will be changing the future. We are working to help you."

The children looked puzzled. One skinny boy with straw coloured hair said, "Are you saying we can change the future? Really?"

"Yes, of course. You have the choice of what your future holds. Einstein proved that time isn't fixed, it expands, and contracts. Time also has a vertical dimension. There are many "lanes of time" running simultaneously. You can change lanes. You can begin in one, and then change lanes to produce a different outcome. This means there are multiple possibilities existing simultaneously in any instant, subject to conscious and intentional choice. Use of the mind."

Many hands shot up. Kate was pleased her words had brought a reaction and interest.

"Questions later please. Listen, you have the power to direct your awareness through this field of creative intelligence. Scientists call it the quantum hologram. Through powerful thought you can activate another strand of time, one in which you are whole and well and already healed, because you were never sick. The same applies to every area of life, relationships, finances and success. Peak performance in every area of life is already a reality, in another thread of time. You've the power to activate any scenario in life that you want."

The same boy put his hand up again. "Do you mean we can change things using our imagination?"

"Exactly." Kate said, and smiled, loving him for his excitement. "The quantum leap to a healthier you, a more abundant you, a more attractive you, a more successful you, a more youthful you, exists in another thread of time, and is possible only if you are able to break the barriers of your current thinking. When you imagine, you tap into an alternative possibility timeline, where what you are imagining exists as reality. Experiencing and feeling that reality puts you into vibrational harmony with the frequency of that timeline. Visualization selects one of the possible scenarios within that timeline to merge with your present timeline." Kate began to feel fuzzy. "That's all I need to tell you for now."

Jacob saw that Kate was getting floppy. She looked as if she might pass out. She twitched a few times. "That's enough Kate. It'll do for the first time," he said. She hadn't passed out before and he wasn't sure if he could handle a new experience. Kate murmured a few incoherent words and slowly came back to reality. It was a start.

CHAPTER FIVE

FRANCINE BREAKS INTO SECRET MEETING

Back in Dorset Francine, Kate's mother, strode briskly along the pathway that ran through the well-kept lawns and immaculate flower beds of her home. She stopped abruptly, turned and paced back along the way she'd come. She did this several times. Anyone watching could see the tall, beautifully groomed, elegant woman was troubled. Francine wasn't satisfied with her daughter's explanation, or the official letter that followed Kate's swift departure. It bothered her greatly. She hadn't for a moment believed the contents of the typed official letter posted through her door.

<*Ms Kate Greene has been offered a job overseas, but due to the secret nature of her work we cannot disclose her address. As her mother we have been asked to notify you of this so that you may rest assured she is well and may contact you in the future. - - -* >

As she had said to her cleaning lady at the time, "We weren't close or affectionate towards each other, but the least Kate could have done was to come and say goodbye. It was all too instant. To go without leaving a forwarding address is unforgivable."

Jacob, her ex-husband had also disappeared. She had hot footed it around to both their houses as soon as she'd received the letter but had found them securely locked up. She had looked into the windows and it was obvious that the rooms had been cleared out. So, this wasn't a temporary move and they were in it together. But where were they?

Francine didn't like being kept out of the loop. An idea hit her and she immediately stopped pacing. Maybe Kate's boss Helga could tell her something. She'd go and see her straight away. Impatient as always, she wasn't going to waste any time on a phone call that probably would end in an answering machine response. She'd go herself, straight round to Helga's big house. It was a weekend, so she'd be sure to find her at home. She knew Helga didn't encourage uninvited guests, but after all they did play bridge there together, and Helga had expressed an interest in Kate more than once. Francine imagined she too would be curious as to what had happened to cause her employee to leave so quickly.

When she arrived at Helga's large, rambling house she noticed several impressive looking black cars parked in the drive outside, hidden by tall hedges which surrounded the residence and kept it private from prying eyes. Francine pressed the gold-plated doorbell and heard the musical chime inside. She rang the bell once more, impatient for someone to come to the door. *Why does it take so long?* She rang again and waited and waited. She rapped on the heavy door and bent down to peer through the letter box. There was still no response. Francine was not one to give up so easily. Her face set she made her way around to the back of the house, but nobody was in the garden. However, Francine was sure someone was in. She stopped for a moment to think. Why else would there be so many important looking cars in the drive? At the back of the house there were more bushes but growing closer to most of the windows. Scrambling through them Francine soon found a seat beneath one window. She carefully climbed up onto it. Being tall was an advantage and with a little effort she managed to get a good look inside.

She let out a gasp of surprise. What she saw wasn't what she expected, though what she expected she couldn't say. She knew Helga was used to holding social events and bridge parties, but clearly this was not one of them. From her vantage point she could see a huddle of at least a dozen dark suited men. It had all the signs of being a board meeting, but as far as she was aware Helga didn't belong to or manage anything more than the bridge club. Francine could hardly contain her curiosity. She rapped hard on the window.

Immediately all eyes swivelled in her direction. They didn't look at all pleased. One or two of them scowled. It hadn't occurred to Francine's one-track mind for a moment that her intrusion wouldn't be welcome. In her opinion men in dark suits meant business, power, and usually money. This was an opportunity not to be missed and her heart leapt in joyful anticipation. Her weak husband was becoming rather a bore and she hadn't had any excitement in years. Through the window she smiled her best smile at the men and through gestures she indicated she'd like to be let in.

She climbed down, moved away from the window and made her way back to the front of the house. She rang the bell once more. Asking about Kate could wait, this was a much more enticing prospect. The front door was slowly opened by the maid. Francine had been to the house several times before for the bridge sessions, and each time she was always taken aback by the grand entrance of the hall which led to a wide sweeping staircase.

"Madam is busy," the maid said, her voice like ice. Francine pushed her to one side.

"She will see me," she said as she took off her coat and held it out.

The maid frowned but took it from her. "Would you mind waiting in the library?" she said. Francine realised she'd been briefed about not allowing visitors and maybe that was why she hadn't opened the door earlier. Being put into the library wasn't what Francine was hoping for, but she had no choice now that she was inside.

For the next hour, she paced up and down the large room which was lined floor to ceiling with books. Every so often she tired of this and sat in one of the deep, rich brown leather armchairs and reached for a book on a side table. More time passed. Would someone ever come to get her? At last she heard a door opening and the murmur of men's voices. This was her chance. She got up swiftly and moved to the library door and opened it. She stepped into the hall. It was clear the men were leaving. The first man looked her up and down with a long, cold, disapproving stare and strode past her. The next one had such a hard, cruel face that Francine looked away quickly so as not to make eye contact. He too walked past, and of that she was very glad. The next ones to go by were engrossed in conversation and didn't even look her way. Francine wasn't about to be beaten, she stepped forward and blocked the way of the stragglers.

"Excuse me," she said, using her little girl lost voice. "I hope I've not interrupted anything. I'm looking for my good friend Helga."

They looked at her with cold unfriendly eyes. She shivered in spite of herself. Too late she realised she'd made a mistake trying to engage with them. They took in her appearance with icy stares.

"Helga is your friend, eh? Was she expecting you?" said a man with sharp features. It was at that uncomfortable moment that Helga appeared. Francine swung round and attempted to greet her, but the chilly expression on Helga's face stopped her dead.

The same man spoke in a tight, clipped voice. "Who is this woman? Who invited her? We asked for absolute privacy and secrecy for this meeting. This *will* be reported."

Another turned to Helga and in a voice full of malice repeated the question, "Who is she? Did you invite her?"

Helga shrank back, away from his energy. "I definitely didn't invite her. She's nobody of importance."

Francine flinched as if struck. She was a little afraid, but also irritated beyond words. Seething inwardly, she tried to control her anger at the manner of his address to her friend, in her own home too. She opened her mouth to speak but shut it again quickly, deeming it wise not to make matters worse.

"Francine, I thought you were asked to wait in the library." Helga gripped her by the arm and ushered her back into the room. She firmly shut the door as she returned to the waiting man.

But Francine was determined not to miss anything. She waited a brief moment and opened the door a crack, just enough to watch Helga as she tried to guide the man to the open front door, but he wasn't about to be put off.

"She can't be a nobody. She knows your first name. I clearly heard her say she's a good friend. What's going on here? Who is she?" Francine could see he was used to getting answers to his questions. She saw Helga hesitate. It was just long enough for him to be even more suspicious. She felt he'd been trained to pick up the slightest sign of a person hiding something.

"She's Kate Greene's mother," Helga said at last. "She plays bridge here at the club. That is how I know her."

He stared at her, an incredulous expression on his face. Francine thought for a brief terrifying moment that he would strike Helga.

"Kate Greene's mother? The same Kate we have been discussing all afternoon? I don't believe it." He motioned to the few lingering men waiting for him in the doorway. "You go on. I will follow later." He turned his attention back to Helga. Francine could see he was furious.

"Helga, you fool. She'll know of course where her daughter is." He turned quickly and strode towards the library door. Francine stepped back and went hastily to the book shelves. Helga stayed out in the hall to escort the remaining men out.

***

Her encounter with what she now called in her mind 'the men in black' shook Francine. She'd heard all about men like them through the internet and TV. A little thrill of nerves mixed with excitement ran through her body as he came in.

"Sit down. Sit down please. There's no need to concern yourself over your unexpected visit." Francine relaxed a little. She liked his soothing tone.

"You have a daughter Mrs Greene." It was a statement not a question.

"I'm not Mrs Greene. I've remarried."

"Oh, I'm sorry. I didn't know." He patted her hand.

"Why would you know? You don't know me, and we've never met before."

"Yes, that's right. But you do have a daughter, don't you?"

"Yes, I have, but you'd never know it. What sort of a daughter goes off without so much as a goodbye? Tell me that." Francine sniffed loudly and dabbed at her eyes for effect.

"But she's got in touch with you, hasn't she?" he probed, sympathy oozing out of him.

Francine by now was losing her nervousness. "Why are you so interested in Kate? What has she done? Is she in trouble? Do you know where she is?" She put on what she hoped looked like a concerned mother.

"We were hoping you could tell us. She may be in some sort of trouble. If we could find her it would help a lot." Francine sensed he was treading carefully.

"Well, she does have a friend Poppy. Maybe she could help." It never crossed Francine's mind to wonder why he was asking, or what Kate had to do with him. She was getting plenty of attention and that was something. Francine told him what she could about Poppy, not that it was much. What she didn't know she made up.

"I hope we'll meet again," she said and flashed him a flirtatious smile. She did so like men in suits, and even scary men in black had a certain appeal.

CHAPTER SIX

POPPY IS DISCUSSED

The Galactic Command Council sat around the oval table once more. Lights from the crystals placed among the small group sitting there shot out bright sparkles every so often, in response to movement and sound. Jamére and Sechem sat close together across the table from Master M.

"You're probably wondering why you've been called here," Master M said. "This time the subject under discussion is Kate's long-time friend, Poppy. I doubt you've given much thought to her. What are we going to do about Poppy?"

They both looked puzzled. Jamére looked up. "Poppy? What about her? All she's interested in are her animals, mainly her dogs. She made it very clear that she didn't want to get further involved in Kate's work. It all got beyond her and scared her a bit."

Master M wasn't going to let this pass. "Yes, we know all that. But she is, after all, Kate's close friend, and very protective of her. Whether she likes it or not, her mind has been stimulated by Kate's talks. Regardless of her previous reluctance to get involved too much, her thoughts will now dwell on more than just her dogs. Without Kate to explain things to her, how's she going to deal with the direction these thoughts are leading her? She's sure to try to find out where Kate is now. If she does then it won't go well, for either of them."

Jamére frowned, then stood up to say his piece. "I agree. Poppy doesn't have the ability to link with us, but if they reconnect with each other, that could be dangerous for Kate. Poppy is well known for never keeping her mouth shut, even when told to. If she reveals Kate's whereabouts, it'll all be over."

It was Sechem's turn to speak up. "I've heard that the woman Helga is trying to get in touch with her. If she does, Poppy could easily be influenced by her, and not to Kate's benefit. We can't let that happen. We must get to her before Helga does. You do know, don't you, that Kate's surrogate mother Francine is also trying to find out through Poppy where Kate is? She is trying to impress one of *them*."

"*Them?* You don't mean one of the Shadow Government's men? Are they getting interested again? We have to do something and soon." Master M thumped the desk. "We'd better get Adam over there. I'll talk to him and get him involved once more. He'll listen to me."

***

Next day Kate arrived home from work at the office and saw Jacob waiting for her on the doorstep. He put his arm around her waist and quickly drew her inside.

"I've something to tell you," he said. His eyes were shining. He was clearly excited.

Kate was taken by surprise over his enthusiasm. She hadn't seen him so animated for a long time. "Couldn't it have waited until I'd at least taken my coat off?" she laughed. "What's the rush?" He helped her off with her coat and threw it carelessly on a chair. Kate looked at him in astonishment. This was so unlike him and he always hung his coat up and expected her to do the same.

"Sechem has been here. I actually saw him with my own eyes. He's marvellous, and so colourful. I didn't know he was so tall. His blue tinged skin colour is amazing. I can hardly believe it. Here in our own living room as large as life."

Kate now understood his excitement for he'd only seen Sechem or the others as if in a mist in his altered state when he was on the spaceship. It simply wasn't as clear as in the flesh.

"What did he have to say? Why did he come?" Seeing the time traveller clearly was fast becoming a normal occurrence for Kate, but she knew Sechem never came to them just for the fun of it. He always had an agenda. Then she heard a rattle of cups in the kitchen.

"Who've you got with you, Dad? Someone's in the kitchen."

Jacob looked puzzled. "There's nobody here sweetheart."

They both went to investigate. To their great surprise they saw Sechem standing by the cupboard holding a full tray of mugs and grinning.

"I understand you always have tea and biscuits before you connect with us," he said. "That's the procedure, isn't it?" He put the tray down. "So, I'm a Nobody. Well I suppose that's right after all. No body." With that he let out a hearty laugh. Jacob and Kate stood there with their mouths open in amazement. They were rendered speechless. Kate recovered first.

"It's lovely to see you Sechem, but why? Why and how can my dad see you too?

"I'm not here as a hologram as before. Let's all settle down in the living room." Sechem picked up the tray again and urged them out of the kitchen. "Please sit. This may take a little time." He nodded to Jacob. It seemed to Kate to be a secret signal. What had they hatched up between them before she'd arrived home?

Jacob turned to Kate. "Please pour the tea. We've something to tell you." He looked around at Sechem. "Shall I go first?"

"It's better coming from you," Sechem replied and chuckled.

Jacob took a deep breath. "Remember I told you that you were conceived on Sirius through Joslene, and that Francine is just your surrogate mother?"

"Yes of course I remember. It's not something I can easily forget, is it? The fertilized egg was implanted in her. That explains why she doesn't like me."

Jacob sighed. "Yes, I remember her reaction when she found out she was pregnant. That hadn't been in her life plan for sure. I don't want to go into all that again. It still hurts that she rejected you so quickly." Jacob patted his daughter's hand.

"That wasn't the only implant that happened concerning you," he said. "I don't know how to tell you this." He hesitated.

Kate sat on the edge of her chair. Surely there couldn't be anything more surprising than what had already happened in her life? She poured the tea and passed the mugs around.

"Do go on," she urged. "Nothing you say can faze me now."

Jacob took another deep breath. "They told me that when you were still a developing embryo, and at the stage when your brain was developing, they inserted a miniscule implant inside the growing brain. It can't be removed in any way for the brain has grown around it."

"You're kidding me," Kate said, and gave a nervous laugh.

"No, I'm not. It's intended to be activated at a time when you can understand and manage the extra capabilities its activation brings. That time has come, my darling."

He smiled broadly and proudly as he watched his daughter's face to see if she understood. Kate was very quiet. It was a lot to take in. They both waited for her to say something. She looked from one to the other to see if they were joking. Surely this was a joke? Their serious faces said not.

"When? What does it mean?" she asked. "Haven't I done enough already?"

Sechem took up the task of replying. "They're going to activate the implant very soon my friend. They'll do it from Galactic headquarters. There's no time to waste, no time to lose. We can't hang about any more."

"What does it mean for me?" Kate got up from her chair and began to pace up and down the room. They looked at each other in consternation when they saw how agitated she was.

"Oh, do sit down, please." said Sechem. "Have another cup of tea."

"You sound more like my dad every minute," cried Kate in exasperation. "Tea indeed!" She sighed heavily. "Get on with it and tell me the worst."

Jacob caught hold of her hand and pulled her down onto the seat next to him. "Kate, remember our visit to the Galactic Council when they told us of the battle between the star races?" he said. "Some powerful races wish to dominate Earth humans, and others wish to continue with Earth's spiritual advancement."

"Yes, I remember, of course."

"Now that the balance has swung towards the positive side for humans, the opposition is pulling out all the stops to counteract the good that has been done. Haven't you noticed the increase in atrocities of all kinds across your globe?"

"Of course I have. Who hasn't? The media is full of it. It's horrible! What has that to do with the implant?"

Both Jacob and Sechem drew in close to Kate, as if to protect her. Jacob took her hands in his and looked at her intently. He squeezed her hands tight.

"The implant will give you special powers. You'll become more your true self."

Kate sharply pulled her hands out of his clasp. "I'm already my true self. How dare you say I am not?"

"No, you're not," broke in Sechem quickly. He saw the distress on both their faces. Jacob turned his head away.

Sechem turned back to Kate. "Your father can't tell you what you need to know before activation takes place. His role will be limited from now on. You'll often do your work without him. He'll be needed to assist you however."

Kate looked down at the floor and seemed glum, so Sechem continued, "How about we have a group session tomorrow evening? That way we can prepare, and maybe The Galactic Command Council will be able to explain better than me. The activation is set to start in a few days. You Kate, need more time to absorb what has been said."

Kate hoped one more day would be enough. It had to be.

CHAPTER SEVEN

ANOTHER COUNTRY

Master M was due to arrive on the Mothership very soon, which meant that officials there were scurrying around a great deal to get ready for him. Meetings of all kinds were generally held in several selected parts of the Mothership. The ship is effectively a self-contained environment where more than a thousand people of a wide variety of anatomically different human races live and work together. All that is needed to sustain life for these residents is produced on board.

Inside the ship are forests, meadows, and vast botanical gardens, as well as residential, recreational areas. Anyone arriving wouldn't be blamed for thinking they'd arrived in another country. The massive craft got the name 'Mothership' because of the role of 'berthing' a vast variety of space craft. Lights of different colours continually played around the outside, as well as inside. Nobody was idle on board. Many space travellers used the Motherships, often called Space Stations, or Way Stations, which would be a more accurate description for these enormous crafts. They weren't what one could consider to be innocuous. All space travellers regarded them as headquarters for other space craft and inter-dimensional movement between worlds.

As well as and apart from the moon, these enormous ships park in stationary gravitationally neutral nodes between planets. They could never ever land on a planet, for if they tried, both the land and the ship would be destroyed by gravity. Mother Ships come in a huge variety of sizes and shapes depending on the specifics of their roles. They are also inter-dimensional portals and as such, from the perspective of the beings that operate them, these platforms are beyond linear space and time and work closely with the Spiritually Ascended Masters.

During his journey to the meeting, Master M pondered on his decisions. He was aware that there was much monitoring of Jump Rooms and Looking Glass devices that were being operated on Earth. This, together with new technology, took human beings to other realms, other times and other places. This could be regarded as good or otherwise. It all depended on who operated them. As well as the beneficial service offered to others by spiritually advanced beings, some self-serving space travellers were also using Way Stations, along with aggressive star species. Their objective was to invade and take over vulnerable and desirable planets. It was these that The Spiritual Galactic Command objected to. They had to be stopped.

Master M's ship docked and entered the larger craft. A respectful line of space travellers of many species bowed their heads before him as he was escorted along a corridor to the special area set aside for spiritual matters. This area was bathed in a soft glow, and calming music could be heard in the background. A variety of peaceful scenes around the walls constantly changed. As a full member of The Spiritual Galactic Command Council, Master M had requested that all benevolent space stations held their meetings in a similar ambience. This was deemed to be essential, and this was where the strategic level debates took place and executive decisions were made.

One such debate was about to start right now. Master M had a special and personal interest in the discussion. Both Jamére and Sechem were present. They were seated so that they could see Master M clearly as he entered and took his place at the head of the table. A respectful hush fell across the room and all eyes turned in his direction.

"I'm sure you are all delighted with the upward swing to a more spiritually positive timeline for the human races on Earth," he said. A murmur of agreement swept through the mixed gathering.

"However, we mustn't sit back and relax our efforts. The dark forces are fighting back. We must do our best to work with those living as humans down there. The future of the human race even can now go either way. So many are still complacent or have given up the fight. They think it's impossible to rectify the ills that are being perpetrated."

Jamére raised his hand and stood up to speak. "We are ready to go and work our magic."

Master M frowned. "You know very well Jamére that change has to be made by the inhabitants on Earth. You can assist, you can direct, but only they can make a difference. We've arranged for your charge, Kate, and her father, Jacob to be involved once more." Master M smiled at Jamére's enthusiasm and waved him to sit again.

"What about Adam? Can he be brought in too?" Sechem chimed in. Kate was his personal charge and he felt he had to look after her interests. "They still have enemies who are closing in on them." Master M held up his hand to silence him.

"This is exactly why we're fully activating her as one of our own, who is incarnated there. Kate's to be totally awakened."

A gasp of surprise went up. "What exactly will that mean for her? We're not clear about this." Jamére asked.

"That will become clear to you when she has her next journey. So far her mind trips have been random and haphazard. In future, they'll occur whenever a need arises. This may or may not be directed by us. Her own mindset will have an effect on what happens and where she may go. It may take her by surprise, so she could be unprepared for her first trip. She won't need to meditate beforehand. It can happen at any point, before she's a chance to settle her mind. It could at times be most inconvenient. To get her ready we'll only direct her next meditation. After that it's up to her to get involved or not. That way it means we'll not influence her choices."

"What about our role with her then?" Jamére and Sechem spoke together.

"Since you've both had Earth incarnations you may be regarded as past citizens of the planet, and therefore have a right to interfere or influence her."

"And Adam?" they both queried at the same time.

"I've already said that's being dealt with." Master M rose from his seat. That was the sign that the meeting was over. They all silently filed out of the chamber.

***

Adam worked quietly at his desk in his private office several floors below the building on Capitol Hill. It was a modest affair with a solid desk and brown leather swivel chair. Without getting up he could swing around to two computers and a printer behind him on another counter. He had no photos on his desk, but pictures of the stars adorned the walls. In one corner of the room a small television screen was on the wall.

He felt a tap on his shoulder. It was so light he almost missed it. What really alerted him was the intense cold that came with the touch. He recognised that energy immediately. He swung his chair around. Standing and filling the room was the magnificent figure of Master M. The colours and light, as usual almost overwhelmed him. The Master was so tall Adam had to crane his neck up to see the whole of him.

"Glad to see you're working hard," the bird man from Sirius said.

"It's so good to see you." Adam smiled broadly and nearly got up to dance a jig. He hoped Master M's presence was in response to his heartfelt but unspoken need to see Kate.

"That's right son." Master M said picking up Adam's thought. "We want you to go to England and reconnect with her. Are you sure you can arrange that, without causing suspicion?"

"No problem." Adam screwed up his face. "There must be a specific reason for you to come down to see me in person, and not send someone else. What's up?"

"Her implant is to be activated. This could cause a lot of adjustment to her understanding about who she is. She'll need you and Jacob to be there when she has her first experience of this. It could be too much for her to handle alone."

Adam brightened. He knew all about the implant and was almost envious of what it could do. But if anybody could handle it she could. He could hardly wait to see her again. Master M decided it was all in hand and left as silently as he came. The seed had been sown, it was now up to Adam.

Adam picked up the phone and pushed a few buttons. "Colonel Fenshawe here, sir. Something important has come up. I'm afraid I'll have to attend to it straight away."

"Where are you off to this time? You seem to go away quite a lot." Adam sensed the Brigadier General was suspicious. He had been behaving himself recently, but his past attendance had been less than satisfactory. He'd failed to adequately account for his absence each time he went away. He knew they'd be watching him more closely from now on. There were too many secrets to keep safe. They might consider him to be the next whistle-blower and could put a watch on him.

"What is it this time?" The Brigadier General asked.

"One of our field men has gone missing," Adam lied. "You know I am not authorised to tell you more than that, sir."

"Go if you must but fill in a form and keep us informed." What Adam didn't know was that after the Brigadier put the phone down he dialled another number.

***

Kate sat by the open window and tried to read a book, to take her mind off what Sechem had told her. What did the activation of the implant actually mean, and why wouldn't they tell her what could happen? Jacob came into the room and walked softly over to her.

"Darling, you look so worried. You know they wouldn't ask you to do anything that would harm you, don't you?"

Just as that moment the doorbell rang. Kate leapt up from her seat and went to answer it. She opened the door and saw a young man with cropped hair standing on the doorstep. He smiled warmly but seemed to be taken aback when he saw her. Kate wondered why he should look so surprised, but she hadn't missed his appraising glance at her slim figure. Slightly embarrassed, she brushed her fair hair back from her face. She was glad she'd decided to put on her makeup that morning.

"Yes?" she asked.

"Excuse me ma'am. You've left your car lights on. Did you know? I thought I ought to tell you or you'll have a flat battery." He smiled again and turned to leave.

"Thank you for letting me know," Kate said quickly. She didn't want him to go till she found out who he was. "I haven't seen you around, and we see most people in this lane." She wanted to know more about the good looking, dark haired newcomer.

"I'm new to the area and I was just wandering around to get my bearings when I saw your car with its lights on. I've just been reposted from America to AWE (Atomic Weapons Establishment) in Aldermaston. I moved in earlier this week. It should be an interesting post." He put out his hand to shake hers. Kate liked the warm feel of his hands.

"I'm Howard, but all my friends call me Howie. Nice to meet you, ma'am." He turned to go.

"I'm Kate. Call me Kate." She didn't want him to leave, so she said. "Come in and meet my dad. He can fill you in about what's going on in this area, since you're new to it."

Kate stood aside to let him pass. He went inside, thoroughly wiping his feet on the door mat as he stepped in. Jacob stood up to meet Howie as he walked into the front room. They shook hands.

"I'll go and turn the lights off in the car. I won't be a minute," Kate picked her car keys off the hall table and left them to introduce each other. When she returned Howie was in the entrance ready to leave.

"Nice to meet you Kate. Have a good day." He touched his temple which reminded her of a salute and walked away down the lane.

Kate turned to her father. "What have you said to him, dad to make him leave so soon?"

"Nothing, nothing at all. Seems a nice young man. He likes you though.

I'd be careful if I were you. He works at Aldermaston you know. Kate, it was no coincidence that we were brought to live here. Surely, you've realised that? You know the interest our space friends have in all things nuclear. Perhaps this young man was sent to spy on us."

"You're getting paranoid."

"What if he turns up unexpectedly when we're visited by Sechem or Jamére? What if he comes around and knocks on the door when you have your journeys?"

"We have a bell now, dad. Remember?

Jacob grunted.

"What if? What if? - Do you mean I can't have friends now? I do have a life." Kate was indignant, and more than a little annoyed by her father's reaction. She stormed off to the kitchen.

"Of course you can, but he's clearly more than interested in you." Jacob called out to her. "He'll be visiting again; you mark my words."

Kate wasn't at all sure what she wanted. She missed Adam, but if he wasn't going to be around, at least she could have male company, apart from her father. Surely there was no harm in that. Howie had a nice clean look about him. She liked his wide brown eyes and round open face. Surely there could be no harm in him.

CHAPTER EIGHT

ADAM ARRIVES FOR IMPLANT ACTIVATION

Adam landed at Heathrow and booked a room at his favourite accommodation. The Broomsquire Hotel off Silchester Road suited him just fine. It had the most wonderful double, four poster bed, and in winter had hog roasts in front of a roaring fire. It was old England for him and he loved it. Best of all it was only 10 minutes' brisk walk from Aldermaston and close enough to Pinks Lane in Tadley where Kate and her father lived.

He hoped he'd be in time for the opening of the implant. He knew what the activation meant but also knew that not everybody could handle something like that. She would find herself entering other times, other places and situations. He needed to get to Kate before she had her first experience with the implant working. The weekend was coming up fast and that was when it would happen. He decided he had to be there when she got home from work and set off for the house.

Jacob opened the door and his eyes lit up with pleasure. "Adam, my boy. How wonderful to see you. Come in, come in. Kate's at work you know. But she won't be long now. She leaves earlier on a Friday. She'll be so pleased to see you. She'll also want to know why you haven't been in touch."

Adam sighed. "I know I haven't been connecting with you, but as you know my calls are monitored even more these days. I was afraid they'd find you through them. How is she?"

It was Jacob's turn to sigh. "She's not as happy as she could be. She's probably missing you. Isn't there anything you could do about that? It is not an ideal situation with her here and you so often in Washington DC."

"For as long as she is doing her journeys we ought to stay apart to keep her safe." Adam said. "That is the reality of it."

They heard the front door opening. They both put their fingers to their mouths in a zip it up motion. Kate walked in and found them apparently just chatting in comfort like old buddies.

Her delight was beyond expression. "You? Is it really you? I can't believe it. I thought I'd never see you again." To his surprise Kate started to cry. Adam took her in his arms and held her tight.

"Well I'm here now darling. Dry your tears." Adam sat her down. "Now let's have a good look at you."

Kate said through her tears, "Is that so you can remember me till the next time you care to visit?"

"Now don't be like that Kate. I come when I can. I'm here now because I heard from Master M that you are to be activated. I need to be here with you for your first time."

"So, I was right. You're only interested in the things I do, and what it may mean." Kate turned away from him. It was time for Jacob to step in.

"Kate be fair. You know he can't always do what he wants. Give him a break. He loves you. You know that. It's because he loves you and cares for you that he's here to support you in your next step into the unknown."

Kate pulled a long face and then despite herself gave a lopsided grin. "Let's get on with it then."

Adam knew Kate wanted to believe him. Whatever feelings she may or may not have for him she had no choice but to take her next step, whatever that might be.

"We'll do it tonight," she said, with more confidence than she felt. "But let's eat first. You know my journeys take a lot of energy from me."

They prepared a meal together and sat down to eat. Hardly a word was spoken throughout. Adam saw that thoughts were racing around their heads. What was going to happen this evening?

"The time is now." Adam said suddenly in such an urgent tone that both Jacob and Kate looked up immediately.

Kate wasn't so sure. "I don't feel any different," she said. "I'm not ready. What if nothing happens?" Adam who'd experienced a little of what she might feel later, knew it wasn't going to be the way she expected.

"What I mean Kate is that first you will need to put yourself into deep meditation. The time to do that is right now. Do it as you usually would. It is then that you'll discover something." Kate looked doubtful. Adam saw her face. "Kate, it's going to be different each time. This is just for starters."

"Have you done these? I mean you personally?"

Adam wasn't sure if he should tell her some of what he'd gone through or leave it to her to experience without any preconceived ideas. No, he wouldn't tell her. He knew she had to do it, and that the time had come. But he did not have the same implant that she had.

He hesitated before speaking and lied. "Yes, I've done it many times. How do you think I got to you whenever there was a need for me to be here?" Adam realised too late he'd already said too much. "Enough of this shilly-shallying Kate. All these questions won't delay the inevitable. This is what you are here for. It's been in the planning since before you were born."

Kate stared at him, unbelieving. "You mean, all that we went through with Helga, the kidnapping, and having to escape? You knew all that before it happened?"

"Yes. How do you think I was able to arrange the escape and your relocation so fast? We had it all planned beforehand. But enough questions for now. We're used to your delaying tactics. Questions, questions, questions." It was about to begin.

Already Adam felt the energies were changing around her. Something was happening in the room. Something he couldn't stop. Solid objects close to her began to lose form and were wavering in front of his eyes.

Kate turned to Jacob. "Dad," she said grabbing his arm. "Stay with me. Don't leave me. I need you as my anchor to make sure I come back. I'm scared."

Jacob took her hand and squeezed it hard. His daughter had been born on Earth to carry out not one task, but many during her life span. Adam saw that with or without meditation, the process had started. He also knew that telling her to use her usual stairs procedure was just to reassure her, and for no other reason. It was simply to get her mentally over the first hurdle. One didn't go into this kind of thing lightly; a certain amount of training was required. Nothing major would be presented during her initial journey. That would come later.

They all heard a sound, a clicking sound. Without any warning, the television set turned on all by itself. Everybody swung around to face it. There was no clear picture, just a fuzzy zigzag. A buzzing noise was coming from the screen. Adam remembered when Kate told him of the first time Sechem had made himself visible through the set. Was this what was happening now? All three stared at the screen, waiting and holding their breath for what it might mean. Static electricity crackled and could be felt throughout the room.

***

The screen cleared and soon they all saw Sechem surrounded by a blue haze. His eyes twinkled. He seemed about to burst into laughter. He was clearly amused at the tension in their faces.

"It is not going to be all that bad, Kate," he said reassuring her. "May I come in?" Without waiting for an answer, he stepped smoothly from the screen and stood before them.

Kate recovered first. She'd seen him do this before. "I thought it was only Jamére who did the tricks," she said. "Why can't you arrive like everybody else?"

"Now where would be the fun in that my darling girl? I don't want to be boring."

"You'll never be that," Jacob moved from his seat at the table and dropped heavily into the nearest armchair. Sechem saw it was getting all too much for him.

Jacob looked worried: What on earth would come next and could his heart stand it?

"Oh, my friend Jacob, your heart is as strong as an ox," Sechem said.

"You read my thoughts too? Oh dear!" Jacob covered his eyes with his hands.

"Oh, don't be so dramatic. My goodness, you should all ease up and relax. I'm here to explain everything to you so you do not take on so. I won't allow Kate to go while she's so stressed. Trust me!"

"I hate it when people say trust me," said Kate.

"I am *not* people," declared Sechem.

"You could say that again," Adam grunted.

"Again? Oh well if you wish. I am *not* people. Now let me get on with the job in hand." Sechem did a little twirl which made them laugh. "Are you listening? Are you sitting comfortably?" he asked.

"Yes, we are," they said in unison and laughed. His strategy to lighten things had worked.

"To begin with Kate, you will put yourself into deep relaxation. I will, or Jamére will, depending on who is directing, tell your mind where you must go, what time base and who you might need to be at that time. You'll hear us either audibly or telepathically."

"What do you mean by 'Who I might be'? Won't I always be myself?"

"You might appear holographically as something other than yourself in order to do what is needed, or to protect yourself. We often use holographic projections when it is felt to be necessary. You'll feel very real and solid, but you will not be. Nothing can hurt you. The sensation of being physical is so strong that you'll forget you're not real, but your mind may manifest what you fear and make that real." Sechem peered at Adam, searching his face for doubts.

"Adam, remember the mind manifestation with the Montauk Chair?"

"Now you're scaring me." Adam shivered.

"Kate, you'll be monitored the whole way. Jacob and Adam will be watching through the Looking Glass. In an emergency, they can call you back."

"The Looking Glass? Emergency?" It was Jacob's turn to be alarmed.

Sechem looked from one to the other. He smiled. "Haven't you realised yet that this is where Kate's implant comes in? It allows her to change into whatever's required in any given situation. To explain further, think of an octopus or chameleon."

"A chameleon, octopus?" the two men echoed and looked puzzled.

"Yes. They don't have to think about changing to protect themselves. It just happens naturally. That is how it will be with Kate. The difference will be that she may automatically revert to her true self, her soul origin. She won't have control over that." Sechem stared at the men and hoped they'd grasped what he'd said. "Now *that* would be something, wouldn't it?"

Adam breathed deeply and looked worried. "I've time travelled but had no implant and can't transform myself. This *is* different." He frowned. "The implant allows her to be like an octopus or chameleon, and change? I don't believe it."

Sechem sighed, exasperated. "Think holographic. Nothing's real, except what you think is real. For Kate it will be reality, and for you watching it'll be real too. Can you handle it? I don't want you to panic. What she'll do is real and will have a definite effect on the situation she'll be in. That too will seem authentic. She'll make vital changes that will have great benefit to mankind."

"What is this Looking Glass thing you spoke of?" Jacob asked and looked anxious.

"You can view what's happening in the time that it happens. It may be the future or the past. You cannot interfere, unless there's an emergency."

"There's that word emergency again." It was Adam's turn to look alarmed. "Where are you going to send her for heaven's sake?"

Sechem realised it was going to be hard work to make them feel easy about what was going to happen, with or without them watching Kate. His colour turned a deep indigo blue and his energy field grew wider until it encompassed them all. He did another twirl, but this time they didn't laugh. Throughout their conversation Kate had remained silent.

"What have you to say about all this Kate?" Jacob looked tense as he asked.

"You're all discussing what I'll do and how and so on as if I'm not here. It seems I should have a say in this."

Adam nodded. "Go on my darling." He put his arm around her as if to protect her.

Kate's eyes sparkled. "If *they* have gone to all the trouble to put an implant into me, for a purpose only they know, then I have to trust that whatever I do is for the best. I'm aware that if change is going to come about on this Earth, then only the citizens of the earth can make the changes needed. I'm a citizen and a human being. So, I've the right, and have been given the capacity to do what's necessary. As an evolving soul, I can't turn away from this. I trust Master M and the Spiritual Galactic Council who've orchestrated this. What can hurt me? Nothing."

Sechem breathed a sigh of relief. "Wise words my dear friend." He turned to the two men. "Your purpose is to see into the Looking Glass so that you can later relate back to her some of what happens during her journey. She may only have a vague memory when she returns. Rest assured they'll start with something easy and simple."

"Thank goodness for that," exclaimed Kate. Sechem realised that she wasn't as confident as she tried to portray for the sake of her two favourite men. She turned to Sechem.

"How will it start and how will I feel?"

"Each time, once you are in a deeper state, we'll give you instructions as to the time and place, without any advance warning. If we tell you beforehand you would think about it, pre-plan, and all that thinking would change the outcome. You'll become whatever you're required to be. You could even be seen as an angel with wings."

"Wow!" said Adam and Jacob together.

"How will I feel?" she repeated, insisting on an answer.

"That depends on whether you use the elevator or spiral tunnel. I don't know yet which one they'll give you to use. Technology is improving very rapidly, and I am not as up to date as I could be. You might feel as if you are being suspended in mid-air, travelling very rapidly, or not moving at all, depending on your perspective. You'll feel an electrical discharge and your fine hair might stand up on end."

"Who's deciding which device I shall use? Who's deciding where I should go and what I shall do?"

"The Spiritual Galactic Command." It was a definite, no hesitation response from Sechem. "They are the ones who wish that the Human Race lifts itself to a greater awareness and eliminate the darkness that still exists on Earth." Absolute silence greeted this declaration. "It will be so," he added.

CHAPTER NINE

THE NET TIGHTENS

The men in black were making enquiries. The net was drawing in on Kate. Two dark suited men wearing dark glasses knocked on the front door of Kate's friend Poppy. The sun was scorching hot. Anybody else would have felt most uncomfortable in such dark suits, but these men seemed quite cool and composed. Some of this composure evaporated as they continued to knock. It brought nobody to the door. One of the men motioned to the other to go around to the back of the house. Not a word was spoken.

One man went out of sight as he worked his way round the building and pushed between the hedges to get to the back garden. What he didn't expect was furious barking that greeted his arrival. Several dogs rushed at him, nearly knocking him over. He panicked and tried to kick them out of the way.

A plump little woman emerged from the undergrowth at the back of the garden, running towards him and waving her arms. "What's going on here? Leave my dogs alone," she shouted. Brandishing a stout stick, she stormed at him. The man put his hands up to defend himself from the furious onslaught.

"Call them off," he yelled frantically and tried to pull his trouser legs free from the yapping dogs' attention.

"You're on their territory, uninvited. What else did you expect? Who are you, and what do you want in my garden?" Poppy was short, but she made up for it in defence of her canine children. No-one was allowed to kick her friends. "Heel, come here," she called to them. They backed off but kept up the snarling.

"We did knock," he said, now free of the dogs. He eyed them warily.

"What do you mean *we*? Are there more of you?"

"There are only two of us. We simply want some information about a friend of yours." Poppy wasn't reassured. She was nobody's fool. She didn't like the look of him and, for her, first impressions meant everything.

"Go back to the front door. I'll see you there." She held tight on the collar of the largest dog Boris but allowed him to lunge forward to make her point. The colour drained from the man's frightened face as the large dog came closer and he backed away and ran back to the front as he was told. This wasn't what he'd expected when he was given his orders.

His colleague was waiting patiently on the front door step. He couldn't stop a smirk spreading across his face as his partner appeared at an undignified run from around the corner of the house. He'd never ever seen him so hot and bothered before. He hid a grin behind his hand.

"We have to wait for her to open the front door," the man said. He wiped the sweat off his brow with the back of a shaky hand. A few moments later the door opened. Poppy emerged. Both men's faces dropped when they saw she had her hand tightly clasped onto the collar of an enormous dog. Its lips were drawn back in a snarl. One wrong move could be very painful.

"Yes?" she said. "Now tell me who you are, and what you want with me?"

This reaction wasn't what they expected. Most people were intimidated by their dark glasses, flash car and smart suits. The glasses were meant to hide their expressions so that people couldn't read what was really going on in their heads. This short-rounded lady was something else, and definitely wasn't intimidated by them. The two men stood there with mouths open. This was not going according to plan.

"Well? Cat got your tongues?"

The hot perspiring one put his hand up to wipe his sweating brow again. In so doing he knocked his glasses off. They fell to the ground. As he bent to pick them up his eyes met those of the dog. Nobody had told him there would be dogs. He'd hated and feared dogs all his life. The cool and composed one decided to take a hand. *He* wasn't afraid of dogs, not him, not at all.

"Ma'am, we're here to enquire about a certain friend of yours. She may be in trouble. Her name is Kate Greene, and we've been trying to locate her." *He* still had his dark glasses on.

He noted suspicion register on the woman's face.

"Kate? What is she to you? You still haven't said who you are." He wasn't used to having questions put to him. He was the one who asked the questions. He had his patter all in place. She certainly wasn't following his script.

"We represent her lawyer. He has some good news for her. She's come into some money from a deceased aunt. However, since we can't locate her, the money may go to The State." He smiled showing a row of perfect teeth. It was the wrong patter. He hadn't thought this one through or done his research. Any friend of this formidable woman would know that Kate Greene had no aunt.

"That's a pack of lies. Get out of here before I call the police," Poppy said as she allowed her dog to lunge forward.

It was too late to change their story. They left in a hurry. What were they going to say to their superiors after failing to get any information whatsoever? They wouldn't be pleased.

***

Poppy had a lot to think about too as she sat in her kitchen sipping her coffee. She was well used to being in control of her life. She knew her decision not to get further involved with whatever it was that Kate was into was the right one. Other worlds, beings from space was a stretch too far for her. She knew exactly where she was with her dogs. She put her hand down to stroke her favourite, Boris, a large wolfhound. But the visit, by what she thought of as 'men in black', had unnerved her more than she cared to admit. Where was Kate? What had she got into that brought such awful people to her door? Poppy was used to getting Kate out of scraps when they were at school together, but this was something very different indeed. If Kate was having a problem, it was one that was not going to go away.

Next day it was again burning hot and sunny, unusual for England. Perhaps global warming was for real after all. What if they were right, and was it man made or just a cycle that Earth was going through, as it had done before? Was it only Earth or the whole solar system? Experts should know the answer, but they too disagreed with each other. Kate would know the answer to that. Poppy realised how much she missed their chats together.

She remembered when Adam had first come on the scene. Kate had been immediately besotted with him and their own friendship had not been the same since. She'd gone deeper and deeper into the space thing and further away from her. She missed Kate and sighed.

She took the leads down from the hook by the back door and took the dogs for a long walk across the fields, so she could think. She walked and walked over her land and after an hour she eventually brought them home. They ran ahead of her as she drew near the house.

Standing on her doorstep tapping her foot in impatience was a lady she'd never seen before. But she knew straight away who it was. Kate had described her enemy and old boss so many times. Skeleton thin and with a steel trap face, it had to be Helga. How on earth did she find her?

She approached this dreadful woman with caution in every step. The dogs quietly growled or snarled, depending on their temperament. Poppy trusted their judgement. The contrast between the two women was almost comical.

One short with well-rounded body, rosy cheeks and merry smile, and the other a gaunt, grey creature with piercing eyes who could send children running after just one look.

"Can I help you?" Poppy opened the conversation with reluctance.

Helga coldly eyed her up and down before replying. "I understand you're a friend of Kate Greene." Poppy merely nodded. "I'm her previous employer and she's due some remuneration of salary. We do not have her present address or whereabouts. I was hoping you could help?"

It was Poppy's turn to deliberately and openly eye Helga up and down. "You surprise me madam that a boss should take it on herself to search for an employee of low status. Is that usual?"

Poppy saw Helga's face go blank at the question and realised she was used to asking questions, not responding to them.

Helga force a smile. "We take a personal interest in all our employees," she said. This did not fool the tubby woman in front of her. Then Helga noticed the dogs and her smile slipped just for a second.

"I understand others have asked you about her. I had to laugh when I was told. Men are fools, aren't they?" she said, in an attempt to be friendly. It didn't work.

It was Poppy's turn to go on the attack. She recognised an adversary when she saw one. She saw one in Helga for sure. "How did you find me and how did you know I was Kate's friend? I'm sure she never discussed me at work. You were hardly on chatting terms. I know *that* much about you."

Poppy realised she'd wrong-footed Helga who quickly recovered.

"You were not hard to find. We learnt that Kate gave talks. All we had to do was to ask at possible venues for names of organisers who'd booked the venues. They *all* complied with our requests."

I'll bet they did Poppy thought. They would say anything when confronted by scary men in black, and she'd already put two and two together.

"I am sorry to disappoint you, madam. But I have absolutely no idea where Kate is, none at all. I'm surprised that any firm would go to such lengths just to give back some salary. What's really going on here? Is she in any sort of trouble?"

Helga's mouth set in a hard line. "We are not at liberty to disclose information about our employees, past or present. It's clear you know nothing about your so-called friend. Helga turned on her heel and prepared to leave. "I'll not disturb you any longer. I'll have to find another way to reach her." She trotted off in ridiculously high heels down the drive to her waiting chauffeured Mercedes.

CHAPTER TEN

HOWIE IS IN LOVE

Howie couldn't get the young woman Kate out of his mind. There was something different about her for sure. But then he knew there would be, given the importance his superiors put on finding her. But he wasn't prepared for the effect that seeing her had on him. It was a pure stroke of luck that he'd been able to knock on the very door where she lived and make an initial contact that way. He saw it as a sign.

His bosses had arranged his posting to AWE (Atomic Weapons Establishment) on the hunch that she'd re-locate to any area where there was a nuclear base, and they were right. They'd noticed that many UFO sightings were near or over nuclear establishments. There weren't that many in the UK and the hunch had paid off. They'd shown him her picture so that he would recognise her if he struck lucky. Boy, had he 'struck lucky'!

"Find her and report back," The officer said at the briefing. He was just one of many men attending the session in Dulce, Colorado, New Mexico. Her photograph had been distributed around the group of men chosen to search for Kate Greene. Gork had commanded that she be found. "She has to be stopped before she noses into our business and changes too many of our plans."

Howard, Howie to his friends, didn't know why she had to be found, but an order was an order. His job was to obey and not question why. His mind went back to the briefing a week or so before.

Silas was holding forth. "This is in the interests of national security," he said. "The order to find Kate Greene comes from the highest ranking, so it's clearly of vital importance. Each of you will disperse around England; for we do not believe she or her father have left the country." He paused and scrutinized the faces of the men. There was no need to tell them of the small spacecraft that earlier in Scotland had saved both Kate and her father from capture.

"You have been given placements mainly in the south of England where she and her father are suspected to be living."

Howie didn't like the look of Silas, but who was he to judge others. He just had to do his job and not question. He watched as Silas gathered his papers together and who glared at them all with contempt before he strutted from the room. Howie filed out with the other men and went to the office to pick up his papers. He'd always wanted to go to England. It seemed to be an easy posting, but he was going to be a long way from his home town of Houston, Texas.

The flight to England was long and tedious, but a day or two later he settled in to his rented accommodation in Baughurst in the county of Hampshire, and his new job. This posting would last only as long as it took to locate Kate. He rather hoped it would take a long time, which would give him a chance to explore England and its famous pubs.

AWE's Aldermaston site covered approximately 750 acres and was engaged in the defence and security of the nation. It wasn't at all what he expected, but his specialised nuclear knowledge put him at ease with colleagues in the establishment. He realised his nuclear 'know how' was why he was chosen for this assignment. He'd fit in and nobody would question his position there. Through the various conversations at the centre he quickly learnt that the continued future of the facility was not at all certain. The public were getting very wary of how the base was being used as storage for American nuclear weapons. The people didn't like this at all and protests were being organised.

Finding Kate so quickly was a bonus. He hadn't known what to expect. He had in his mind what he thought a spy ought to look like and what he saw when he met Kate didn't match up in any way. Her slim figure, fair hair and open, honest blue eyes took him by surprise, even though he had her photograph securely in his papers. Most of all it was her warm smile that enchanted him. As if his bosses knew what he was thinking his mobile buzzed, demanding attention.

"Howard, what have you discovered? We know you haven't been there long, but have you got any leads yet? We are drawing blanks with the others so far."

Howie hesitated. It was too soon. They wouldn't expect anything from him this early. Something held him back as a vision of her face came into his mind.

"Nothing yet, sir," he lied. But an order was an order and he couldn't hold off indefinitely. The trouble was he just couldn't see her as a threat to his country. First, he would find a way to get to know her better. He'd keep an eye on her.

"I'll keep making enquiries. Something will turn up, sir." He ended the call. He'd just disobeyed an order for the first time ever in his service.

A few days later Howie saw the notice pinned on the board as he went for his lunch in the work's canteen. It screamed at him like a neon sign. DANCE THIS SATURDAY at Heath End Village Hall. He quickly took a note of time and place. This could be the opening he'd been looking for. He'd found an excuse to see Kate again. He could decide for himself if she was indeed a threat to national security, as they'd said.

That evening he prepared to go around to her house and ask if she would go with him to the dance. He dressed hoping to impress. Surely, she'd like his freshly cut hair. He sensed she wouldn't like untidy or sloppy dressing. He changed his shirt many times before deciding on the right one. He felt like a schoolboy asking out his first date.

When he arrived, her car was in the drive. Her car lights were off this time. He cursed aloud when he saw two more cars. One of them could be her father's who he knew lived with her, but the other one? There was nothing for it. He had to bite the bullet.

He ran his fingers over his short hair, put his shoulders back and knocked on her door. It took a little while before he heard someone coming. As the door opened Howie's jaw dropped in dismay. Standing before him was a tall, smiling man. He hadn't expected to see a fully uniformed American colonel. Instinctively Howie saluted. Thoughts were racing through his mind, none of them reassuring. The young colonel was speaking.

"No need for that young man. I'm not on duty. I've only just arrived, and I haven't had time to change."

Howie realised that the good-looking officer was as surprised as he was at his appearance on the doorstep.

"I thought you were someone else," he was saying.

Howie wondered who he was expecting. It couldn't be Kate since her car was already in the driveway. Howie was quite a bit shorter than Adam and had to look up at him.

"I was hoping to see Kate," he said, hesitating. "Is she in?" Howie realised the salute had given him away as a military man and cursed inwardly. Had he blown his cover?

"I'm sorry. She's not back from work yet. Can I give her a message?"

"But her car is here," Howie objected. Was she unwilling to see him? After all they'd only met once.

"She often walks to work," explained Adam. "Who shall I say called?"

Howie's head was full of questions. He was disappointed. Was this handsome officer her partner? Was he living with her? He obviously had a key to her home. But then he reasoned with himself. If they were married, an officer of his rank would live in a much better house than this, and she'd probably not be working. No, he decided they weren't married. But he seemed to know a lot about her movements. An awful thought struck him. Perhaps she was a spy after all and she gets information through tying up with him, a military man. He ought to report back. He'd found her out after all.

"No, no message," he mumbled and turned away and went back down the path, his shoulders drooping. Adam closed the door on the young man.

***

Half an hour after Howie's visit, from the window Adam saw Kate swinging jauntily along the lane towards the house. Her fair hair was lifted by the wind. It seemed she'd had a good day at work and was happy with the way things were going. He was happy too. He was back with her. She'd had two exciting journeys already. So, the plan was working. What troubled him was that he still had to play the role of colonel. He always had to report back to base so that his bosses wouldn't get suspicious. It was getting harder to avoid the tails he guessed could be put on his movements. He knew the General was doubting him but dared not probe too openly since he also knew Adam was on a special secret service mission. This was his second visit to Kate since the watch on him had been intensified.

Kate saw him as he opened the door for her. Delight climbed her face as she rushed up the path and into his arms. He pulled her inside and shut the door. There was no need to fuel gossip among any neighbours who might be watching. He was aware his big black Mercedes had already caused a stir.

"Where's dad?" she asked, getting her breath back following his kisses.

"He's in the back garden."

"This is a lovely surprise Adam, but it would be great if we could have some advance notice." She grinned. "Then we could arrange some alone time."

Adam stroked her hair. She always knew what he was thinking. Thoughts were not enough for him anymore. Would they ever have proper time alone? He doubted it. As if to prove a point Jacob walked in at that moment and they drew apart.

"Ah my darling girl. You're back. Great to see Adam, isn't it? In full uniform too. Very impressive, but it doesn't do much for being unnoticeable."

Adam groaned. "I was just explaining that to a young man who called. You were in the garden Jacob or I wouldn't have answered the door. You should have seen his face. He even saluted me." Jacob and Kate exchanged concerned looks.

"I came straight here in a rush Kate; I haven't had time to change yet."

"Young man? What young man? Who was he?" Jacob asked, immediately on the alert? His second sight flared into action. Something wasn't right.

"Calm down, Dad. It was probably the man who told me my car lights were left on. He was quite nice." She smiled remembering his face. "He's harmless."

"Nobody just passes by in this lane unless they live here. It's almost a dead end. He must have had a reason to pass, or live here." Jacob's suspicions were still on red alert.

"You're getting paranoid, Dad. It isn't like it was in Dorset with bugs hidden in phones and everything. They don't know we're here and we are in no danger. I've an ordinary respectable job and we are living respectable lives, as far as anyone knows. Stop worrying."

Adam's brow furrowed. "He's right Kate. They picked up on you before, remember."

"But that was Helga's doing," Kate objected.

Jacob frowned. "Coming here in uniform doesn't help Adam. I'm not easy about this."

Kate looked from one to the other. "It's time to put a stop to all this unnecessary worry. What are you here for this time Adam? We know enough by now not to expect that your visit is just to see us. It's not simply a social visit, is it?"

Adam knew that what she said was correct. Kate was about to take yet another leap into the unknown. He had to be there for her. Where would it take her this time? Kate would only know when she got there.

***

Sechem saw to it that preparations were in hand in the little house in Pinks Lane for Kate's next journey into the unknown. Lights were turned low in the front room and the cushions were plumped up on the sofa and chairs. Just one solitary table lamp cast soft shadows over the furniture and walls. Everybody in the room was nervous, for this was the first real test for Kate. Would the implant work after so many years of non-use? Nobody knew for sure. It was after all an experiment in time and space.

They'd all had a good meal beforehand to give them energy. Adam and Jacob sat a little further back, facing a blank wall. Kate sat too, but alone, right up close and facing the same wall. She'd chosen a comfortable chair where she could truly relax and go deep into herself.

She quickly went into trance. Jacob and Adam watched anxiously as the wall before her began to shimmer. This grabbed their attention to such an extent that they failed to notice that Kate's body was becoming misty... a shadow sitting in the chair. The shadow seemed to smile briefly, then it rose up and walked into the wall. Kate was through it into another world.

Jacob held his breath and sneaked a quick look at the now empty chair, and back at the figure moving towards a strange tunnel world mirrored in the wall. He gingerly extended his hand towards it, expecting it to pass through easily, but his hand met a hard surface. He resigned himself to being only an onlooker. Together they continued to watch Kate carry out her mission.

Sechem began his instruction. "Kate, listen carefully to me. You're to enter the tunnel. It'll be on some other world, maybe yours. Just report back to me. We're not sending you for your first effort to a dangerous, strange world. If you try to enter a world that's not sufficiently compatible with your own physiology, for you to breathe and survive, an alarm will be activated. That'll be enough to deter you from making the trip. You can still force your way through, or even be forced through by other things. If that does happen, resist else you could go somewhere that might immediately kill you. Do *not* go anywhere where you feel you are forced to go. I'll be with you all the way. Report to me as you go. This is a training run remember. Good luck."

They all heard Kate say. "Thanks for the warning. I can hear a hum. I am going through some sort of a whirling tunnel. It's spinning fast. There's a fairly loud humming sound all around me."

Sechem asked, "Are you off the ground, or do you feel as if you are still standing on something solid as you go through?"

"I'm being magnetically levitated. I'm suspended in mid-air, in the tunnel. I'm solid. Oh my gosh! I'm hurtling through at a fast rate now. Everything's flashing by. . . it's slowing down at last. I've arrived. I can stand but I have to be careful or I'll fall. I'm struggling to keep my balance."

"Good. I'm still with you, even though you can't see me." Sechem reassured her though he knew he couldn't always be with her in future trips. "Keep talking to me," he urged. What are you dressed in?"

"I'm dressed in a silver suit and am standing quite still in front of some doors. I'm strongly reminded of lift doors, elevator doors. I don't need to press any buttons. They are opening as I approach. I am going inside now. Oh dear! There's nothing to hold onto. As soon as I enter, there's movement. I can't tell if it's movement up or down. It's just vibration. I feel a little nauseous. It's the energy around me that's vibrating. I've no means of knowing if the lift is moving up or down. *A pause*, It has stopped now. Doors on the other side of the lift are opening. I'm stepping out."

"You're all right. Keep going, keep reporting." Sechem breathed a huge sigh of relief.

"All I can see are green fields. There's a low, very orange sun, such as you'd get with a sunrise or sunset. It's very low on the horizon. Everywhere is very flat. I can't, no — I mustn't stay in one spot. I must walk forward. I'm still in the silver suit. Nothing's changed there.

"You're doing well," Sechem reassured her.

"My senses are on full alert. I'm straining to hear something, anything in this unreal world. I hear clicking sounds. It's like an insect noise perhaps, or a creature of some kind. There's a little movement over to the right. I'm slowly turning my head to look. I can't see anything, but the clicking is definitely there. Suddenly something has popped out of the ground, a head of something. It's taking a good look at me. It stares at me. It's lizard like and it's this that is making the clicking sound. It pops back down. I'm not afraid. I'm going over towards it. I can see the hole it's come out of.

"What do I do now Sechem? Oh my gosh! There's somebody or something behind me. I hadn't noticed him coming up. It's another person dressed like me. It appears to be a silver suited human being, but much taller than me, very male. He is putting his hand on my shoulder."

"Stay calm," Sechem said.

"He's not unfriendly. He is just making sure I feel him and to know he's there. Sechem, he's not a mirage. My goodness, it's not a mirage. I'm turning around to face him now. He doesn't have a helmet. His face is warm and friendly. He's difficult to describe. He has a sharp nose, bushy eyebrows, nice mouth, a little bit on the full side. The sort I wouldn't mind kissing. That's an irrelevant thought that popped in. Sorry about that Sechem."

Jacob and Adam heard Sechem laugh but couldn't see him.

"He doesn't say anything. He's steering me away from the hole and walking me over to what looks like a flight of stone stairs going down. How ridiculous is this! They're constructed steps going down into. ... if I was in my own world I'd say this is a silo hidden from the surface. That's where we're going, I think. We keep going down. It's not steps all the way because we finish with the steps, and then there's just a downward path. He still has his hand on my shoulder, not that I'm going anywhere. Where would I run to? There's blue lighting along the floor; we turn a few corners which shut off the outside completely."

"Keep going Kate," Sechem said.

"I feel this journey's going to be long. There's another lift. Dull grey doors. We get in that and we go down. This time I can feel the downward movement. I see there are cameras mounted in this lift. We're being observed, not specifically just for us but for whoever uses this lift. These cameras are in place all the time. So, someone in a control room somewhere must be observing whoever enters. The lift shudders to a stop. The doors open automatically, and we get out.

"I can't be holographic, can I Sechem? He can see me and I can feel him."

Kate sensed Sechem's nod and was reassured. "Keep talking, Kate."

"The tall silver suited man is at last speaking to me. 'You've gone into inner earth where the activities on the surface are viewed on a screen. Those who inhabit this inner earth cannot, will not, or dare not go to the surface. So, you may do this for them. Because your mind creates realities, it's your mind that can bring changes so that they may feel safe again. The world needs peace, more now than ever in its history. Teach others to collectively use their minds to do the same by creating peaceful scenarios. Teach them to bring peace into the hearts and actions of mankind. This is how you'll be working whenever a situation needs to be adjusted. You'll have many adventures.'

"He is taking my arm and guiding me through a gap in the undergrowth. It's astonishing, Sechem. I wish you could see it. But you can, can't you?" Kate smiled. "There are thick forests and lush grasses. Growing plants, flowers and beautiful trees growing down to a shoreline. A crystal-clear lake stretches for what seems to be a very long way. The temperature's warm. As I look up I can see a red sun in a blue sky. I really like it in this place."

"Are there any people here?" Kate asked the man.

"Oh yes indeed. But they're a little afraid of you and me and are hiding."

Kate frowned. "Why? I wouldn't hurt them."

"You are a 'Top-sider'. Remember they're viewing what goes on in your world. As a result of what they see they are naturally afraid. Can you blame them?"

"I want to stay here and meet them."

"I understand, but this is your first time, so that won't be possible. I'm sorry."

The man started to fade in and out of her vision. "I can't see clearly. I am finding it difficult to focus my eyes."

"What's happening Sechem? I'm beginning to feel very odd and a bit dizzy."

"You're returning to your world."

***

Awestruck, Adam and Jacob watched. The scene they'd viewed slowly dissipated, until all they could see was a solid wall. Kate had returned to her chair. Sechem was nowhere to be seen. He'd done his job. With all their past experiences nothing had prepared them for what had happened.

Jacob said, "I thought this was supposed to be an initial easy start for her. What's going to happen when she goes further, and the tasks become difficult?" Kate looked at them, puzzled by the looks on their faces. Gradually memories of the last few minutes seeped back into her consciousness.

"Do you understand what you've done and where you've been, my darling?" Jacob stroked her hand. "Well done sweetheart. I'm so proud of you. How do you feel? What's with the silver suit, Adam?"

"Jacob, slow down with the questions," Adam said patiently. "The close-fitting silver suits are used in teleportation because tight fitting outfits can go with the body. Loose garments can get caught up."

"So, the tall man with the bushy eyebrows is a time traveller too? He had a silver suit." Kate said. A flush crept up her face as she remembered her desire to kiss the stranger.

Adam nodded. "That was an easy run, just for starters. You won't always have Sechem on hand. You'll soon do more alone, without any help at all. The implant worked admirably."

Jacob breathed a sigh of relief. "Well. That was a success, wasn't it? How about we celebrate?" He helped Kate up from her chair and led her gently and lowered her into an armchair away from the wall. None of them knew what to do now. Anything else would be an anti-climax after what they'd witnessed. Jacob brought out a bottle and glasses. They needed something stronger after that experience. He was thoughtful as he poured their drinks.

"Kate, it would appear that you went to inner Earth. I wonder what time frame that was. I suppose we should ask if it occurs again."

Adam looked up in surprise. "I doubt if Kate will have the same thing more than once. It was a training run, remember."

"Some training!" said Kate.

Jacob poured himself another drink. "I read some time ago Jules Verne's 'Journey to the Centre of the Earth'. Was it true I wonder? Is there a whole new world waiting to be explored, a place where living beings inhabit the depths of our planet, a place that cultures and ancient civilizations knew existed and still exists today? That's why we should've asked what time frame."

"You mean, I should have asked," said Kate. "You were not there. I was."

"I stand corrected," said Jacob and hiccupped loudly. "But I know more than you my darling daughter." He chuckled at the idea. Kate realised he was beginning to be a little drunk. "Have you heard of the Macuxi?"

"Dad, I don't think you should drink anymore. You are getting a bit tipsy."

"I must tell you a story that's true and not fable. It may well have a bearing on where you've been."

"Let him tell it, Kate. He won't be put off." Adam said as he made himself comfortable in an easy chair. He took the bottle out of Jacob's hand and helped himself to a drink.

Jacob leaned forward, his elbows on his knees. "The Macuxi Indians in Northern Brazil tell a story through oral traditions. They're still around today, near the border with Venezuela. They say that before the year 1907 they were entrusted with secret knowledge of a gateway to the underground realm of inner earth. They entered a cavern and walked for thirteen to fifteen days until they reached the interior. The Macuxi were allowed to visit this hidden land and interact with the giants residing there. They were also promised that if they carried out their guardianship duties faithfully they'd be allowed to reincarnate in the peaceful realms of the inner world.

"Unfortunately, the white man of Europe came and stole the lands from the native inhabitants of North and South America, and it was necessary to close up this portal to protect the hidden lands from the destructive tendencies of the conquering white nations. The Macuxis were warned to flee to the inner realm. Those that stayed suffered at the hands of their conquerors and still live on today with the memories and oral traditions of a paradise lost. That is the story anyway," Jacob said.

Adam said, "It's still happening today. The land grabbers are still trying to get them off their lands."

Jacob hiccupped and put out his hand to silence Adam. "I must continue their story while it's fresh in my mind."

Kate realised that when her father became a little intoxicated his mind linked more freely with other worlds and it loosened his tongue.

"So," said Jacob. "The Macuxi say they are descendants of the sun's children, who created fire, as well as diseases. They also believe they discovered *Washacá*, the Tree of Life.

Macuxi's lands still have some diamonds today. In the beaches of the inner lands, there's an abundance of diamonds, just like there is in some carbon mines of serpentine, from ancient volcanic shafts which are today those tunnels to the interior of the world. Years later, the Garampeiros started to arrive, to pollute the rivers with quicksilver, and to destroy with drugs the minds of the Macuxies that stayed behind. They also clouded their minds with whips and polluted their race by raping their women."

"It's an age-old story. Perhaps the diamonds are the reason land grabbers still want them off the land." said Adam.

Jacob grabbed the bottle back from Adam and poured himself another drink. "Well during June or July of 1946 there was a huge collapse in the tunnel, destroying almost all the stairs. Today there are only some steps at the beginning of it, and there's a huge and un-climbable pit, where the wind blows from different directions. Some old Macuxies who escaped the foreign whip, still live counting their age in moons, and have not forgotten the Lost Paradise."

Adam sighed. "Could this be just another legend? Or is there something more to the mysterious Macuxi tribe? It's said that the Hollow Earth story exists in many ancient civilizations and cultures around the world."

"What do you think Kate? Is this the place you went to?" There was no reply. Kate was fast asleep in the armchair.

***

What none of them realised was that Kate's journeys had created electromagnetic activity around the house and this had been observed. Young Howie had decided to try again and ask Kate to the village hall dance. It was dark by the time he arrived at her home. The three cars were there, but the house itself appeared to be in darkness. He hesitated. In those few brief moments of doubt something happened he couldn't explain. Lights of many colours began to play like a heat shimmer all over the house. It was above and all around the building. He could swear the earth itself rumbled. But that couldn't be, could it? A faint hum invaded his senses. He lost his balance and almost fell over. Howie put a hand on one of the cars to steady himself. Prickles ran through his body as if he had an electric shock. He shivered and shook. Howie had no idea how long this went on. His mind closed down.

Then at last it was finished. His head cleared again. The house lights came on. He looked at his watch. To his astonishment well over two hours had passed. He couldn't call on them now. It was too late. What should he do? If he reported these happenings the place would be swarming with men who wore no uniform, and who answered to nobody. They'd take over and he'd be moved back to base. He was sure of that much. He'd never be able to discover what it all meant, and he'd never find out if Kate was indeed a threat. His doubts about her had been strengthened by the appearance of the colonel. Howie was used to having everything clear and laid out for him. This was anything but clear. Yet again he reminded himself, orders were orders. He almost ran back to his digs and knew he would not sleep that night.

CHAPTER ELEVEN

THE GOLDEN ONE

The Mother ship was busy once again. This time another much revered and spiritually elevated being was expected. Time travellers, Sechem and Jamére chatted while they patiently waited for the arrival of The Golden One. Master M presided over this meeting as he did many of these council assemblies. This was just such an occasion where they were going to discuss the state of the human race once more.

Also on the agenda was the situation regarding Kate and Jacob. Much of Sechem and Jamére's time while they waited was spent conversing with Master M about the latest developments on planet Earth. All around the walls of the circular chamber they were in was a continuous floor to ceiling screen on which could be seen a moving picture of various parts of Earth. The pictures shown could be changed to any area of interest or time frame at any time. They were never idle.

Soft gentle music began and The Golden One arrived surrounded by angelic beings. He was escorted to the chamber which was set up for him. He seated himself and prepared to address the group. All eyes turned to him and chattering stopped. There was an expectant hush throughout.

The Golden One looked out over the assembly and each one present realised he was seeing into their souls. His voice was calm and gentle. "What have you to report Master M? Are there enough good souls to turn the tide towards a more spiritual direction on planet Earth?"

Master M, the Bird Man, bowed his silvery head in deep respect. "We have put our two best time travellers on the job and they are doing very well." He pointed to Sechem and Jamére who beamed with pleasure from their position at the table.

"However, the changes overall are fragmentary rather than global. These two are working with Kate, the Transformer and her father, Jacob. You may remember them from a previous meeting."

It was the Golden One's turn to beam with pleasure. "Yes, of course we remember. We are following their progress closely."

Sechem spoke up. "With your permission Great One, you are not the only ones following their progress. They may be in danger. Can you not safeguard them?"

"You know full well we can't interfere. Only those who've had earthly incarnations can interfere. It's up to you to do what you can. You do realise of course that every success, no matter how isolated, contributes to the greater collective vibration of human progression. What you're doing may well turn the tide from disaster to a happier future. We all wish for the human species to be spiritually advanced enough to join the other races among the stars. We don't wish you to become disheartened. What you're doing is making a huge difference.

"The planet Earth you're currently working on is invaluable for the development of the souls incarnated there. The range of emotions among humans is vast. Not all races have the ability to feel the way they do. Believe me when I say we wish they could. This is why you have such a long queue lining up to incarnate on Earth. All the things you might conceive of as being wrong are in fact stepping stones to great soul advancement."

He turned his gaze on the two space travellers. "You, Sechem and Jamére have a role to play just as much as Kate, Adam and Jacob, and you'll all advance as a result."

The Golden One looked around at the serious faces. "Cheer up," he smiled broadly at them. "You'd think the world wars on the planets were never going to end by the look of you."

The two time travellers brightened at his words. If he was smiling so would they.

Jamére felt it was time to speak on another matter which had been bothering him, and nothing much bothered him as a rule. "I'd like to find out more about those star visitors who do not mean well for the development of human beings. I understand they're holding important and dominant positions in a secret government on Earth that is well below the radar of the elected governments. The general public are becoming more aware of our interstellar space craft orbiting Earth but are almost totally blind to some visitors from space who are already on the soil of Earth, and who work against spiritual development. These spiritually inferior species from other worlds have integrated themselves into positions of real power. What can we do about them?"

The Golden One smiled patiently. "We are well aware of this of course. Again, we remind you that we can't interfere from our level. As we all know it will be for the citizens of the planet to wake up and admit what's going on and do something about it. They often put their heads in the sand when any subject is too difficult to accept. When they are able to realise that there are both well intentioned and self-serving species from other worlds visiting and residing on their Earth, things will begin to change for them. They've more to fear from each other than from off world visitors. It's about time they understood that."

Master M gave a polite cough, more to get attention than anything else. He hated to interrupt the Golden One. "I agree. It is time we told of large social groups from off the planet regularly visiting and residing on large restricted areas in North America. Charles Hall wrote a three-book series entitled "Millennial Hospitality" in which he described his personal experiences at Indian Springs, Nevada, and of interactions with the tall white extra-terrestrials, in the mountains north of Indian Springs, Nevada. He said many USAF personnel frequently encountered them at close range in and around the buildings on the various ranges during both day and night time operations. In answer to a question during an interview he said, 'They used the base as a place for their deep space craft in the way the US Navy would use a base in the Pacific. They used the base to refuel, repair and refit their deep space craft.' Because of long distances in space they need a base on a planet like Earth where they can get supplies, make repairs, etc. Since deep space craft arrived and left on schedule, this meant they were engaged in commerce and don't have any ulterior motive to colonize the Earth or dominate governments. Charles Hall argued that the tall whites like to keep to themselves, they just want to maintain friendly relations with the US government so they can continue to use the base. He frequently saw the tall white extra-terrestrials accompanied by UASF Generals and other high-ranking USAF. A Tall White female who called herself "The Teacher" explicitly stated that all they really wanted was for people to enjoy them, while they were here."

Master M paused and waited for a reaction from The Golden One and others listening. "It is time to speak out."

Jamére changed the subject. "Speaking of time, how much time do we have before a division of the human race begins?" he asked. "And does it have to divide, or can the whole human family go forward and advance together?"

The Golden One looked up and everyone there saw the sadness on his face. "I am sorry to say the division has already started on its journey into two levels. This is why it is vital for everybody to think in a positive way." The Golden One raised both his arms in supplication. "More kindness, more tolerance, more love is needed. It's not too late for many to switch over from one timeline to the other. A decline isn't a happy place to experience." He pointed at a scene of bloodshed now showing on the screen. "They need to start acting as one united species and care for each other as much as they care for themselves, and I may add, for their football games. They're not going to survive if they don't. If the Earth becomes sick, then so does the human race."

The Golden One thought carefully and paused before continuing. He looked at both Sechem and Jamére to see if they were up to the task of helping Kate. "Your charge Kate will meet many people and she needs to put her teachings over to those she meets on her journeys. You will do alright with Kate," he said at last. "Just teach her more about Timelines."

The gathering moved on to other matters of discussion and Master M indicated that the two friends were to leave. Jamére and Sechem left the hall together. They'd soon meet up again with their charges on Earth. There was much to do before diverging timelines permanently divided the human race. They both remembered that visionary author H. G. Wells had predicted this, and in 1895 he'd written about this division of the human race in his novel *The Time Machine.*

CHAPTER TWELVE

BLIMP = Biological Live Interstellar Mind Projection.

Kate was focussing on having more experiences while Howie was struggling with his priorities of allegiance. She knew she had to wait until she was alerted, and there wouldn't be any warning, but patience was not her strong point. What if the signal came while she was at work? They wouldn't do that, would they?

It was during this time that she began to have messages of a different kind. One intrigued her because it was simply one word, BLIMP. She puzzled as to the meaning when other words flashed through her mind '*Biological Live Interstellar Mind Projection*'. BLIMP was clearly an acronym. What did it mean and was she supposed to investigate? Her dad was the one to ask. As if he'd heard her thought Jacob walked in from the garden at that very moment.

"Hi sweetheart. Got any food going? I'm starving."

"Sit down, Dad. I have something to ask you." Kate told him what she'd received.

"What do you think it means, dad? Food can wait." But, having said that she still walked to the sink and filled the kettle. He followed her and sat down at the kitchen table. He began to twiddle with a knife. Kate saw him frowning. He was clearly thinking about how to respond to what she'd asked. He must know by now she could take whatever he had to say.

He stopped fiddling with the knife. "I have knowledge my darling that I've not shared with you. Please sit down." Kate sat with a worried expression.

"You know I'm sure, that the mind is extremely powerful. Your own experiences prove this. Other minds are also powerful, but not all operate to a spiritual base. There are forces on this planet that have a different agenda. There's indeed a programme called BLIMP. What this does is project into life, programmed life forms through Nano biological machines. Some things people see and thought to be of the space family such as greys and or reptilians are grown in this way and are not natural. They're not, absolutely not extra-terrestrials, for they are made here on Earth through this programme." Kate's hand went straight to her mouth as she gasped in horror.

Jacob reached for her hand. "Darling, they aren't to be confused with actual greys or reptilians. These programmed entities are used to induce fear, false abductions and sightings."

"How will we know the difference?"

"That's the problem," Jacob said.

Kate found it hard to believe. "Why would anyone do this terrible programme, and who's doing these things?" The tea was ready. She poured it into the mugs and passed one to her father.

"Biscuits?" he asked as he spooned in generous amounts of sugar. Absently she reached for the tin and brought it down from the shelf. Jacob helped himself. "We've already spoken of those in shadow governments and their military, haven't we? Fear is their weapon. You've already experienced what they can do and know how widespread their power is."

Kate nodded. She had to agree.

"I don't for one minute think they can harm us, Dad. We have Sechem, Jamére and Master M watching our backs. We know *they* are not projections of our subconscious."

Jacob laughed out loud. "That's my girl! But what about multiple consciousness? Have you thought about that?"

"Ooh! That's a big one. Why do you ask?" Kate sipped her tea thoughtfully and wondered what was behind the question.

"Well my sweet, you are going to have to be many different characters in your future work, and as a result will be experiencing various consciousnesses."

"No, it won't be like that," Kate objected. "I'm still aware and conscious of you here when I'm working out of body, and know I have to report to you. I know you're watching. Therefore, I'm two different people at the same time and conscious of both."

Jacob smile in triumph. "That's what I mean. Multiple consciousness."

"You're wrong, dad. Not multiple, just two, with the principle one as Kate. The other is playing a part. Don't you see?"

Jacob took another sip of hot tea. "Hmm! I suppose we ought to take into account the subconscious, the deep unconscious, our dreamtime consciousness and so on. It's a question I don't have answers to." He drained his mug and held it out for a refill. "But my darling girl you'll be changing a lot when you travel out of body and will experience many forms. That's what I mean."

"Dad let's just focus on the one we are experiencing at this moment and let the others take care of themselves. We'll get into parallel universes and parallel lives next. I've enough to deal with in this life as it is."

Jacob looked at her as she filled his mug again. "I'm just trying to find what it must be like to be someone else, and how you might feel. You're entering that stage after all."

Kate bit her lip and was thoughtful. Who was she really? What consciousness did the biological life forms called greys, and or reptilians have who were programmed through Nano biological machines? Did they have any minds or souls?

***

Adam had to return to his base in America all too soon. There was no way he could be absent too long without fabricating a story that would hold up under investigation. He sat across the table from Kate in Badgers Wood pub in Heath End, Baughurst. Each Saturday the pub had live music, but today it was Sunday and quieter. This pub had a great reputation for large meals, and best of all he'd have alone time with Kate before he had to leave her. Jacob had left them in peace and stayed home. The smell of good food set Adam's gastric juices running. He was hungry. He held Kate's hand tight across the table. He didn't want to let go. Would they ever spend their lives together? The order they'd placed at the bar arrived. There was silence while it was delivered.

"Go for it. Enjoy." The waitress winked as she put the plates down. She left them to it.

They spent the next few minutes tucking in to a delicious meal. Mouth full, Adam put off telling Kate he had to leave straight after the meal. Later there'd be no private intimate time together.

At last he braved saying what he had to say. "I'm going to have to go back to DC straight after this." Kate's expression dropped. He saw her eyes welling up, but she said nothing. She carried on making an effort to eat. "Say something Kate," he implored. He reached for her hand. She pulled it away. He could see how angry and upset she was.

"Is it always going to be like this?" she asked. "You there and me here? We never even get to spend one night together. It won't do Adam. It just won't do." Her lip trembled. They finished the meal without talking. Adam paid the bill and they left the pub walking in awkward silence to his car. They pulled up sharp when to their surprise they saw Jamére was there leaning against the car door. They both looked around in alarm. Could anyone see him? The car park was full and people were everywhere. His colourful garb and impressive height would surely be noticed.

“Oh, stop fussing, do. Only very psychic people can see me, and then not all of them,” he said and blew them a kiss.

“What are you doing here, Jamére? Where’s Sechem? You’re usually together.” Kate asked. Adam saw how annoyed she was that even here they couldn’t be alone.

Jamére drew himself up importantly, as only he could. “I’m here to be with you Kate for your next trip.” He paused for effect. “Sounds like having a drug experience, doesn’t it?” and burst into wild laughter. “Trip! Get it?”

Adam knew that Jamére saw they didn’t smile and seemed depressed. “What’s the matter with you two? It’s not that bad. It’s easy really. And I shall be with you, so no need to worry. I’m as good as Sechem.”

“I have to leave in half an hour,” Adam said. “Kate won’t have me.”

“You mean, you’ve asked her to marry you and she’s refused? Oh, my stars!” Jamére waved his arms about, raising his shoulders and gesturing with palms upraised like a Frenchman in an ‘I don’t understand it movement’.

“No you fool. I must go back to The States immediately. Let’s get Kate home.” He opened the car door.

“Can I come too?” Jamére climbed into the back of the car without waiting for a reply. They wouldn’t be alone even for the short ride home.

***

They made the arrangements, as they’d done for the previous trip. This time it was just Jacob sitting in front of the blank wall, well behind Kate’s chair. He twitched with nerves. Anything could happen and if it went wrong he was the only one there who would be able to call his daughter back.

Jamére said. “I’ll be with you Kate. You won’t see me, but you may converse with me if you wish. I won’t be far away. Remember this is still training for when you do this by yourself.”

“Where am I going this time?” Kate asked. “Will I be myself?” He didn’t answer her. “Get ready and relax. Go deep Kate. It’s a learning,” was all he said.

Kate focused, and went deep into her meditation until she heard in her head, as if in a dream, “You are pure energy.” Jacob watched as the wall became a haze, a mirror. He saw his beloved daughter rise and walk into the haze and disappear.

Kate begins to talk to Jamére.

"I'm like a whirling dust devil at the top of stairs. I'm a vortex, a spinning column moving down, down, down. I must always go down to the source, that inner being. I'm watching it, and yet am it at the same time. I get to the bottom and swirl around, covering all parts of the space here. As I go I'm gathering energy, picking up energy from the surroundings. I move into the passage, gathering speed and even more energy. I'm beginning to grow larger and am getting hotter. Strong hot energy now! Moving along, gathering speed as an energy, and getting brighter. I'm white, glowing white. I stop at an entrance. I wonder what's going to happen now. I hesitate in front of the opening. I'm a fast whirling column of energy.

"I move in. I don't know how I am to become the 'Kate me' again. It's odd because I recognise at last, this energy, this me, is just consciousness in movement. I'm aware of all things. I'm aware of taste, of everything. I'm acutely aware. It's hard to find words I can use to say what's happening. I have to describe it all. It's my training. That's what my role is, to describe being in both places at the same time.

"This is what energy does. It can take a form that you can recognise, but at the same time it's aware of everything that the inter-dimensional world holds, feelings, all the senses, acute awareness, but without using ears, eyes and touch. Without anything that makes up physical reality, the awareness is still sharp and clear.

"Having realised that; what this experience is trying to tell me is that all energy forms that we connect with as human beings, all forms, however presented, are acutely aware of what it is to be human. We understand emotions, all the senses, and thought processes, and understand them from our own viewpoint. We are observers with complete understanding. There's nothing we don't know. This is why it's said that each leaf, each blade of grass is known, because there's nothing we can't be aware of. I think that must be very hard for some of the things that go on in this planet."

In her head a voice replied. "Because we are no longer in solid form it doesn't mean that we don't suffer as you do at the hands of your fellow humans. Each ill deed jars against the Life Force and is painfully experienced by all. We in the spirit world put out a hand to calm and comfort as one would to calm an animal quivering with fear or distress. Sometimes this is effective, sometimes not. Don't become hardened to the blows of life but deal with them from a position of strength, not weakness or submission.

"This is why we say we suffer as you do. We aren't distant from you. We don't distance ourselves from humanity, and this includes all spiritual energy forms. We're not specifically speaking of this form or that, whether we're from your planet or elsewhere, whether we're Masters, or souls in other dimensions. We as pure energy know all. We are speaking of pure energy, the Great Knowing, the Great Awareness. Put this out to others so they don't feel that they're alone or ignored in any way. They *can* communicate their feelings and needs to this energy and it is recognised. Animals are becoming more aware, and more closely aligned with the thinking of humans. We are aware." The voice faded.

Kate stayed in a space that she couldn't define in any way. She felt she was in a void, as pure consciousness.

Then she began to panic and called out in fear. "Jamére, where are you? I don't know how to get back." She couldn't recognise herself anymore. No silver suit, no form of any kind.

"Stay calm Kate. Think of your body. Think of your home," Jamére said. "Think of your father. You *will* return. Stay calm." Kate stayed quiet and thought of physical things. She began to feel colour, sensations, awareness of something more solid, awareness of breeze on the skin, awareness of sight, sound, awareness of the physical senses coming back. She hadn't really gone anywhere; she'd simply experienced not being in a form, and being just a mind, intelligence, energy. She'd simply vanished. Her vanishing, her going had no place in time, no time in space, it simply was. Life was continuous.

She slowly became aware of the wall, and the chair. *It's all in the mind*, she told herself.

Jacob had fallen asleep. He was being gently shaken by Jamére. "You missed it," he said softly. Jacob opened his eyes just at the moment his daughter took form in her chair. Another journey was over.

"Next time will be different again," Jamére cautioned. I won't be here, nor will Sechem. It's all going to plan. Goodbye for now." So saying, he vanished – poof!

Kate saw that her father was put out. "He might have given me some insight as to what happened," he grumbled. "Do you remember anything, darling?"

"I was simply energy," Kate quietly replied. "Let's have a cup of hot chocolate. It will ground me, and then I must go to bed. I have work tomorrow and I'm tired."

***

The energy in Helga's office at the satellite firm was anything but peaceful. Helga was more than upset over Francine's unexpected appearance at her meeting with such an important group of men. A nerve in her jaw twitched. She wasn't just mad, she was furious. She stomped around the room in a rage. She shuddered at the memory of how flirtatious Kate's mother had been with the top man there. Whatever was she thinking of? The stupid bitch! If she'd any sense the woman would stay well clear of such people. Even she recognised these men weren't to be trifled with. Silas standing by the door watched her with narrowed and amused eyes. He opened his mouth to speak when she stopped him.

"Don't you dare bring up the subject of finding Kate and her father," she stormed. "It's not the right time." She swept a pile of papers off her desk in a further fit of temper.

"You couldn't have known the mother would turn up like that," he said, in an attempt to calm her down. "It wasn't your fault." Helga was more than surprised at his calming tone. He was usually scathing over anything she did wrong.

"Well, no I couldn't have expected any disturbance of that kind. The meeting went well, despite her uninvited appearance, and anyway we were almost finished."

"What was decided at the meeting?" he asked, trying really hard not to look interested. Helga wasn't fooled and smiled to herself. He only wanted to know what he'd missed. She saw that Silas was peeved that he hadn't been invited. After all he was superior to her. He wouldn't forget that slight in a hurry. She usually had to do most of what he ordered her to do but had no influence over the men who came to her house, and he hadn't been invited. She smirked in satisfaction.

Helga visibly puffed up her bony chest and decided to gloat in knowing more than him. "They're going to bring in psychic remote viewers to see if they can pick up on her movements. They've been very quiet for some time, but that won't last. Kate is bound to start interfering again. I'm to join the team." She scrutinised his face for his reaction.

"Oh!" She watched him pull a face. "Is that all?" he asked.

"They've sent a group of men around the country to seek her out. They're good at their job. Something's sure to turn up soon." Silas wisely kept his mouth shut just for a minute.

He hesitated before asking but couldn't help himself. "Do you think I could be included in this team? I could be of enormous help, because I know the kind of things she is likely to do," he finished lamely.

"I'll see," was all she said. It felt good to get one over on Silas.

***

CALLING EARTH – II

Next morning Kate woke up fresh and eager for more. She had the bit between her teeth after the last journey. On her way to the bathroom she remembered how it felt to be pure energy and smiled in contentment. It had changed something in her. She skipped in delight along the landing. She could be anything and it would be alright. But she still missed giving the talks she'd done before their move to Tadley. There had to be a way to spread the knowledge of a greater, more wonderful world that she knew could be had by all. How was she to do this without attracting the wrong kind of attention? That was the problem.

As if in answer to her unspoken question Sechem arrived that evening. Jacob was lounging on the settee watching television and Kate sat reading at the table. They both looked up in surprise as a scratching sound of static came from the television. The screen became zigzag and fuzzy. As he'd done before Sechem appeared on the display, and as cool as could be he stepped out on to the carpet. It was becoming his favourite method.

"Good evening," he said politely, and bowed as if appearing in this way was perfectly normal.

"Are you holographic or solid this time?" Kate laughed. She remembered the time she had attempted to put her hand into his energy field and had been zapped as a result. Then again since her implant had been activated her own energy had changed as a result. She could be anything and do anything. She decided to give it a try and reached out to touch him. This time he felt perfectly normal and solid.

"Blast!" she exclaimed. "Now I won't know if you're holographic or really there." Sechem laughed in his delightful bubbly way and wagged his finger at Jacob.

"Jacob, don't you try it. It might hurt you." Sechem laughed some more and settled himself in a chair. Kate moved to sit next to her father.

"Now let's get down to what you are to do next," he said. "Regarding spreading the information to a wider audience, it's easier now that you can mind travel and meet other minds in their own subconscious time. You may know of the super psychic star children here on your planet. You'll need to connect with them through your mind. You can teach them how to work together, with you, or in their groups. They'll then be able to spread the knowledge for you."

"Wow!" said Jacob. "Where do I come in?"

"You as always are the monitor and can safeguard your daughter if she gets into trouble while you watch on the Looking Glass wall."

"I fell asleep last time," Jacob cried. "What if I do that again when she needs me?"

"Get plenty of sleep beforehand," recommended Sechem who didn't appear to be at all concerned. "She may do some of her journeys alone anyway," he added. Then he surprised them both. "Let's do it now," he said in a manner that suggested there was to be no argument.

Kate leapt up from her seat, eager to go forward without any delay. "Oh, great. It's a weekend after all. There'll be plenty of time." She began to re-arrange the chairs.

Jacob stopped her. "Leave them. You are forgetting one thing, my darling," said Jacob. Kate looked up surprised. "Tea first, as usual. It doesn't do to break the pattern." They all laughed, and the three of them went to the kitchen.

Sometime later, refreshed and ready, Jacob set out the chairs. Kate settled down comfortably and went into her trance state. Her focus and intention were completely about connecting with star children. She'd never forgotten her meeting with the young souls waiting to find suitable parents to which they could be born. She also recognised that star children would be the evolved souls she'd spoken to before. They'd volunteered for the task of making a huge difference as to how the human race could proceed. As she held her intent the energy around her changed. She felt a rush, like a strong wind force pulling her forward. Images flashed by swiftly. She couldn't hold them. They became a blur.

Sechem and Jacob watched entranced as Kate faded from their sight. They stared into the glass wall, straining to see. This time Kate knew Sechem had to stay out of it. She was to get stronger and be able to do everything and anything without him. She was going to set up remote schools for super psychic star children. Many of them would be far more advanced than she was, both psychically, and in soul development. Being newly incarnated to Earth as children could dampen their abilities. It was her job to bring them back to becoming aware of what they could do. In a way, it was what Sechem had to do with her when he first made contact with her. It was now her turn to do likewise for them.

After the first rush of images and colours Kate became aware of where she was. She'd arrived. She looked around at her surroundings. To her astonishment she saw she was inside a large circular room full of glowing vibrant colours and shapes. They vibrated and changed hue as figures moved about. She tried to see through the colours and distinguish the forms in them. As they became clearer inexpressible joy flooded through her. Were these the elevated souls she was here to teach? She doubted she could teach *them* anything. *They* could teach her much more than she could. Kate bowed low to them in humble greeting. As she moved she discovered she was not in her usual human form. She ran her hands over her tall and colourful body. She put her hands up to her head and realised it was much larger and elongated than before. She wore a gold close-fitting hat and a long golden tunic.

She gathered her senses. It was time to speak. "I'm a star member of the Bird Tribe," she declared to them all. "I've come to prepare you for your lives on Earth. It will not be easy. You'll feel emotions you've never before experienced. Emotions can only be experienced in the moment that you are aware of them. Although past, present, and future are one, I can't tell you exactly what it'll be like for you, but we can go to a possible future just to see. It will be like viewing a movie."

Kate waved her hand at a screen on the wall. Immediately it came alive with scenes and landscapes that moved before their eyes. Then suddenly it changed to show horrific pictures of torture, abuse and cruelty by human beings, on both animals and people. The viewers shrank back in disgust. Before their eyes hordes of desperate people fought each other, climbing over the bones of the dead and grabbing whatever they could find. They saw helmeted men in riot gear, carrying guns, ready to shoot anyone who crossed their path. They heard the incessant buzz of clouds of black flies hovering over dead animals and people.

A lone child of about eight wandered crying through the stinking mess and looked totally lost. In his arms he carried a small baby. His tearful face was clearly seen by them all. The watchers looked away unable to stomach what they were viewing.

"This is the result of war and conflict that is not stopped by people in the early stages." Kate looked at the souls around her who would be incarnating and who would be the special children, to see if they understood. They would perhaps be the ones to stop such a terrible future.

One of those watching put a hand up. "Is this really what we are going into?"

"No, my dear. This is just a possibility if things do not change, and if people do not take a stand against tyranny while they can. So many put their heads in the sand and pretend that the terrible things that are happening on their Earth are not happening at all. It's all a conspiracy theory meant to create fear, they say."

Another soul put a hand up. "Yes, I agree. I've seen that too. So many feel they have too much to lose if they rock the boat and speak up. What they do not realise is that those in power do not have the best interests of those they control. They fear losing their power and control and will not stand by for what is right for all."

A rustle of movement followed this statement. Kate's eyes opened wide, entranced as the colours and iridescent figures seemed to merge with each other. Kate wondered if they were discussing what to do.

Eventually a glorious soul in sparkling colour separated from the group and stood out saying, "Maybe some of us will be whistle-blowers. After all, if they kill us we can come back here. We are always safe." He looked around at the group. They all nodded in agreement.

Kate relaxed and smiled with a fondness she had never experienced to such a degree before. "As gifted and very psychic children on Earth you may be misunderstood," she said. "*You* will be the awakened ones and you will be uncomfortable to many, especially to those in power. You will be given various names by those who understand. They may call you the Indigo children, Rainbow children or Crystal children. By those who do not understand you may be labelled as ADHD (Attention deficit hyperactivity disorder) and may be given medication that will slow you down and dumb your minds.

Kate waved her hand at the wall. This time the screens showed people helping others and showing enormous courage and kindness. They all watched with close attention and saw men and women handing out dishes of steaming food to a line-up of hungry people.

"They don't get paid for this," Kate told them. If they didn't care those people would go hungry. They have nowhere to sleep and nobody to care for them."

A watcher said, "That service alone is not enough to save the world though, is it? We can do more, much more."

Another scene appeared on the screen. A dog surrounded by ice struggled for its life in freezing waters. On seeing this a little group of people attached a rope to one of their party. He crawled across the ice knowing it could break under him at any moment. Cracks appeared as he drew near the animal, but he carried on. Cheers rang out from the onlookers as he grabbed the dog and pulled it from the hole onto the ice. They pulled on the rope and hauled them both in to safety. He'd saved an animal in need, even if it might have put him in danger.

A little cheer also rang out from those watching the screen. Then it changed again. Startlingly clear they looked on as a team of surgeons worked on the frail body of a child. They had been there for hours but were determined not to give up.

"Not for them the clock watching that so many engage in. They stay until their job is finished, no matter how long it takes." Kate said. "That is dedication indeed."

Once more the picture changed but one of the watching group said, "It's enough. We don't want to watch anymore. It is too upsetting."

Kate frowned. "Engaging in small acts such as those shown can eventually lead you toward more global acts of courage and love. Simply getting involved with a volunteer opportunity at the local level can open doors to bigger projects involving human rights and opportunities, such as taking a stand against an unfair social or economic practice. You could make a public presentation about something you believe in or stand up for a person who is being picked on." She paused. "I too get upset when I see cruelty or neglect." Kate was close to tears and turned her face away from them.

They moved in closer. She felt them touching her with such love she could hardly bear it and her tears flowed.

She looked up at the glorious souls surrounding her and knew they would be alright. She gathered herself together and said, "You may feel empathy now, but it's not the same as first-hand experience. That's why there is no substitution for incarnation. It's the difference between watching and doing." It seemed to Kate that the moving figures took on more defined forms. Was she imagining it?

Kate knew she had to carry on with the message. "When you are there and when you are children, don't spend one moment in fear when there are so many rich opportunities that await you. Fear is a limiting emotion. Clear it. You'll find that there are far more exciting and fulfilling emotions to enjoy," she reassured them. "Earth is unique because of its genetic makeup, from its wildlife, fauna, oceans, and skies. The range of emotions is vast."

She saw them smile at her and at her efforts to prepare them, but she had to continue, even though they were more able than she. Perhaps it was herself that she was convincing and not they.

"Your unconscious is connected to the universal matrix. It knows the answers. The awake and conscious mind is always thinking and busy. Analysis and interpretation abilities of the mind cloud over what the unconscious knows. The unconscious doesn't have the barriers that consciousness has. It knows the truth without imagination overlay."

Was it her own imagination again, or were the great beings here taking on yet more form as she spoke? They were now recognisable as being humans, ones that she could see clearly. She had to carry on. Kate remembered what she had told the teenagers earlier, but although this was a different group of souls she had to tell them too. Kate looked at them as they solidified even more. It wouldn't be long before they went to Earth. She was running out of time.

"As natural psychics, you may not be aware of *how* you do things. So, you won't always get things right. If you find yourself going into thoughts of not being worthy, things not being right, or thoughts straying, repeat to yourself 'SWITCH OVER TO A POSITIVE LINE. SWITCH OVER TO A POSITIVE LINE' and recite that until your mind is filled with all the positive things you'd like it to be. That includes being with members of your family, staying with those you love in a positive way, having sufficient for your needs. Whatever your dream world is, switch your thoughts to that dream world. Every time you drift back to a negative, switch back to a positive line of thought. Say again to yourself 'switch back to positive line'. You'll be telling your subconscious where you want to go, and the subconscious always obeys. You'll do remote viewing into the future. You'll see in your mind's eye the future as you wish it to be. You *will* create your future by taking your mind ahead to it."

One of the shining lights raised a hand. "What if we find a situation too difficult for us? It's so long since we fought dark energies. We're not used to doing this anymore."

Kate, as the Bird Tribe family member, thought hard about this question before answering. "Recognise and accept that you are of the light and of a higher vibration. Know for certain that a lower vibration, a darker energy cannot, absolutely cannot enter your being, physical or spirit form. A darker energy cannot enter the light, unless you fear it can. Fear can allow entry, as fear is in itself a negative energy. A heavy dark vibration is the weaker force and if it's put into a lighter, stronger vibration it will destroy itself, or will have to transform into light. Rather in the same way as a weak fuse cannot be put into a strong current. You do understand that, don't you?"

Kate saw that some of the group were losing their gloriously coloured forms, and as they moved they were slowly morphing, becoming new babies. She had to hurry now while they could still understand.

"When you find yourselves in difficult situations, and with those who don't understand you, and you don't think you can stand it anymore, you may have feelings of wanting to go back to your real home, that of the stars. Remember what you're there for. Focus on what you'd like life to be."

Kate felt she was losing their interest while their concentration was on their own transformation that was taking place before her eyes. But she had a job to do and she was going to do it regardless. She moved closer to them.

"There are other human races elsewhere that operate in a much-improved manner to those on Earth. But then I don't need to tell you that, do I?" This brought a laugh from those who were still visible and even a childish giggle from some who were changing more quickly.

Kate tried to grab one form, but her hand went straight through the body. She felt almost desperate now. "Please also note how many good, honest and loving individuals there are within the human races on Earth. I ask that you help them and direct them to a more positive timeline. They don't all need to travel down the negative timeline that is being directed by those who wish ill upon them. It's your job to point out that there's a positive timeline they can travel down. Show them how to avoid crossing or merging with the negative line that's *already* doomed to failure."

Kate saw with dismay that a few of the quickly changing souls had disappeared. They had already started their new journey on the Earth. She had to be quick. She took a deep breath.

"You *will* create your future by taking your mind ahead to it. Create with as much feeling as you can. Be passionate about it. Feel the passion as you create great things. It may be gradual, and many of you may move back and forth between dimensions. There will be difficulties for some of you in fully grasping the events that had transpired before your arrival. It may be like a dream from which you're waking. It will be a new experience emotionally, because no planet full of conscious beings has ever had this much help before. We only see probable futures, because they're rewritten every second. Nothing is certain."

Kate paused and looked around at the remaining glowing volunteers ready to help planet Earth's inhabitants. Would they be recognised as astounding souls, or be ignored? The colours around her began to fade. Kate became aware of her own changing energies. She felt tingles all over her body. She watched dumbstruck as her limbs began to disappear. Next thing she knew she was rubbing her eyes and yawning in her own chair. Another mission accomplished, or so she hoped. Would it always be like that, she wondered? She looked around for Sechem. He was nowhere to be seen. Jacob helped her up.

CHAPTER THIRTEEN

POSSIBLE DISCLOSURE

Rumours were circulating back in Washington DC where Adam was working. Rumours and hopes of disclosure about the existence of space beings, not only visiting and circling our planet, but also working with certain covert military elements of the governments. It was all the talk on the internet. Was disclosure going to happen or not? News that hadn't reached mainstream news before began filtering through internet sites and was gaining momentum. It reported events that had occurred at least over one generation before, and maybe even earlier. Much of the current population had no inkling of what had been going on within the confines of a secret government.

The internet and whistle-blowers were at last successfully leaking evidence that could not be stopped. One such story was that President Eisenhower had had the unique experience of physically meeting and talking with aliens. In 1954, it was reported that five spaceships landed at Edwards AFB, and the space travellers asked to meet with the President. Eisenhower was rushed to the base where he met and talked to Pleiadians. They demonstrated the manoeuvrability of their spaceships, and instantly made themselves invisible. They did this by swiftly transferring their bodies to their normal vibrational frequency.

Kate knew this was how Sechem, Jamére and Master M managed to disappear so effortlessly. It was perfectly obvious to her that many space vehicles did the same. Kate discovered through researching the various internet sites that President Eisenhower and his companion, Robert Saunders, were invited on board the spacecraft. The Pleiadians said they wanted to begin an education programme for the people of Earth, to make mankind aware of the universe and its ET existence. It was not Eisenhower's way to make impulsive choices or decisions, so he asked for a great deal of information. Extensive discussions were held with the Pleiadians. For the next three days Eisenhower virtually disappeared from public view while he and his top aides discussed what their response would be.

The biggest threat regarding any decision was the economy. Economists warned that alien intrusion would put an unknown factor into their reality. It was a major consideration. Having alien technology show up would probably put their economy in disastrous financial jeopardy. Additionally, there would be a strong negative reaction from all religious leaders.

Eisenhower warned the space visitors that this would cause panic on Earth.

He pleaded, 'We are not ready for that yet.' The Pleiadians understood, and left the bewildered President and his entourage standing, awestruck and silent.

Although Kate discovered these facts through an open internet, she had no way of proving any of it. Should there ever be disclosure by the government, the records and proof were there to be had in full. It seemed to her ironic that a growing number of people around the world, are denying the truth for fear of a possible threat it may pose to their comfort and survival in their personal lives. Nobody likes change. While these same people are beginning to realize that their continuing support of the existing system along its current path, may at some point in the very near future, lead to inevitable destruction of the planet.

People had forgotten so quickly what John F Kennedy had said in a speech delivered to the American Newspaper Publishers Association on April 27, 1961, *quote*: 'Our way of life is under attack. Those who make themselves our enemy are advancing around the globe… no war ever posed a greater threat to our security. For we are opposed around the world by a monolithic and ruthless conspiracy that relies primarily on covert means for expanding its sphere of influence on infiltration instead of invasion, on subversion instead of elections, on intimidation instead of free choice, its preparations are concealed, not published. Its mistakes are buried, not headlined. Its dissenters are silenced, not praised.' *End quote:* It was quite a speech and so prophetic.

How true that is today, Kate thought. She wondered how he knew so much. Was this why he'd joined the ranks of those who had to be silenced? Then she remembered the Biblical reference:

And when ye shall hear of wars and rumours of wars, be ye not troubled: for such things must need be; but the end shall not be yet. . . nation shall rise against nation, and there shall be earthquakes in diverse places, and there shall be famines and troubles . . . these are but the beginnings of birth pains.
Mark 13:7-8

In remembering she felt calmer in the knowledge that all would be well in the end. She had to hold onto that thought. There was to be a positive outcome after all the trauma that the Bible was referring to.

***

Howie was also thinking hard while Kate was pondering on these questions. Was Kate a threat to national security? Was she really a spy? He had to find out, and soon. Time was running out for him. If his superiors decided enough effort had been spent searching in his area he'd be withdrawn. He would try again to ask her to the dance.

The street was quiet, but the evening was still in its early stage. People were settling down after work and no doubt were preparing meals before a night of television. Her car and only her car was in the drive. The lights were on in the house. It was looking good. She'd be alone. Howie decided to be straight and upfront in his approach. He knocked firmly on the door and also rang the bell, to be sure. Determination was his stance. He'd nothing to lose by this approach. Kate opened the door. She had oven gloves on and a smudge of flour on her cheek. She smiled warmly at him. This was good. He melted.

"Hello Howie. What a nice surprise. I'm sorry I wasn't in when you called last time." This was encouraging, thought Howie.

He didn't hesitate. "There's a dance on Saturday and as I don't know anyone in the district I was wondering if you'd come with me." He blurted it out before he could make a fool of himself. "It's at Heath End Village Hall, not far from here."

Kate's smile spread over her face as she looked at him. Howie blushed. He felt shy.

"I haven't been to a dance for ages and ages," she said. "I would love to come. Will you excuse me Howie, I have something cooking and I don't want to burn it."

"I'll pick you up at eight," he said. Howie felt like skipping as he walked away. Now he'd discover what she was really like, and if they'd got it all wrong about her.

***

Saturday arrived quickly. Jacob watched as his darling daughter got ready for the dance. She hadn't been out to enjoy herself for such a long time. He didn't want to spoil things for her, but and it was a big but, he couldn't shake off the feeling that something wasn't right. His second sight was buzzing, but he couldn't put his finger on it. He'd no right to stop her going. He wondered what Adam would think about it. He should be here more often, and then there wouldn't be this temptation that was sure to come her way.

Along with Saturday came heavy rain. It gushed and splashed along the gutters and the road was awash. Jacob watched Howie arrive in a small battered car. He opened the door and let a dripping Howie into the house.

"My original plan had been to walk, but a friend lent me his car," Howie explained. "The hall is near enough. In my short dash up your drive the downpour has already soaked me, as you can see."

Jacob said drily, "Best laid plans often go wrong." Kate came into the room all dressed up and ready. She reached for her raincoat and Jacob helped her put it on.

"Here, take an umbrella with you," he said. "You'll need it."

"Come on Howie. A drop of rain won't hurt us." Kate grabbed his arm as they prepared to rush to the car.

"Have a good time my darling," Jacob said, and watched from the window as Howie held the large umbrella over her as he helped her into the car. He's at least a gentleman, Jacob thought.

***

The old borrowed Austin pulled into the car park. Clutching the umbrella Kate and Howie dashed through the downpour from the car into the hall. It was already packed with dancing bodies and the music drowned out conversation. They disposed of their wet coats and joined the throng on the floor. Howie went to get drinks and while away Kate was whisked off for her first dance by a portly gentleman.

Kate started to enjoy herself and danced with quite a few men of all ages, some of whom she recognised from around the village. Howie badly needed to find a space when he could get her into conversation. He was concerned that his bosses would discover he knew where Kate Greene was, and he hadn't told them. He started to sweat. It wasn't going to be easy with so many people around. The volume of music made it impossible to talk and time was passing. So much for plans he reflected. He stood to one side with a glass in his hand and watched her on the dance floor.

It was time to take matters into his own hands. He threaded his way through the dancing couples towards her, took her from her partner and waltzed her away. "I think we need some air," he said to her startled face. He steered her out to the covered veranda, picking up a full glass on the way.

"Howie, I was dancing," she protested.

Howie thrust the glass into her hand. "I need to talk to you," he said. "It can't wait any longer." Kate stared at his flushed face and looked puzzled. Howie realised his behaviour needed some explanation, but he was deadly serious and wouldn't be put off.

"Sit down, stay calm and tell me about it," she said and looked around for a seat and pulled him onto it.

He took a deep breath. It was now or never. "Are you a spy?"

"A spy?" Kate gave a nervous laugh. Howie was relieved to see her amazed expression. So, it couldn't be true what they said after all.

"Whatever made you think such a thing? How on earth could I be a spy? I don't have any contacts with governments, or anything like that? You're mad." Her face flushed. Howie felt uncomfortable now. Maybe it hadn't been such a good idea to broach the subject in this way after all. He'd already sensed her father didn't trust him. He'd already asked him how he'd just turned up in a side street that had no exit. Jacob had asked him where he was going when he just happened to see Kate's car's lights on. Howie hadn't been able to give a good enough answer to that.

Kate stood up. "I'm going back to dance," she said. "I'm angry with you, Howie. How could you think I could ever betray my country? You must be crazy."

Howie grabbed her arm. "Don't go. Tell me it isn't true," he pleaded.

Kate tried to pull away. "Stop it Howie. You're hurting me. I don't have to justify myself to you. Who do you think you are?"

Howie could see how furious she was, but he'd detected something else. Was that fear he'd seen fleeting across her face?

"I need to know Kate. Tell me it isn't true," he said again and pulled her right up close to him. It was the wrong move. Kate struggled to push him away and started to cry.

"How could I be a spy? I know nothing about world affairs. Politics don't interest me at all. Naturally I'm interested in what happens to this planet, like everybody else. But that doesn't make me a spy. Let me go. You're frightening me."

She was crying now but Howie couldn't stop himself. He still wasn't convinced. "What about that American Colonel at your house then? And there were queer funny goings on over your house the other evening. Explain that then."

Kate flared up at that, angry now. "What is this? The third degree? I don't have to explain anything to you. Who I have in my house is none of your business." But Howie was quick to see how rattled Kate was.

"I'm going home. I don't want to see you near my home ever again. Spy indeed!" She stamped hard on his foot and he let her go. Kate ran and threaded her way back through the dancers on the floor aiming for the exit. Howie was right behind her.

"I am sorry. I didn't mean. . ."

She spun round on him. "You didn't mean what? To accuse me of being a spy? Leave me alone."

"I need to explain. I've been sent." Kate stopped dead in her tracks.

"Sent? Who sent you? You are mad."

They were at the cloakroom now and collected their coats, not saying a word. Howie desperately wanted Kate to think well of him after his rough behaviour.

"Walk with me and I'll tell you. I have to explain."

"It's raining, Howie," Kate reminded him.

"Hardly at all now. It's almost stopped. And we have a large umbrella. I can pick the car up later." Howie wasn't going to let this chance pass that easily. They left the building and started to walk. He opened the umbrella and took hold of her arm, gently this time. "I'm a military man. I was detailed to find you." Kate stopped walking.

Howie frowned. "I don't know what you've done, or who you really are, but I like you. I really do. But I'm confused."

Kate took a deep breath before speaking. "You knew my name before you knocked on my door? How did you know it was me? I'd never seen you before in my life."

"They gave me a photo of you. I recognised you immediately when you opened the door. Believe me it was pure chance that it was your car lights that brought me to you. It must have been a sign we were meant to meet." He smiled, more to himself than to Kate.

Kate gasped. "No, I don't believe that. You mustn't think that way." They walked on, not talking for a while, neither knowing how to deal with the awkward situation.

The umbrella tipped. Water ran off and went down Howie's neck. Kate stopped walking to close the umbrella. "It's stopped raining altogether now," she said. It broke the uncomfortable silence between them. "Howie, where are you going with this mad idea? I haven't done anything wrong. I don't understand why you're interrogating me this way."

"I don't know what to do, or what to believe." Howie was confused. He really liked Kate, and he'd heard about innocent people being targeted before. They continued to walk slowly until he stopped her again. He turned her to face him and looked her straight in the eye.

"Kate, I want to believe you. Do you swear to me you're not a spy?" He'd never been so serious in his life before. He realised he was holding his breath.

He watched Kate weigh up how she should answer. He'd never understand if after all her denial, she did tell him of their illegal activities.

Kate's lower lip trembled. "Whatever they have told you it's a lie. I've never in my whole life done anything to harm this or any other country or any other person," she said. It was the truth. "On my mother's life," she added for good measure.

Howie let his breath out. "I never really thought you were a spy, or someone who could deceive," he said. "But what do I do now? An order is an order, and I have to report back."

"You can still report back and say you haven't found the spy they're looking for. I'm not the person who is a spy, and they are looking for a spy. It's not a lie." Howie didn't want to argue with that reasoning. He gave a worried nod. They walked back to Pinks Lane in silence and said goodbye on the doorstep.

Kate peeked into Jacob's room when she got in but saw he was in bed fast asleep. There was no need to disturb him and he'd only say, 'I told you so and start worrying.' Kate spent a restless night tossing and turning. What now? Would they be discovered? Would Howie stick to his story?

***

Jacob got up bright and early the following morning. It was a clear sunny Sunday; the birds were in full song and all was right with the world. Jacob intended to make the most of the day. Kate was still in slumber land. Unusual for her, he thought. She probably got in late after the dance. He decided to take her a cup of tea and then he could hear her news of the evening before.

He knocked on her door. No answer. He knocked again, harder this time. He'd no intention of letting her waste a day off, dance or not. It was such a beautiful day. "Come in," he heard at last. He carried the tray in and set it down beside her. What he hadn't expected was the look on her face. Worry and fear was etched all over it.

"Dad don't be cross with me. You were right about Howie. He's been sent to find me."

Jacob's heart thudded with fear. "I don't understand. Sent to find you? Who sent him?" Kate told him the whole story. Jacob listened in silence till she'd finished.

"I don't think he'll say anything, Dad. But we can't be sure, can we? Can we trust him?" Jacob took off his glasses and cleaned them with the bottom of his shirt. It was a sure sign he was thinking deeply before speaking. Kate waited, watching his face carefully.

"I think we ought to have him round here and talk to him a bit more. We can't ignore this, or let it go without doing something. Invite him tonight before he has a chance to change his mind, and before he can say what he knows. Have you got his number?"

"Yes, Dad."

Jacob shared her concern. He'd take charge and look after his precious daughter no matter what it took. "Let's go for a walk to where we were first brought here, in the woods near Aldermaston. You must remember that day Kate? It'll clear our heads."

Oh, *he* remembered alright. It was also where he was returned by space ship after his visit to his love Joslene. He so missed her now. Would he ever be able to go back to her? He was certain Kate too would remember that day when she'd found him wet and shivering in the bushes after they had returned him to Earth.

Kate dressed quickly in sweatshirt and jeans. They set off in her small car. They soon arrived, parked the car and strolled arm in arm through the trees until they reached the spot of his return. With the sun streaming down it was hard to imagine a space craft setting down in the clearing without anybody noticing. Then he reasoned there was hardly anybody visiting this small wood these days. Maybe someone could be found there occasionally walking their dog. Jacob began to wonder if he'd imagined it all. It was impossible to turn back those events. Their lives had changed forever. After walking for a time Jacob declared they'd had long enough to clear the cobwebs. They drove home each of them wrapped up in their thoughts. How were they going to explain things to Howie that evening?

***

Kate phoned Howie and he enthusiastically agreed to come. Kate was nervous. She wished Adam was there to help with a plausible story that would satisfy the young man. As the day went on Kate couldn't take her eyes off the clock, looking at it time and time again. At last it was time for him to arrive. She was sure he'd be punctual. Even so she jumped when the doorbell rang. Jacob went to answer it, giving her time to calm down.

It was immediately clear that Howie was even more nervous than Kate. He sat stiffly with a straight back on the very edge of his seat. "It's good of you to invite me here given the situation," he said politely.

Jacob stepped in to break the tension. "What would you like to drink? Tea, coffee, or something stronger?"

"Coffee please. Black, no sugar." His eyes followed Kate as she went into the kitchen. Kate's psychic senses picked up on his thoughts. She knew he still had nagging doubts about her.

As she entered the kitchen Kate staggered back, surprised and shocked. Standing there, leaning against the units in full regalia was Jamére. He didn't appear to be a hologram and looked quite solid to her. Was it just her rising abilities and heightened vibrations causing the illusion? She blinked hard. She didn't know which was which anymore.

Pulling herself together she faced him. "What are you doing here? Your timing couldn't be worse. You must leave immediately." Kate shook. What if Howie walked in? What if he saw this magnificent creature? She could never explain that away.

"Don't you be fretting wee lassie. He can't see me or hear me. You are needed on a mission this evening. It's important."

"As I said your timing is the worst it can be. I can't do a mission this evening. I just can't, and that's that."

Jamére rested his arm on her shoulder. Kate realised he wasn't going to be put off. "In the future you'll be called on at the most inopportune moments. You must learn how to deal with this. It's part of your training. You have to do this, lassie."

Kate looked at him. She could see he was deadly serious and for once was not smiling. "Stay here and don't move. I have to take in the drinks, or they'll come looking for me. Stay here!" Kate picked up the tray and carried it to the front room. Jacob and Howie were chatting about sport and the differences between American and English football. Kate was pleased to see they'd found safe ground.

She put the tray down and handed out the mugs. As she turned to sit down her face dropped in alarm. Suddenly Jamére was standing behind her chair. Jacob too looked surprised but held his tongue. Howie saw nothing unusual and Jacob managed to keep his eyes from straying to where Jamére stood.

For the next few minutes Jacob told Howie how he had taken early retirement, due to ill health, and how they'd moved here so that he could live with his daughter instead of being alone.

More comfortable now that Kate realised Howie couldn't see Jamere, she said, "You know Howie, Kate Greene is a very common name. I've often been told I look like someone they know. I think your bosses must have mistaken me for someone else." Howie nodded, and to her absolute astonishment immediately fell asleep. He was out stone cold. She turned just in time to see Jamére waving his arm at the sleeping man. Streams of colour were coming from his hand and circling Howie.

"What have you done to him?" she exclaimed in horror.

"I told you lassie that you've a mission to attend to. Let's get on with it. Before he wakes up," he said with a twinkle in his eye. She saw Jamére was enjoying himself immensely.

***

Secure in the knowledge that Howie wouldn't see a thing Kate placed herself in front of the wall as before and set her intention to travel to wherever she was needed. She'd no idea what would happen next.

"You won't always have a wall," Jamére whispered in her ear. "Training, remember?"

Kate began her descent into another world, knowing Jacob and Jamére were watching and recording what she told them.

I'm in silver, a beautiful gleaming silver suit, not at all dull. Oh, it's so bright. I appear to be very slim. Going down now! I'm standing on a pad, just descending like in a lift. I feel as strong as a man. As I look down at my feet I can see I'm totally enclosed in this shiny silver outfit. The way down is — it's difficult to call them stairs because it's like being on an escalator and I don't have to move. It's taking me down while I'm just standing in one place. It's like a lift, but I'm only on just a small pad. Quite interesting really! In fact, it's more than interesting. You stand on a little square of something, like a footpad, and it goes down. I can't describe it better than that really. I feel I'm passing down several levels.

The downward movement stops. I've landed. As I step off the pad strong men surround me. I don't know if they're here just to show the way, or to guard. They're all equally dressed in silver, same as me. They're hefty. They look like guards. They point the way I must go.

They say to me, "Forget your usual routine, and just follow where we direct you."

I walk along. There's not much to see. It's very white and sterile, clean, no windows; a clean pristine world. I could almost be in a tube of something. Oh, I *am* in a tube. I can actually hear my footfalls, but it's not hard or loud. It's soft, a muffled sound. I keep walking. I come to another silver suited guard and he points me in a different direction. So, I'm after all following my routine, which is to turn right.

There's a .... I don't know what to call it *(pause)*.... it's a red panel which opens automatically as I approach it. I don't have to do anything. It slides to one side and I step in. It slides shut behind me. I'm looking around, but I can't see much. There are little lights everywhere. They're not bright but light up where they are positioned, not much more. They're in different colours. I feel they're coded, a bit like traffic lights, or marker lights, where colours mean different things. I move on and feel a waft of air. I am relieved that I can feel air.

I call out to nobody in particular. "What am I doing here and where am I?

I must keep walking. At the end of the walk there's another door. No numbers or notices on it, just a plain brown door. I'm in a hurry now. I feel an urgency to hurry, as if I mustn't be late. But I am still cautious as I come closer to the door. It too slides open. I step in and find I'm in a big meeting room type place. There're lots of others here, men or women, it doesn't matter which and it is difficult to tell gender. They're all in silver suits. It's a meeting of some kind. I can't see the faces very clearly, nor would I want to. They're moving around talking quietly to each other. They beckon me over. I know somehow that this isn't the first time this has happened. I'm expected and am one of them. I'm a reporter.

That's interesting. I suddenly realise where I am. I'm back at star headquarters reporting on the state of the human race. This is very serious.

One of the men responds to my thought. "*Yes, it is very serious*."

"How can this journey help me with what I'm being asked to do?"

"You must continue to note and report. We'll take the information off you while you sleep. It's then we have easy access to you. In the meantime, during the day don't worry, because you are absorbing detail every time you look around. What you see is being relayed back. For us it's like watching through a television screen, using your eyes as the camera."

"This doesn't help me much, does it?"

"You'll see it will fit in very well. Give it time. It will fit in. You're an ambassador."

"Who am I an ambassador for? Earth humans, or those present at this meeting?"

"It works both ways you know. Clearly, you're a human, but are equally clearly not human. That should give you something to think about."

"Oh, Okay. But that doesn't answer the question."

"You are still too concerned. For the meantime let us use your eyes to report."

"But I'm not doing much. I just mix with ordinary everyday people."

"That's just what we need to have reports on. Not the stuff that's constantly seen on your media, such as wars, bombs and suchlike. Dreadful things! We need to see ordinary human lives, decent people in the main. We need to see them through your eyes, with the camera of your eyes, for that's what will sway the difference in *our* thinking. Each time we see or feel a loving, positive action or thought it swings the balance towards the Human Race travelling to a positive future for your world. "

"I wish I could understand that."

"Move among the people and talk to them. We're observing everything that goes on. We form our opinions based on the characters and the way these characters behave towards each other and to you."

"I'll do my best." Kate promised.

Jacob and Jamére watched as the strong male aspect of Kate walked back through the wall and sat down. Kate returned to her own form and had a good stretch.

"Well, Jamére I don't see that was a mission that was so important it had to disrupt the evening." She quickly looked over to Howie and was relieved to see he was still asleep.

Jamére gave a half smile. "I told you it was training to see how you would handle a surprise request. This time it was with my help. Another time I won't be there for you. It was also necessary for you to hear what we had to say at the meeting."

Kate was astonished. "You were there all the time? I didn't see you or feel you."

Jamére grinned. "You don't know everything."

"Shall we wake him up?" Jacob nodded towards Howie who was snoring loudly. Jamére waved his hand over the sleeping man and then vanished.

Jacob gently touched Howie on his arm. Howie slowly opened his eyes and looked extremely embarrassed. "I'm so sorry sir. I seem to have nodded off. I apologise. I hope you don't think me rude."

"That's alright lad," said Jacob. "You must be working very hard."

"Yes, sir, it must be that. I'm so sorry." He stood and had a good stretch. "I hadn't realised how late it was. I'd better be going and get a goodnight's sleep."

Jacob patted Howie on the back. "That's right my boy. You'll feel better in the morning." Thankful it had all gone so smoothly he escorted Howie to the door.

Kate gave a huge sigh of relief as they both watched his go down the path. What would come of his visit they couldn't tell.

CHAPTER FOURTEEN

RENEWED EFFORTS

Silas, puffed up with his own importance, stood with Helga and Marco to the forefront of a group of military uniformed men. They all stood to attention when Gork, the dark one entered. A sigh of palpable relief spread through them when they saw he was wearing his customary large, dark glasses as he turned to face them. Through them the giant looked over the subdued gathering of people in the room and let out a snort of scorn. The traffic outside could just be heard as a hum above the noise of many machines clicking away in the next department. The blinds were drawn closed across the windows shutting out any stray light from the outside world. Several of those present in the gloom of the room had long since realised that the dark one did not enjoy the light.

They had not yet found their places at the boardroom table and were standing in a confused group. Anxiety was etched on the face of every one of them. They were glad that the dark one stood in the deeper shadows. They hoped never to fully see his face or his dreadful eyes again as they once had.

"Sit down," he growled. It was a command. They hesitated and shuffled to the chairs placed around the table. "It would seem that none of you has been successful in finding Kate Greene or her father Jacob. It might please you to know that despite your ineptitude I've had more success." The face of the monster changed to what with a stretch of the imagination could be called a self-satisfied smile. All it did was to reinforce the rumour that he might not be human.

Silas hoping to gain favour spoke up. "Congratulations, sir".

"Congratulations?" the creature bellowed. "Congratulations? For doing *your* job?"

Silas shrivelled and sank low in his seat. Helga smirked at his embarrassment. Marco kept quiet. He'd learnt from his experience at the last meeting.

"We've been able to pick up her energy signal. She's clearly active again. So far she doesn't appear to have visited again, or done any damage to our nuclear sites or underground bases. It's only a matter of time before she does. We're worried about the information she may pick up and spread to the general public. Our problem is that we still don't know where they're both hiding. Her energy signal changes constantly, so she seems to be in many places and not just in one spot."

The giant figure again turned to Marco, Helga and Silas. "This is why we've called you here. You must use your own psychic abilities to track her down. Do it! Redouble your efforts." He stood up and turned his back to them. "You three may go." It was clear that their presence at the meeting was no longer needed and they filed out.

Feeling rebuffed it was Silas who spoke first as they walked down the corridor. "We must get more information from her friend Poppy and her mother. You, Helga have no choice but to let me join the team of men who came to your house. Marco, stand by."

Marco merely mumbled something unintelligible and stood to one side, like a bodyguard.

"It appears that you've taken charge Silas," Helga said in a huff. "My team of men, as you put it, will be the ones to decide if you join them, or not. It won't be my decision. They are way above me in rank."

"I realise that. But you can recommend me." Silas wanted to be acknowledged in the higher realms of espionage. He yearned to be one of them. "It's time you put your connection with satellite companies to good use. You know what I mean." He knew Helga did know what he meant.

Silas wasn't about to let her off that easily. "The men who went to your house have control of satellites and their uses in ways you don't want or can't delve into. They're not innocuous satellites. They're often used for mind control, if what I suspect is true. If you know what's good for you, don't probe too deeply or start asking questions. You're just a pawn, and you know that all too well. Concentrate on honing your skills at picking up on Kate's energies."

Silas smirked as he saw how Helga hadn't liked being addressed in that manner.

"I've done that already," she said, "but that was when Kate was working nearby. I've no idea where she is now."

Silas smoothed his hair and grunted. "Get in touch with the mother Francine once more. That should be easy enough for you. After all she plays bridge at your house, doesn't she?"

***

Kate wasn't totally satisfied with her latest journey because to her mind it hadn't achieved much. If Sechem and Jamére were correct she'd be having her journeys alone from now on and maybe, just maybe she could run it her way. Everything they'd already done was simply preparation for what was to come. It was training she knew, but for what, and why her? She sat on the rickety bench in a shady area of their small pretty garden pondering how she could get started. The birds were singing their hearts out and bees were busy with the flowers. All was well with their world. But they only needed to focus on their own part, that of keeping the hive alive and healthy. Her small endeavour in keeping Earth alive and healthy should be her only focus too.

She remembered that she could probably only do space or time travel as an individual when her implant was activated. Maybe that wasn't right. Who or what activated it? Was she mind controlled? Kate nibbled on her bottom lip as she thought about it. She had to find out, and who better to ask than her father. She got up from her seat and went indoors to find him.

As she entered the kitchen she realised that her father had been watching her from the window. She could see from his face that he'd picked up on her thoughts. She'd forgotten how psychic he was and how in tune they were with each other.

"Come and sit down my darling." He took her hand and led her into the front room. "What's bothering you this time? From the look on your face it's not a trifling thing. You're such a worry bunny."

"Sit down dad. I want to ask you a serious question, and I want a straight, honest answer."

"I always give you honest answers, sweetie."

Kate took a deep breath. "Am I mind controlled through the implant?" There, she'd said it. "I've heard of some people who have implants and what it could do to them. It seems to me that none of it was good for them."

Jacob took off his glasses and began wiping them. It was a clear sign to Kate that he had to think carefully before answering her. She couldn't wait and said, "There was one man I've heard of but have never met, Kieron lee Perrin who said he was multi implanted in 1975 and considered himself to be a Cyborg. After all it was you who told me that Helga is mind controlled, but is it through an implant?"

Jacob looked up and gave a half smile. "Do you remember the mind controlling satellite you destroyed? There are multiple other ways to control the minds of others. Have you never heard of the HAARP installation in Alaska?" Kate looked puzzled.

"No, I haven't come across it but will look it up now that you've mentioned it." She looked thoughtful. "Especially if it's involved with controlling others." Kate made a mental note to do some research.

Jacob frowned and put his glasses back on. "Oh, it does much more than that my darling. But we are getting away from your question, aren't we?"

Kate nodded. She could see by his expression that her father was taking her question seriously.

"Rest easy, my darling daughter. There are many ways an implant can be given. More and more people are being duped and encouraged to have microchips inserted in them for a whole variety of reasonably sounding purposes." He leaned over and patted her arm. "Kate, do you really think your biological mother and I would allow anything to be done to you that would be harmful?"

"No of course not, but . . ." Kate got up from her chair and started walking up and down the room like a caged animal. Jacob reached out to her and pulled her down on the sofa to sit next to him.

"But nothing. It's important to think about who's doing the implanting and why. As you well know there are good people, and not so good people. You call them black hats and white hats. You've met some of both. There are also those who arrange for implants with the very best intentions to assist and do good in the world. These people only mean to help and don't mean any harm whatsoever. The list is endless.

"For example, there are Cochlear implants to help deaf people hear again, dental implants to give teeth back to a denuded mouth, implants to track those with Alzheimer's so they don't get lost, spinal implants, heart implants. Animals get micro-chipped so that if they get lost or stolen they can be traced. Do you want me to go on?"

"I get the message dad. But you are avoiding the *real* question in my mind. Stop fooling around and be straight with me. What about my own implant?"

Kate saw that her father didn't find it easy to explain, but he'd no choice any more.

Jacob sighed. "Positive implants that you are thinking about, such as yours, are different from negative implants used for mind control. The positive ones are made of pure light. They're in sacred geometry shapes and comply with all requirements of being "in service" to love and light of the Divine Plan."

"Kate wasn't satisfied with that. "How can mine be activated if it's just pure light? How can pure light be switched on and off?"

"There you've said it, my darling. Lights can be switched on and off." Jacob got up and switched the wall light on and off to demonstrate.

"But you're using something solid to do that. Your hand and the solid switch itself."

Jacob was getting nowhere. He tried again.

"You're forgetting the work you do yourself. When you go into a higher vibration you are still able to affect third dimensional things. You've demonstrated that again and again. This is just as true for anyone else. Just think how spirit beings are able to move objects in a physical world, and how some people are able to feel their touch. And think how psychic surgeons from a higher vibration are able to heal those still in a physical body. But that's not what I'm trying to say. As you know the mind is powerful and can create. It can activate just by intention and thought."

"So, it *is* mind control after all."

"Yes indeed. Yours! Control by your own mind. We, all of us, collectively agreed before you were conceived that you would be happy to be a guinea pig in this experiment."

"So now I'm an experiment. This is too much." Kate flopped down onto the nearest chair and stared with troubled eyes out of the window. It was such a normal world out there.

Jacob went to her. He'd done a bad job of explaining, and he knew it. He turned her away from the window and drew her to face him.

"Now listen to me, you silly girl. You personally agreed to this. Nobody's controlling you. You're the only one that can activate your implant now that it is turned on, nobody else."

"The experiment? What's that all about?" Kate felt light in the head.

"The experiment is that only you and the team can activate this implant inside you even though it had a time set when this was to be put into action. Remember it was inserted while your brain was growing inside the embryo. It's not foreign to you and is part of you." Kate listened carefully, but still had many questions. This after all was her life, not his.

"Then, tell me this. Why did I have to have it activated by others? Why couldn't I do it myself?"

"You agreed that we, your parents would know when you were ready to take full control. All the journeys and tasks you've already been given were preparing you to go it alone. It's a bit like passing your driving test." Kate brightened, understanding a little more, but she still had unanswered questions.

"Why is it an experiment? Others have implants so it's not unusual."

"It's an experiment in that it was inserted in the brain while it was developing. This had never been done before. This is why it will be your intention and thoughts that activate it. Yours is an advance model that will enable you to mentally, vibrationally and inter-dimensionally travel through time. You can and will change body form according to the need and urgency of any given situation. No other, that we are aware of has these capabilities, except of course some creatures of the deep such as the mimic octopus, squid and cuttlefish." Jacob paused for breath. "Of course, the exceptions are avatars, high celestial masters such as the Master Jesus, but these do not have implants." He laughed at the idea. Smiling he looked fondly at his daughter. "You will be called upon my darling."

"Is there anything else you haven't told me?" Kate was getting used to these bombshells in her life. Where would it end?

"You can decide, if you wish, to be monitored through the implant for your protection when you have your excursions."

"Excursions, my eye! Is that what you call them? Just as if I was on holiday?" exclaimed Kate. But after a short while she broke into laughter.

Jacob began laughing too. For both of them it was a release of emotions. "My darling child, the positive implants are used to communicate better, and to offer assistance if needed. A scout ship can often do this, and they too can morph into different shapes. They can also activate areas that have been unused in people or which have become dormant in the DNA. So you see my dear, positive implants are beneficial to many who have them. Does that make you feel any better?"

Kate nodded and realised that she was about to enter a whole new and exciting time in her life.

CHAPTER FIFTEEN

FIRST CALL FOR HELP

Early next day Kate stood before the mirror in her bedroom, admiring the reflections of the morning sun that painted the walls in soft colours. It was going to be a good day. She breathed in the scent of spring flowers that drifted through the open window. Then she was startled by a voice in her head.

"Come quick. Hurry! We need you here, now." Kate didn't recognise the voice. It wasn't Sechem or Jamére, or even Master M. What was she to do? She looked around her for ideas. Clearly she had to do something. Jacob was out for his early morning stroll. He'd be out for a long time on such a lovely day. This was a call for help, one she couldn't ignore.

"I'm coming," she said in her head and hoped they, whoever it was, would receive her thought.

"Hurry up." The voice had a desperate edge to it now. Kate quickly tuned in, the speed in which she so quickly entered her deep altered state took her breath away. It had never been so fast before. She wondered if this was due to the heightened abilities the implant gave her. She was so quickly in connection, it had to be.

"I'm coming. Hold on," she said and began to disappear from the room.

Next thing she saw were earthen steps covered in rattan leading down to a native village. Should she tread carefully? Caution might be a good idea. Kate's ears strained to hear anything that might give her a clue as to why she was called. There was a slight buzzing sound that meant nothing to her. Something large she'd no time to see whizzed by her shoulder. It was fast, so fast.

A movement caught her eye. Then it was gone. Small shuffling sounds were on either side of her. What was she to do? She kept walking. The steps were well worn, as if many people had been this way before. She rounded a bend. It was then she saw a native long house further down the path. It reminded her of a typical native meeting place where decisions are made and where everybody congregates. Kate had no idea what period of time she was in, or what part of the world this was. All she knew was that somebody had called for help and she must go to them. She'd entered a completely different world, and Kate had no idea what or where that world was. But step in she must. There was no going back. Once she stepped in there'd be no changing her mind.

Too late she realised she was being followed by many natives, local people were following her. They wanted to see where she'd go and what she would do. They were intrigued. Hands from either side tried to grab her, but they didn't quite make it. Kate knew that if they caught her they would pull her away from the path. But they didn't quite catch hold of her. They were trying but couldn't quite reach. Kate's heart hammered in her chest as she recognised the stench of dark energies. She kept walking. She was just a little afraid but something inside her urged her on.

Kate continued to walk through undergrowth, along an obscure path where not many had been before. She realised she'd been sent ahead so that the others could follow. Those who wouldn't take the lead; who'd refused to take the lead. Somehow, she knew they looked to her to do that.

At last she reached a village. The entrance to it was almost hidden, like a gap in the undergrowth that she had to squeeze her way through. She went down on her bottom and went through feet first. The others stayed outside. They were still waiting to see what she was going to do next. She almost felt them holding their breath. On the other side of the entrance it was light and airy. This was nothing like where she'd just come from. She felt comforted knowing she was protected by her implant and that she could call on her friends if necessary. Was this yet another test, or the real thing? She'd no way of knowing.

There was nobody and nothing there. It was as if she was in another empty world. Nothing was recognisable. Then thankfully she saw a bright pin point of light ahead, so that was clearly an indication of where she must go. She walked towards it hoping it wouldn't disappear. She was alone and felt very lonely. She was unquestionably in some part of what she guessed might be Africa.

As she neared the light she saw it was coming from a village with many huts. Kate walked up to the first one that she could see. It had the light that had guided her here, holding steady over the roof. Stooping she squeezed through the low entrance into a dark interior. It was very black. She couldn't see anything at first, but as her eyes adjusted she noticed two children on the far side, a boy and a girl. They were in front of a large group of children, all staring wide eyed in her direction. They were nervous of her, a stranger. Kate realised they'd probably never seen a white person before. They crouched in fear against the far wall of the hut. She couldn't see any adults, just children. Kate didn't try to reassure them for she realised they wouldn't understand. Instead she sat down cross-legged in the centre of the earthen floor and waited for curiosity to get the better of them. A long time passed in silence.

Eventually the two children in front struggled up from where they'd been huddled together. They began to inch nearer. Kate knew it was useless to try to speak to them, for they wouldn't understand. She saw they were both crippled, maimed. They weren't born like that. They'd been maimed. One was minus a foot, the other one minus an arm. They weren't in good shape. Kate wondered if it had been mines that had caused their injuries. They crept very cautiously towards her, eyes big and round. Because Kate didn't move they looked more reassured but were still nervous. She tried not to look directly at them because it would be too confronting. She kept her eyes down, looking at the ground but watching them out of the corner of her eye.

She waited and tried not to breathe too loudly. After a while Kate very slowly extended her hand towards them. She very slowly raised her head and looked at them and smiled. But still they were not sure. The boy's lips trembled, and she thought he would cry. Kate kept her arm extended. The little girl bravely put out her hand and touched Kate's fingers to see if she was real. She explored Kate's fingers with her little hand, the one she had left. She began to feel the hand more, then her arm and shoulder. Because Kate didn't move she came in closer and tentatively stroked her face. The smell of damp skin and the dirt on her body wafted over Kate. The little boy watched. He didn't want to be outdone by his sister. So he too came forward, touched Kate, and prodded her with one tiny finger. He soon grew bolder when he realised she wasn't going to harm them. He shuffled in a circle around her feeling her clothes, her hair and skin.

After a while they were calmer and trusting enough for her to open her arms and give them a hug. Kate drew them into her and rocked their little bodies of skin and bone back and forth. They started to cry, a whimpering sound. Then they began to sob. The sobbing got louder and more intense, deep, deep sobs from the very core of their being.

Kate looked up and was surprised to see that adults were there after all. They had silently moved into the hut. She looked up and smiled to encourage the men and women as they stood hesitating in the doorway. They cautiously came further into the hut, as many as could crowd in. They'd heard the crying of the children and had come to see what had caused it. They ought to be used to it by now she thought.

Kate was then told in her head, "They're not used to it, for when there's deep suffering there's no crying. There's silence and patient resignation. They go beyond crying."

The people saw that she too wept with and for the children. She called out to her spirit friends for help. "I don't know what I can do here, except to be here and give them something from the outside world that isn't going to hurt them. This is a place that's not reached by world aid associations, for this place is hidden and isn't easily reached by the outside." Tears ran down her cheeks.

A reply came at once. "Ask spirit if you can bring some hope, some light by being their contact. Ask for the rainbow bridge to reach down to this place, and for it to be a bridge for the angels and the light, so that they can travel this bridge when they wish to leave. Ask for something better for them. You're to take them. You're to lead them to the bridge and to encourage them to go over it to the arms of the angels."

She watched with awe as a rainbow bridge materialised and filled the hut with light. Kate did as she was instructed. The adults fell to their knees and covered their eyes. One by one all the children got up, stretched out their arms and walked into the rainbow. It was done.

Was this part of her work? Next thing Kate knew she was back alone in her room standing in the early morning light. No time had passed. Had it all been a dream? It was then she realised her cheeks were still wet with tears and her slippers had mud and straw on them.

CHAPTER SIXTEEN

DISCOVERED

Helga was ecstatic and almost did a jig around the office. She stopped herself just in time. It would have been quite a shock to anyone walking in and seeing the boss acting so out of character. They couldn't know that she'd just received a call from headquarters. The team had located Kate and her father. She jumped in glee as she heard the news. What was even better, they were still in the country under their own names. How foolish they'd been. Retaining their identities made it all the easier. Now she and the heavy team could get to work. She'd managed to rid herself of Silas by recommending him for the position in espionage he so eagerly desired. Her private nickname for him was Slimy Silas. He could be slimy somewhere else now. She'd never enjoyed the way he bossed her around. She was still stuck with Marco however. He could be useful though and would do whatever she told him to do.

Her phone rang again. She recognised the number immediately and her heart jumped in happy anticipation. This time it was the leading man from the team that had held the meeting in her home. Helga's ego was suitably bolstered, and she could hardly stop herself from grinning. Here was the top man asking for her help. A finger to you Silas, she thought as she picked up the phone.

"Madam, here are the location co-ordinates. Get yourself down there. No more excuses about not being near enough to track Kate Greene's activities. Your expenses will be covered. We have booked both you and Silas into the Broomsquire Hotel. It's close enough for you to do your work."

Helga plucked up courage to ask a question. "How did you find them? Have they been active?" There was a distinct hesitation on the other end of the line. Were they going to tell her anything?

After a few moments he answered. "We've picked up her energy signal through our own remote viewing spies. They were trawling and got lucky. She'd already strayed into the area of Jump Room technology." Helga's ears pricked up. As soon as he said it Helga knew he'd made a mistake. She hadn't been told about Jump Rooms. She didn't know anything about them. She definitely wasn't meant to know of or be included in these things.

Helga was on it straight away. "Jump Room technology? What is that? Why wasn't I told?"

He hesitated again. There was silence for a moment or two. It was just long enough for Helga to get suspicious once more. What wasn't she being told, and why not? Did Silas know about this and she didn't? That would be unthinkable.

"That information is on a need to know basis and you do not need to know," was all he said. Helga decided not to push it, not yet. For now she had a job to do and she'd do it well.

She packed her bags that night and set off for Broomsquire Hotel in Tadley. She'd no idea how close to her quarry she was going to be. It didn't take long to drive there from Dorset and was pleased to discover it was only twenty minutes off the M4, the main highway. Once she arrived she'd have plenty of time to make sure her room was in a secluded position away from any distracting noise. She needed peace and quiet to tune in to her quarry's activities.

She pulled into the private carpark and was disconcerted to see the hotel was not a modern complex but a rather old-fashioned establishment that from the outside looked more like a pub. Resigning herself she entered the cosy reception area and was met by a smiling lady, who she assumed was the receptionist.

"I'm Amanda," the lady said. "Welcome".

Helga looked the receptionist up and down with a cold stare and gave her name. "I have a reservation. My room must be away from disturbance of any kind," she stated, in a tone that stood for no argument.

Amanda hesitated. "Our main rooms are at the front and overlook the main road. The only room we have left that is suitable is at the back. It's not as comfortable as those nearer the front," stammered the nervous girl behind the desk. This guest's steel trap face frightened her.

"I'll take it anyway. Make sure I'm not disturbed for any reason." Helga collected her key and stalked off. It was time to set her psychic abilities in motion. Kate would soon be in trouble.

***

Kate saw that her father was concerned over something. He fiddled with this and that and couldn't settle. He picked up his newspaper and then put it down. He did this several times until Kate felt she had to say something.

"Are you going to read that paper or not?" she said. She was amused to see her father so distracted. It wasn't like him at all. Then she saw his troubled face. "Dad, what's the matter?"

Jacob put the paper down once more. "I don't know darling. Something is up. My second sight is firing on all cylinders, but I can't put my finger on it. Where on earth are Adam and the boys?" He'd long ago taken to calling Sechem and Jamére, the boys. "Why aren't they here when we need them?"

"That's not fair, dad. They always turn up when it's important to be here. You know that. Anyway, nothing's happening. I agree, it's a bit too quiet, but that's a good thing, isn't it? We haven't heard or seen Howie for quite a while now either."

"Yes, and we still don't know if he's said anything" Jacob replied. "I don't like this feeling that there's something going on. You haven't had any journeys without telling me, have you? You wouldn't be that foolish."

Kate went silent. Her father didn't know she'd had her latest adventure without him. She hadn't used the wall mirror or sat in a chair before it.

"Well," she confessed. "I had an experience recently. You were out when it happened, and I truly didn't plan it. I haven't had time to tell you."

Kate told him her story and worried about how he'd take it. However, Jacob laughed and chuckled in delight. He grabbed her around the waist and danced her around the room.

"My darling. It's working. You're having your journeys without me having to be present in order to be safe. You were safe, weren't you?"

"Well, there were some entities trying to grab hold of me, but I passed them easily. No worries."

"Maybe that's why I'm having these uneasy feelings," he said. "You must be careful. Not all spirits here or in space have good intentions. You must know that after everything that's happened."

Kate could see by her father's expression that even as he spoke he knew everything wasn't all right. His inner senses were still warning him about something.

He frowned. "Why haven't we heard from Howie since he was here? Did we frighten him off? I don't see how we could have since he fell asleep so quickly. Let's hope he's all right."

***

Howie wasn't alright. Jacob was correct. Something was amiss. Howie was shaving early one morning when his door burst open. Two men wearing green combat clothes rushed in and grabbed his arms.

"You're coming with us," they said. "Back to headquarters for you my lad."

"What's this all about?" Howie yelled as he struggled to get free.

"You'll find out when we get there. Get dressed." was their only reply.

The two heavily built men bustled him into a car and drove at speed to Blackbushe airfield in Yately, Hampshire. Howie saw the sign as they entered the airfield and remembered how a business jet had crashed there in July 2015, killing the sister and stepmother of the former al-Qaida leader Osama bin Laden. He knew Blackbushe airport was originally an RAF base. An unmarked private jet was waiting for them on the tarmac, engines running.

They climbed on board and settled into their seats. Not a word was shared with Howie during many long hours' flight.

Howie's stomach grumbled. He was hungry. "Can I have something to eat?" he asked. "I haven't had any breakfast."

One of the men handed him a packaged meal. Howie ate. Nerves had made him ravenous. He dropped off to sleep eventually until one of the men shook him awake as landing lights of an airfield came into sight. Howie realised they weren't going to land at a civilian airport. Flashing their credentials, the men escorted him through a building out to a darkened vehicle. It was raining hard as they drove in silence through streets crawling with traffic.

They pulled up in a quiet street. As they brought Howie out of the car he caught a glimpse of a notice on the wall of the building as he was rushed in through a side entrance. He realised he was at the U.S. Dept. of Defence on Wisconsin Avenue, in the Bethesda area of Maryland. It was an impressive building. He could hardly keep up as they hurried him along corridor after corridor.

It wasn't long before he stood in front of his superior officers. Standing in the darkened room was the one person he hadn't expected and had hoped never to see again. Silas stood next to an ageing general and was busy giving him a light for his cigar.

The general tilted his chair back and puffed on his cigar as he scrutinized Howie.

"What do you know about dancing?" It was an unexpected question. Howie didn't know how to reply. The puzzled look on his face amused the general. Howie realised this man liked to play with his victims. Suddenly he slammed his fist down hard on the table. Howie jumped.

"You were seen dancing with Kate Greene. The lady we'd been looking for all over England. Why did you not report back? What are you up to? You'll be court-martialled for not obeying orders." The general's eyes narrowed as he waited for Howie's reaction.

"What have you to say for yourself?"

Howie gulped. He tried to maintain a blank expression. *Do not let them know what you are thinking. Do not let them see fear*. His training taught him that. But the training couldn't stop the sweat running down his neck, or his knees knocking. He had to think fast and that wasn't his strong point. Neither was lying, but he had to do something now, and quickly. If he didn't it was a court-martial for sure.

"I didn't know she was Kate Greene - Sir," he muttered with as honest a face as he could muster.

"You were given a photograph of her," the general shouted at him and thrust her picture in his face.

"I- I-lost the photo on the flight to UK. I couldn't remember her face." Howie stumbled over his words.

The general leaned forward. "Come closer boy. Don't take me for a fool." He grabbed Howie's lapels and pulled him even nearer. Howie felt the man's hot cigar breath and tried to draw back. The sergeant standing by the door stiffened in readiness to jump in. He looked alarmed. This general was well known for brutality. Howard was just a lad and was easy meat for a man like this general.

At that moment Silas who'd been watching from the side stepped forward. He smiled but it came out like a smirk of enjoyment.

"I think we can turn this to our advantage sir. Are you able to see her again Howard?"

"Not from here," Howie replied, without thinking first. He thought it was a stupid question.

"We can send you back. No court-martial, providing you follow our instructions." Silas said.

The general was beginning to catch on. He snapped his fingers at the man by the door.

"Take him away sergeant. We'll deal with him later." The sergeant looked at Howie who was visibly shaking by now.

"Come on lad, it's not as bad as you think," he said. He led him out of the room. Secretly he wondered what those two devils had in store for the young man.

Alone the two men discussed the situation and how they could turn it to their advantage.

"Well, Silas, what have you in mind? Speak up man."

"I've history with the woman and her father. I know how to deal with them better than anyone else. Why don't we send Howard back? I could go too. If he says nothing to them, they'll be none the wiser. They'll assume he's kept quiet about their whereabouts. Their guard will be down." Silas smirked in satisfaction. "If he stays friendly with them he can report back to us on what they are doing. With his help we can bug their house, as we did before in Dorset. With Helga in the area it should be easy for her to psychically pick up on their off the radar activities."

"Hmm! I suppose it could work." The general said. "They've no idea we know where they are, so they won't try to escape as they did before. Gork, the Dark One will be pleased."

In spite of himself Silas couldn't help a shudder at the mention of the dark one who shall always be feared.

He sidled over to the general's chair. "Your cigar has gone out, sir. Would you like another?"

CHAPTER SEVENTEEN

EARTH INHABITED BY OTHER RACES

The Spiritual Galactic Command Council was holding their regular meeting in the circular chamber reserved for them on the Mother Ship. The walls of coloured lights shimmered and flowed like waterfalls. As usual the table seating was set as a circle so that all attending could see each other.

The one known as Osishoo, aka Master M, was dressed from head to foot in white and gold and was the first to speak. His large glowing eyes swept the gathering. He smiled with pleasure. Everyone present knew he was respected as a highly placed spiritual soul, rather than just by name.

"We mustn't forget the reason for our meetings, and why we're calling on those currently incarnated on Earth. There has to be harmony in the Universe, and as you all know Earth is inharmonious at times. If this gets worse, our priority will be to save Earth, not the human race, which can always start again. Our intention is to save both. We earnestly hope to encourage humans to remember their heritage of spiritual values and act accordingly.

"We've gathered to discuss the future programme, of allocating guidance and direction for those on planet Earth. You are here to give guidance to those who are willing to accept it. All of you have a large part to play. There's a need for direction and enlightenment as have never been needed before. You'll direct wisely, and with authority that which has been earned through many lifetimes of experience and self-learning."

A gentle murmur ran through the assembly of spirit guides, space lords and representatives of interested races who had travelled from various star systems. Everybody there had been drawn to planet Earth to assist in its development and spiritual journey. It was a glorious assembly of so many colourful and varied races from other worlds.

Master M raised his hand to silence the murmuring. "The planet Earth is in difficulties. We have a responsibility to do something to assist it, before it loses all life-forms. It is already losing so many it can upset the whole balance of nature. However, we don't have the right to exert our will over any individual, even if that individual is bent on destruction. We can merely present the possibilities so that mankind may make decisions necessary to avert disaster, or at least lessen the impact of its actions. Moreover, we also have a responsibility to all planetary systems, not only to that of the local universe."

The glorious figure turned around to face the wall behind him. He waved a hand at it and the entire wall became a huge screen. Depicted there were many stars, galaxies and planets. "I'm to make it clear to man in a language he can understand that man isn't controller of the Earth or of the universe. He's not in command. There's a higher authority. This same authority has instructed me to act in kindness and love to further the creation to its best advantage, not for destruction. I'm also given the responsibility of looking for the greatest benefit to the whole of creation, not only for one portion of it, such as the planet Earth."

The booming voice vibrated throughout the entire assembly. All eyes were on the screen and they watched transfixed at the awesome movement of planets, galaxies, new stars, dying stars, and clouds of cosmic dust.

"The souls of man do not reside on the planet Earth alone. They reside on many other levels and on many other planets besides. Therefore, we have to look to the greater whole. At times, some adjustment is necessary for the smoother running of the entire system. I have the authority and the responsibility to maintain this. I'll do it with love, compassion, and understanding. But I'll also do it with a firmness that will not be shaken. It's for each individual here to understand the overall system, and his or her role in it."

Many heads nodded in agreement of his words. They had long ago realised that what happened to Earth affected other spheres in space, especially with regard to damaging nuclear weaponry in space.

"We are showing you this representation not for amusement, but so that you may take heart and know that there's to be a continuation of mankind, even if it is elsewhere, other than Earth." The scene faded, and the murmuring began again. After a while the energy in the chamber returned to a sense of calm once more.

Master M turned to Sechem and Jamére. "How is it going with Kate and her father? Has she managed the implant activity as well as we expected? We haven't had any reports from you for a long while."

Sechem and Jamére stood up together. They stopped themselves just in time from bowing to him. They knew he didn't appreciate a show of subservience or affected reverence. He considered all were equal. The great birdman smiled fondly at them and patiently waited for their response.

Sechem spoke first. "Kate is outstripping our expectations. Her training is complete, and she's already taken her first journey completely alone. What should she do next?" Sechem hesitated. "I feel great concern for Kate since I was responsible for waking her up. She's now on her own."

However, Master M knew more than they did. "Next she'll delve into more areas that are away from public knowledge. She'll be directed by us."

Jamére put his hand up. "What is she expected to do with what she discovers? Will she be safe?"

Master M frowned slightly. "On that point, we've noted that her position has been discovered. It's time that she began to teach others to do what she does. That way if anything happens to her the work can continue."

Both Sechem and Jamére looked at him aghast. They protested. "You think so little of her that she's expendable? What's more, only she has that particular implant. She can't teach others who haven't got it."

"Master M looked at them with a patient smile. "How do you know she is the only one with it? You don't know everything. She can still teach others to travel in the mind if they can't do it physically."

Jamére spoke up. "Can we bring in Adam again? There's this guy Howard who's taken a fancy to her, and she's lonely. Who knows what may happen if they're left alone too long. She likes him too and if Adam stays away as often as he does . . . well, it's anybody's guess as to how it could turn out.

The great one was thoughtful. He closed his eyes to consider his words before speaking.

"You are of course aware that Adam has other work to do as a 'Trojan Horse' within the secret government? He's been busy reporting back to us on their plans and we've been able to avert some global disasters as a result. Have you never wondered why some nuclear missiles have not been successful, or that rockets have misfired?"

"We thought that was Kate's doing," said Sechem.

"His reports enabled us to direct her and others to take action. So you see his work is equally vital. His position there is important. Should we really remove him from Washington?"

Sechem and Jamére were silent. There was no answer. It wasn't their decision to make.

Master M stood up. It was clear the meeting was over. The two space travellers waited until he'd gone. They left the hall together.

"All we can do now is keep young Howie and Kate apart, if we can," declared Jamére.

"Let's frighten him," Sechem said. "I'll give him a dream he'll not forget in a hurry."

CHAPTER EIGHTEEN

SHADOWS

When man again shall conquer the ocean
and fly in the air on wings like the birds;
when he has learned to harness the lightning,
then shall the time of warfare begin.
Great shall the battle be twixt the forces,
great the warfare of darkness and Light.
From The Emerald Tablets

Jacob was busy cutting the grass, but his mind was on other things while he pushed the mower up and down. He didn't notice the shadow creeping up on him until the last moment. He stopped in his tracks and stayed as still as he could. He wasn't sure how he felt about this unknown presence. His psychic sense had deserted him for once. This alone made him uneasy. He moved forward. The shadow moved with him. He knew it wasn't his own shadow for the sun was in the wrong position.

Jacob said a quick silent prayer and resisted the urge to turn around. He'd heard about the shadow people and knew they'd disappear the minute he looked. He had some knowledge of shadow people who are usually attracted to one person or location for unknown reasons. People they visited often saw them as dark silhouettes of human-shape, generally male, that preferred to watch someone unseen. They flee the moment they are noticed. Was this what was happening here in this quiet garden?

His second sight hadn't sent any warning signals to him, so he knew whatever it was couldn't be harmful in any way. Should he turn around? He hesitated. In that moment, the shadow swiftly moved. It was facing him. Now *that* was unusual. It appeared to be watching him, studying him. They watched each other, neither knowing quite how to proceed. Jacob felt he was in a time warp.

He'd heard of the theory that they were some sort of other-dimensional beings, whose dimension of origin occasionally overlaps with ours. Could this explain their fleeting nature? Other believers and paranormal authors couldn't agree among themselves whether shadow people were evil, helpful, or neutral. Some even speculated that shadow people might be extra-dimensional inhabitants of another universe. A significant number of people believed that shadow beings act as benevolent guardians, watching and guiding us.

Jacob's concern was why was it visiting him now? What was its purpose? Was he seeing it because his own psychic abilities made it possible? Was it an inter-dimensional being, a time traveller, or something else? He decided he'd nothing to lose by asking. Kate always told him to ask if you wanted an answer. If you didn't ask you didn't get a response. It was her mantra. He smiled at the thought of her. Was it his imagination, or did the shadow smile back?

"Who are you and what do you want?" It came out as a whisper from Jacob. He waited. No sound, not a peep. He repeated his question. Suddenly his mind was filled with a jumble of thoughts. He couldn't make any sense of them, until he realised with a flash that he needed to switch over to a telepathic mode. He knew how to do this. Just intend to receive and listen to your thoughts. It worked.

He received. "You and Kate are being shadowed, but not just by us. Those who would hurt you are seeking you out. We've seen them at work."

Jacob's heart plummeted. "I thought we were safe. Who are they? Who are following us?"

"You are of course aware of remote viewers and psychic spies."

"Yes." The response and memories came ringing back into his mind. Was it his imagination or did the shadow jump about?

Jacob received more unwelcome news. "That's how your daughter, Kate was picked up originally. It was by pure chance that time. Her mind journeys aren't unknown. Why do you think there's so much interest in her by forces of the dark? She goes into restricted areas where she's not welcome. Now she's working again, and her energies have been noticed. Watch out!"

Jacob thought fast. "Can you help?" But the telepathic link was breaking up. He heard just in time, a whisper.

"We're only shadows." Then it was gone. The shadow was no more. Jacob carried on mowing the grass.

***

Kate was unaware that she might be followed on her way home from work. No longer was there the previous stress in Dorset caused by being with Helga most of the day, and her present job was easy with no pressure she couldn't handle. As a result, a false sense of security lulled her into calm. She felt very safe knowing Jamére, Sechem and her dad were on hand if she needed them. She wished she could say the same for Adam. Oh, how she missed him.

She let herself in the front door and changed out of her office suit into jeans and a red sweater. She felt more comfortable in these clothes and relaxed. There was no sign of her father indoors as she prepared the evening meal. She was eager for another journey, with or without Adam.

"Dad?" she said as soon as Jacob walked in from working in the garden. "Shall we do some more mind travelling this evening? I really feel like it, and it'll make a change from being asked to do one. *We* can decide for a change."

Kate and Jacob settled down for what they often called 'a session'. It would be just the two of them this time, but it seemed to her that Jacob was uneasy.

"Shall we have our meal before we start?" Kate was eager to get going but knew her father's preference of eating beforehand. To her utter amazement Jacob merely shook his head.

"Not tonight, if you don't mind. We'll eat later." Kate sensed something was amiss. For her dad to decline food was seriously out of character. The chair was put in place and they settled down to wait. Kate took herself down quickly and Jacob watched intently as she walked into the mirrored wall. It was becoming routine.

Kate saw she was wearing a long, plain gown in green. The stairs were constricted with a rail on either side. The narrow treads were rough-hewn wood, nothing polished. She went deeper and deeper into herself as she carefully went down each step. She became aware of rustling noises on either side of her and felt she wasn't alone. Reaching the bottom, she saw she was outside, and standing on a hanging swing bridge high over a forest canopy. At the far end of the bridge were a lot more wooden steps to take her down onto soft ground. Careful not to trip she climbed down until she got to undergrowth. It was like being in the base of a pit. There was not much space to stand. Just discernible was an opening in the side that she felt she could get through, even though it was covered with branches and brambles. If she'd been any larger she'd have had difficulty getting through the gap. She tried to squeeze her way through, her gown catching on the brambles, but it was impossible to move forward. In desperation she looked for another opening, and there it was on the right, just a clear gap in the undergrowth.

As soon as she stepped through she found herself in a strange world, a completely different vista, nothing like the one she'd left behind.

Kate called out to the space. "Take me where I need to be, show me what I need to see." As soon as she asked she saw a row of little blue lights on the ground, marking the way. It was just enough for her to see her way and no more.

"Where am I going, where am I going?" she called again.

"You're entering another world, another time, another dimension." Came a voice in her head.

Kate tried to go forward. But there was a barrier, a wall, an invisible wall. It was enough to stop her. She realised she needed to ask permission.

"May I enter through this veil, this barrier?"

"Enter." As the word came, Kate found she could walk through as if it didn't exist. It closed behind her. She was indeed in another time and was grateful that there was soft air she could breathe. Everything shimmered in blue, but out of focus. She waited for it to become sharper, but it stayed flickering. Kate thought, *maybe it's because I'm not used to it. My view of it hasn't yet adjusted.*

Suddenly Kate saw large, tall human beings. For an inexplicable reason, she hadn't expected humans. They were mostly male, though there were some beautiful females. The voice was speaking to her.

"This is a vision of what can be in your future. This isn't fixed. It's an aspect of a possible world, which is why it moves back and forth and seems to shimmer. Realise this time hasn't yet been set. The large size of those you can see relates to the strength required to exist in this world. Only the strong will survive, and we mean physically resilient. Those who aren't robust cannot endure this reality, and so will pass on. What you're seeing is a possible future. As we've said, it's not set.

"I had hoped to see a future that was more likely." Kate said.

"There are many possible futures. You know this already. This is but one. Know that if things don't go well, those who survive will need to be physically strong. It'll be survival of the fittest, and not according to the mentality, or technology, or the ability to see ahead. It will be survival on a daily basis."

"Can't you show me an alternative future for us as a human race? Please, a more positive one."

"You'll need to go in a different direction."

"But it was ***you*** who led me on this path by giving me the lines and lights to follow."

"We showed you the way, but you didn't have to follow."

"I'm asking you now to show me another way." Kate felt disgruntled. This was not what she'd expected.

"Go to the mind's viewing room. Do as you've been instructing others. Change it into something better. See a view that's as bad as it can be, then change it for the better. It is good practice for you. Isn't this what you've been teaching others?" Kate had to admit it was. She knew she had to walk her talk.

"This is what you'll do on most of your trips. The various scenarios will be individual, separate, and each will have a reason to be changed. Collect a group together to do this. We constantly stress that you Earthlings yourselves must make the changes. This is the way it can be done."

Kate's mind couldn't accept any more information.

"Thank you," she told the voice. "I'm tired now."

Kate came back easily into her natural state, grateful that she could return to her world without having to retrace her steps. She hadn't enjoyed seeing the future, where one had to be strong. Kate recognised the truth of what he, whoever he was, had said. She saw too how relieved Jacob was to see her return. He must have felt some of what she'd experienced.

"I didn't see a thing this time." he said. "Did I sleep through the whole thing as before?"

Kate looked at his worried face. "It was alright, dad. I'm fine. Don't worry so much."

"Now we can eat," Jacob said firmly. "I need to put my mind to something easier to handle. I'll cook what you've prepared," he said. "You rest. Eating will keep us grounded."

***

Jacob got up from his seat and stretched. His brow creased and he was still concerned about the shadows watching what Kate did, and where she went. Who did they represent? His thoughts couldn't get away from his meeting with the shadow, and the warning given in the garden. At the back of his mind he suspected it could be the secret government sending their spies. Then he laughed at himself using the same shadowy words with very different objectives; *that which shall not be seen.*

Did both kinds of shadow people realise that Kate not only remote viewed, but because of something in her was able to virtually travel, to the place she was remote viewing? She could physically affect various things that needed changing? Did they know that Kate was teaching others while in their own subconscious state? She showed them how to remote view and how to take themselves non-physically into many places and scenarios, so that they too could change things. However, without having her implant they could only go so far in projecting themselves and needed to use their minds and set the intention.

Jacob realised Kate didn't want to rest at all. She followed him into the kitchen and watched as he cooked the vegetables she'd prepared for their meal. Perched on a stool she fiddled with a spoon. She tapped it repeatedly on the table until it got too much for Jacob.

"Would you please stop that, my darling? It's getting on my nerves. Why don't you go and sit down and relax in the front room?" Kate blew him a kiss but ignored his suggestion, her mind elsewhere.

She went to him and put her arms around his shoulders. "I love you, Dad."

"What was that for?" Jacob was surprised but pleased.

"You are always so calm and supportive, whatever I do. I don't deserve you, Dad."

He looked at his daughter, surprised at her outburst. What was bothering her now? Her display of affection was always welcomed, but it reminded him of when she was a small child, suffering under her mother's lack of love of any kind, which had almost amounted to cruelty.

"What is it, my darling?"

"Dad, after we've eaten can I ask you some questions? Serious questions. You may not know the answers, but I have to ask."

"Let's eat and we'll both be energised for whatever you have in mind. Food will be ready soon." Jacob hoped his inquisitive daughter wouldn't ask uncomfortable questions about her star mother, Joslene. He wasn't ready for that.

***

They ate in silence, each wrapped up in their thoughts. Fully replete, they began to clear the table. It had been an eventful day. At last Jacob felt Kate pluck up courage to bring up what had been bothering her. Washing the dishes could be dealt with later.

"Dad, what if I had a group here so that I could teach them how to do what I do? Would you mind?" Jacob stopped what he was doing and held his hand up in a gesture that clearly said, hold up there. He turned to face her with a set expression.

"I don't think that's wise sweetheart. It'll attract too much attention. Think about how narrow this lane is. With many cars arriving on a regular basis there's bound to be talk around the village. Remember, darling, it was your activity before that brought unwanted notice to us."

"But. . ."

"No buts! It won't do."

"But during my latest journey I was told to gather groups and teach them to change what they wouldn't like to have in their future world into something better."

Jacob realised his daughter wasn't about to give up.

"You've already done that during one of your journeys. Have you forgotten so quickly?" He argued.

"I know quite well that we have to *create* the future we want to live in?" Kate said. "However just knowing isn't the same as going into the future, using the mind and changing things. That's what they told me to do." Kate frowned. "It should be easier than this."

Jacob saw how frustrated his daughter was. She was like a dog with a bone when she got her teeth into something.

"Darling, nobody said it would be easy. You are part of the future. How you think, how you feel, and how you act matters far more than you realize." He took the dishes to the kitchen and put them in the sink. Kate followed him.

Jacob ran hot water over the plates and began to wash them. "Holding group meetings here is definitely not the way to go about things," he said. "What if a call comes in the middle of a session? What will you do then?"

Kate frowned. Jacob saw she wasn't appeased with these answers and was changing tack.

"Dad, you know the various races in our space family, don't you? How do we know which ones are good, and working to help us? How can we recognise those who are working against us?"

Jacob looked at her in surprise. "That seems to be a daft question. You should go by the feeling they give off when you meet them. Use your special senses and trust them. We're surrounded by multiple different groups of intelligent, humanlike ETs. They've been interacting with Earth throughout our entire recorded history. To some degree they can anticipate what needs to be done, how to do it, how people will react, etc. We owe them a greater debt than we can ever repay."

Kate picked up the tea towel and began drying the dishes. Jacob could see by her thoughtful expression she wasn't about to drop the subject.

She put the plates away in the cupboard. "Dad, how many off-world species are there? I know I've seen some of them at the Galactic Council meetings, but they were so few. Can you tell me more about them, Dad, please?"

Jacob drew her into the front room and sat down on the comfortable settee. He patted the seat beside him. This was going to take some time.

"Come and sit near me, darling." Kate did as she was told and snuggled up to her favourite man. "This could take a while. I'll give you a little history. Are you sure you have enough focus to hear some of it?" Kate nodded.

"Sirius system is the one most connected with you, since your mother came from there. Master M is also of the bird tribe, the most dominant species on Sirius. The Sirius B race was having a war with the Orion Draco. Thank goodness that's over now. The humans on Sirius B had some sort of goodwill union between the beings in the Orion system. Together they created what we now call the Tall Greys, as offspring of a hybrid race, created to stop a war between the Orion's and Sirius B, so that they could have peace amongst themselves. Many representatives of Sirius B have been interacting with the surface population of this planet throughout human history, and their DNA is prevalent in human beings." Jacob watched his daughter's face carefully. Satisfied that she could handle some more he leaned back.

Kate listened, her face alight with all the new information. "Is this where Sechem and Jamére fit in? They're very clearly human in form, even with their bright colours."

Jacob put his arm around Kate and continued. "I am simply giving you a brief outline, not the whole picture. I don't know it all, my sweet, but Sirius A, as I understand it, is the home of the blue lodge, and the mission of the 144,000 ascended masters to Earth. Maybe they're connected with them. Sirius A is the Beacon of Light for a cluster of stars in this local sector of the galaxy and was holding the light when the Archon invasion happened and filled the quadrant of this galaxy with trillions upon trillions of dark entities. If you understand what's going on in the solar system, you'll understand who's behind the wars arising all over the world."

Kate felt a dark shiver running through her body at the idea of trillions of dark entities existing on Earth. She snuggled even closer to her father.

"Because of Sirius A and their light, we're still alive and here today. You can be proud of Master M, Sechem and Jamére. There have always been sentient beings on Earth because they were the so-called guardians responsible for creating life on this planet. They started to evolve biological life from viruses, microbes and on and on. They were here billions of years ago."

"Those dark entities? Are any still here?" Kate looked around the room and looked worried.

"I'm surprised at your question Kate. You already know there are forces beyond this planet that are behind the dreadful things that are occurring here." Jacob said. "As Bill Clinton said, and I quote, 'There is a government within a government that I can't control.' Who is supporting the shadow government and those who have ambitions to control the world?" Jacob gave a big sigh. "Who do you think controls the shadow government?" He sighed again. "There are dark entities of the human kind, as well as space beings. Human beings are entities too remember. There'll always be people with different views to their neighbour, so we can be sure there are differing views between star systems too. We can't throw all Pleiadians, Sirians, Orions, or all ET's with grey skin into one pot."

"How do we protect ourselves from these dark entities?" Kate looked so worried that Jacob held her tight.

"Darling, don't you know that each of us is a divine being with full love intention of the I Am Presence. If you connect with that love and practice it, you won't be manipulated by any other being with bad intent. Put more attention on your connection with your own higher self, and your own power of manifestation. Dark can't enter light, for if it tries it'll be destroyed or transformed. Do you think you're of the light, or of the dark?"

"What a question. I'm of the light of course."

"Then what are you worried about?" Then Jacob remembered the warning from the shadow in the garden.

CHAPTER NINETEEN

EVERY MOVE IS NOTICED

Eyes that you do not see are upon you. Every move is noticed. Where your actions are to assist someone else, the eyes light up with joy and delight. Then they know that all is not lost upon the planet Earth and the heart is lightened.

From spirit

Jacob was awakened early next morning by a hammering on the front door. He got out of bed, thrust his feet into his slippers and pulled on his dressing gown. He hoped the knocking hadn't disturbed Kate. It had been a long hard night and she needed to sleep and recover.

"I'm coming, I'm coming," he called as he hurried to open the door. His mouth dropped open in enormous surprise to see Howie, meek wouldn't hurt a fly Howie. He was shaking all over and looked very very scared.

"Come in lad, come in. What's the matter? You look as if all the demons were after you." Jacob pulled the young man inside and shut the door. He led him to a chair and sat him down. He saw how pale Howie was and how his hands were trembling

"Tell me what's happened to get you in such a state, but please keep your voice down. Kate's still sleeping. We had a late night and she needs to catch up on her sleep before she goes to work tomorrow." He went to the drinks cabinet and poured a large glass of whisky. He thrust the glass into Howie's hand. "Drink this, it'll do you good."

Howie downed the drink in one go. He held on to the glass as if it were a lifesaver. "I had a dream. No, more than that, it was a nightmare."

Jacob looked at him, incredulous. "How old are you? You've come banging on our door at this early hour because of a nightmare?"

"But it was real. I was there in the middle of it. Kate was there too, and she got me out of it."

Jacob almost laughed, but the fear on Howie' face was real. "Howie, how could Kate be there to get you out of a nightmare? She was here, sleeping soundly in her bed."

"You don't understand. She was with me in the nightmare and she saved me. They're after you both. The shadows." Howie put his head in his hands. They were still shaking. Jacob's face blanched at the mention of the shadows. His senses came on full alert at this reference. At this point Kate came into the room rubbing her eyes.

"What's all the noise about? Howie? What are you doing here at this hour? Where have you been this last week?"

"Darling, this young man has had a bad nightmare, and you were in it."

Kate suppressed a laugh. "A nightmare? He came here because of a nightmare? Unbelievable!"

"Darling girl, can't you see how upset he is. He's come with a warning. Don't you see? This is some of *their* doing." Kate's face dropped in dismay. But Howie heard that last sentence. He took his head out of his hands and looked up at them.

"*Their* doing? Who do you mean?"

Kate quickly parried the question. "Don't you think you'd better tell us about this nightmare," she said gently. Jacob passed him another whisky.

Howie gathered himself together. "I was naked in a large room with strange looking, scary creatures. They were all staring at me, as if they wanted to eat me. That was menacing enough, but then a huge man, if you could call him a man, came towards me. He was massive and not quite human. He looked at me with dreadful, burning red eyes that seemed to go right through me. I screamed and screamed. I was in pain all over. As I cried a lot of shadowy creatures surrounded me and tried to pull me to pieces. It was then that Kate came to my rescue. She faced the dreadful, tall creature straight on and appeared to talk to it." Howie looked at Kate with obvious admiration.

"Go on Howie," Jacob urged. He was impatient to hear more now.

"She wasn't afraid of it at all. I watched as it backed off. She turned to the shadow people and ordered them to leave me alone. They were afraid of her for sure, but not too afraid to say she'd better beware. They said they weren't finished with her yet. They shrank back and disappeared. Then I woke up." He waited, anxious for their reaction and emptied his glass, his hands still shaking. "They were afraid of you Kate. That surprised me, even while still in the dream. What was it they were afraid of?"

Jacob felt he had to change the way the conversation was heading. "You know Howie that dreams, or nightmares often reflect our own fears. They are not meant to be taken literally. These images surface while we sleep and are meant to show us how we should take notice of what we fear and do something about it."

He watched Howie's reaction to what he'd said and guessed what was bothering him. Was Kate a spy or not? He knew Howie didn't want to believe what they'd told him in America, but he had to obey their orders.

Then without thinking Howie blurted out, "Kate, are you a spy or not?"

His question took them both by surprise. Kate stared at him. "I'm not a spy, but they are worried . . ." then she stopped, and put a hand over her mouth. She looked at her father for help.

Jacob nodded to her. "He needs an explanation, Kate."

Kate squeezed her eyes shut before looking at the young man. "You see Howie, I dream. Like some people I've developed the ability of becoming conscious in a dream. Some people call it lucid dreaming. I'm able to do things in the dream that aren't done in normal reality. In them I can fly, move objects with my mind and teleport. My dreams are very real to me. Because of what I discover in my dreams others are worried that I might talk about it and tell what I've learnt from my experiences."

Jacob knew she was lying and that they weren't ordinary dreams at all. But she could hardly tell Howie how she travelled.

"I don't understand," Howie drew his brows together in puzzlement. "There's no proof attached to dreams, so nobody would take any notice anyway. I don't know what they're worried about."

"Howie, my dreams take me into places they would prefer I didn't know about. They are worried that I might blab to others."

Howie thought for a minute. "That doesn't make sense. Nobody is going to take notice of somebody's dreams."

"That's enough," Jacob said abruptly. "I think that's enough information for now. Let's change the subject, shall we?"

"Alright, if you say so" said Howie. He seemed pleased to have got his own experience off his chest. He didn't look so shaken now and had stopped trembling. Jacob saw he was more than a little drunk with the two whiskies. He knew Howie liked to stick to beer, and never much of that either.

Howie hiccupped loudly, then stared at Kate. "What about your colonel friend? Where does he fit into this?"

"Howie, do stop calling him colonel. Just use his name. His name's Adam. He comes into it because he's a friend and happens to visit from time to time. No more than that. Dad, can you explain to Howie please?"

Jacob realised that they'd better widen Howie's knowledge, if only to stop him thinking they were dangerous spies out to destroy countries.

He refilled Howie's glass and handed it to him. "Get that down you my boy. We have a connection with those you might call ET's, but which we call our space family. We're trying to acclimatise people to an extra-terrestrial reality, ahead of any official disclosure announcement." Jacob watched as Howie's expression changed into one of disbelief.

"You're kidding me, aren't you?" Howie gave a faltering laugh.

Jacob continued and ignored the comment. There was no stopping now. "There's abundant evidence that we're being contacted, that civilizations have been monitoring us for a very long time. Disclosure is just around the corner, my boy. Their appearance is bizarre to say the least, from any western point of view. These visitors use technologies relating to levels of consciousness, they use toroids and they use counter-rotating magnetic disks for their propulsion systems."

Howie smiled happily and perked up. "As an E-4 Specialist in an army division I am much more in tune with technology. I am more than comfortable with that sort of language," he said and sniggered. "ET's take a bit longer to accept."

He shifted in his seat and looked around for his glass, now empty once more. Jacob noticed and gestured towards the whisky bottle, nodding as he did.

"Yes please." He reached for the bottle, but his hand missed it." Howie was becoming a little tipsy by now. "Please go on," he said, and hiccupped again. Kate and Jacob smiled at each other. It was going better than they expected.

"I'll give you some facts you can verify for yourself."

Jacob filled Howie's glass, and his own and continued speaking. "Gordon Cooper, Former NASA Astronaut, Aeronautical Engineer and test pilot was one of the seven original Astronauts in Project Mercury, the first manned space program of the United States, and Howie, do you know what he said?"

Howie shook his head. "No, I don't know what he said."

Kate put a restraining hand on Jacob's arm. "Don't drink any more, Dad. It's still morning."

Jacob shook her hand off his arm. "Now my boy. As I was saying."

There was no stopping Jacob. "In my opinion, I think they were worried that it would panic the public, so they started telling lies about it. And then I think they had to tell another lie to cover their first lie, now they don't know how to get out of it. It's going to be so embarrassing to admit that all these administrations have told so many untruths. It would be uncomfortable getting out of the fact that there are a number of extra-terrestrial vehicles cruising around out there."

Howie gave a loud burp and held his glass out for a refill again.

Jacob filled both glasses with the last drop in the bottle. He shook it to make sure it was empty. "Extra-terrestrials are beings from another world," he stated in a matter of fact manner.

"Of course," agreed Howie with a stupid grin on his face.

Jacob looked at him and swayed a little on his feet.

Kate sighed. "Dad I am going to the kitchen, and I'll leave you to it," and walked away shrugging her shoulders. Before she left the room, she saw him stagger. "Dad, I don't think you should drink anymore." It wasn't only Howie who was getting drunk, but also her father. Who knows what he'd say in that state? Giving up on him she went to the kitchen to make strong coffee.

Jacob ignored her comments and peered closely into Howie's face. "They've come to Earth to teach and procreate life on this planet. How about *that*, young man?"

Howie giggled like a school girl and nearly fell off his chair but righted himself just in time.

Amazingly clear in what he wished to say Jacob wagged a finger at Howie. "They're both human and subhuman, my lad. They're the Bootes in the southern constellation." Jacob hiccoughed loudly.

"Boots. Why do they want boots?" He laughed like crazy at the idea of aliens in boots.

Jacob chuckled too. "They came to procreate themselves through genetic engineering. They're without reproduction capability you know. Poor things don't know what they are missing. They don't have digestive systems like humans." He paused and looked around for something to hold onto, waving his arms around like a blind man trying to feel his way. He couldn't seem to find anything and gave up.

Howie squinted at him. "Go on, Pops. Tell me more. Where are they now?"

Jacob leaned over to pat Howie's arm and nearly fell over. "They mainly live underground here, and on other planets. Imagine that my boy."

Howie roused himself and tried to understand. "I don't get it," he said with a stupid grin on his face.

Jacob was on a roll. "They're not the only ones around from space. There are Norwegian-like space people, which look human like us in every way, but are more intelligent." He laughed. "That's not hard to be, is it?" and slipped as he leaned over the coffee table and almost landed on the floor. "They're our guardians, the Pleiadians. They're everywhere on Earth. Fancy that! They're among the human race and live in the mountains, the deserts, and the oceans.

They live in underground cities and bases." Jacob put his finger to his nose and tapped the side of it. "Shush! The governments know where they are, they communicate with the ETs about abductions of humans."

"Explain yourself, sir." Howie tried to stand and failed. He fell back on his chair laughing.

Jacob took no notice; all caution had fled from his brain. "My boy. They're the Galactic Federation, or Council of Light, from the Pleiades, Orion, Bootes, Alpha Centauri, Zeta Reticuli, Comsuli, and Pouseti. A UFO cabal and the Illuminati have been keeping them secret."

At that moment Kate walked back in and listened for a moment, taking in their condition. She stamped her feet. "Enough! I said stop it now, Dad. How much have you been telling this young man?" She moved around to Howie's side. "Dad, I think he's had enough. Look at him. He'll fall off his chair in a minute." Howie lurched to one side and was only saved by Kate's arm.

Jacob didn't want to stop. "But there's so much more. The list goes on and on. Lord Admiral Hill-Norton, Former Chief of Defence Staff, 5 Star Admiral of the Royal Navy, Chairman of the NATO Military Committee no less, said, and I quote, <There's a serious possibility that we're being visited, and have been visited for many years by people from outer space, by other civilizations. Who they are, where they're from, and what they want should be the subject of rigorous scientific investigation, and not be the subject of 'rubbishing' by tabloid newspapers.>"

Kate put her hand over her father's mouth. "Enough! We'll have to put him to bed. We can't let him leave in this state. How much whisky did you give him? He'll have a terrible hangover when he comes to. And so will you by the look of you." Between them they hauled him to Jacob's bedroom. He collapsed on the bed grinning like an idiot, and then passed out cold. It wasn't long before Jacob too collapsed onto the nearest chair and was snoring loudly.

Kate was worried. She knew Howie could only take just so much information, drunk or not. Her father had overdone it for sure. She could see that the young man may not be satisfied with their explanation that she wasn't a spy, but merely had an interest in other worlds sparked off by dreams. She'd already discovered that Howie was a stickler for obeying orders and liked knowing where he stood. Anything that didn't come into this category he had to question. It was his nature; he couldn't help himself.

That night she tossed and turned in her bed. Sleep was impossible with all the thoughts buzzing round and round in her head. She wondered if perhaps their location had already been discovered and that Howie's superiors had sent him to report back on their activities. She shuddered at the thought and bad memories surfaced of how Helga and Silas had made her life miserable when they were in Dorset. Then she remembered Howie's dream. What was it that scared him so much that he'd had to share it straight away?

***

In Washington DC, the old general had been watching Adam carefully but wasn't able to catch him out in anything. Perhaps he was wrong about him after all. He knit his brows, puzzled. If only he could find out more about his recent past. Adam was a young man who had risen swiftly through the ranks. This was mainly due to his amazing knowledge of the stars, and his obvious desire to have a part in space exploration. He'd been given the highest clearance to secret files and locations and was able to share with those who had agendas not open to public knowledge. But something had changed in him recently and he couldn't put his finger on it. From being a nervous worrying man, he had become more assertive. The general couldn't understand why he had to be absent so often. '*You're not privy to that information*', they said whenever he queried the absences. He'd had to be content with that. The problem was he wasn't content at all. Was this young colonel being groomed for Jump Room activity? Why wasn't his own teenage grandson being chosen? It was time to call in a friend who owed him.

His friend didn't hold the rank of general but had a nose for gossip and kept this nose well immersed in scandal. They arranged to meet at Club Quarters on Capitol Hill where it was discreet and quiet. After handshakes and a few drinks, they got down to the purpose of the meeting.

The general didn't waste any time. "I want you to find out all you can about Colonel Adam Fenshawe," he said. "I'll make it worth your while." After a few more drinks, and another handshake, they parted and went their separate ways.

The timing was unfortunate, for this was the moment that Adam received the call from the Galactic Council. "We've heard that Kate and her father have been discovered. We want you to go back to England and see what you can do to keep them safe."

CHAPTER TWENTY

SECRET ENERGY SOURCE

Time changes not, but all things change in time.
For time is the force that holds events separate,
each in its own proper place. Time is not in motion,
but ye move through time as your consciousness
moves from one event to another.

From The Emerald Tablets

That night Kate was to experience yet another dream that was more real than not. It was getting hard for her to know the difference between dreaming and daytime events. She wondered if sleep was where the real training was given. She remembered every fine detail, unlike most dream states. She climbed into her bed grateful that the day was over. Here at least she could forget the problem of Howie. At last after a restless start she fell into dreamland. It came almost immediately and was so similar to the process she used to go into trance that she thought that was what was happening. Maybe it was.

Her stairs were padded and felt like she was walking on air cushions.

"Why are the stairs like this?" she asked in her mind.

"It's so that your entry will be unheard, silent. Nobody will know you are coming. Everything is deliberately muffled," came the thought.

As she descended there wasn't a single sound. There was a stillness all the way. At the bottom, every surface continued to be well padded in a soft blue colour. It was soundproofing, and she realised it was not just for her but for others, so that the outside world, the general population would be unaware of what was going on.

Kate called out hoping somebody would hear and respond. "I'm here for something, so show me." At once she realised she was in a narrow tunnel and searched for a way out. She came across a door set deep into the wall. It was almost invisible. She pushed on it, because there was no door handle or lock and realised it was kept shut by suction. She had to push harder and harder until she got it to open through to the other side.

"Show me what I need to see," Kate shouted.

She looked down and saw a pair of ear-mufflers at her feet. She put them on, somehow knowing that what was to come would be noisy. The mufflers were good and thick and now she could only hear her own thoughts. As she walked she saw many men in uniform constructing what appeared to be an even deeper underground base. Kate suddenly had a coughing fit which preventing her from connecting by thought and delving further. She knew she had to overcome this semi-physical barrier that she felt was set up by another unknown force. But her inner knowing was working well.

Suddenly she heard in her head, "They don't wish you to investigate. That's what is happening here. Irresponsible forces are delving deep into the Earth to source an as yet unknown energy related to the core, the magnetic core of the planet. They wish to harness it, but it's dangerous work. Once they discover how to harness it they'll use it, not necessarily for the benefit of the inhabitants of the planet."

"Why are you telling me and what's the purpose of me knowing this?"

"You are, as you have been told, an observer and need to report this back to your home base."

"I would have thought they knew of this already."

"Remember you're a citizen of Earth and have the right to report back as an observer. Your role is to report back, to give this confirmation if you will. The military on your planet are delving into matters which could, if mishandled, damage the planet and its inhabitants. They're playing with fire."

"I'm completely confused now. If it's you who are telling me this, then why don't you report this yourself? Anyway, you said they already knew."

"We've already answered that question many times. As citizen of planet Earth, you must make the moves and get involved. Now we've told you it's not possible for you to say you didn't know. You must inform the public too, before it's too late. Once they've been informed, they also cannot say they weren't told."

Kate groaned. Who on earth would ever believe her, and after all it was only a dream. Wasn't it?

Kate came out of the dream at last. She had lots to think about. Not wanting to wake Howie or Jacob she padded softly along the landing in her slippers and went downstairs to the kitchen. Maybe a hot drink would help clear her head. As she went past the door to their room she heard them both snoring loudly and was surprised she'd fallen asleep so quickly with all that going on.

Then a possible reason dawned on her as she remembered how Jamére had put Howie to sleep with a wave of his arm. She looked around wildly but saw nothing. Relaxing, she boiled the kettle and made her drink. Just as she put her lips to her mug a hand touched her on her back causing her to spill some of the hot liquid. She spun around. It was Jamére.

"Jamére! What are you doing here? You mustn't creep up on me like that."

"Did you enjoy your dream? Good one, wasn't it?" He laughed aloud.

"Shush! You'll wake the others. Be quiet."

"How many times do I have to tell you lassie that they can't hear or see me, unless I decide to let them?" Kate sighed.

"But they could hear me talking to you, couldn't they? You haven't thought of that, clever clogs."

"How do you know you're not still dreaming Kate? You yourself said it was difficult to tell the difference these days." He chuckled.

"You tap into my thoughts too, do you?" She sighed. "Why have you come? You must have a reason."

She saw Jamére hesitate. Her mind raced ahead of his. Perhaps he needed to teach her more about teleportation. She might need it in an emergency.

Jamére sat down on a stool. "Kate, have you heard of teleportation?"

"Yes of course. Who hasn't? Isn't that what I've been doing all along?" Kate frowned, puzzled at his question.

"This is something different. Currently you always prepare for what you do and then go in with absolute focus and intent. That's true, isn't it? What I want you to experience, so that you are not frightened, is something else we may do, or later you may do, with *our* permission and expertise. Would you like to give it a go?"

"When have I ever said no?" Kate said drily and took a sip of her drink. She knew he'd do it anyway. Most of all she trusted him. "What about my father and Howie?"

"They'll sleep for ages yet." Jamére said. "Don't worry about them."

"While it's happening, I want you to speak to me and tell me of the experience, so I know you're alright. Do you understand me?" Jamére looked into her eyes to make sure she understood. Kate nodded.

"We'll go outside in the garden to do this for the first time."

Jamére also knew of the shadow people and knew that he'd protect her from those dark others who'd been sent to stop her. They moved out of doors into the darkness. After a short while a screen image appeared before Kate. It was a holographic image of a theatre. Kate hesitated and slowly entered the image.

"Speak to me Kate. Go with your feeling."

Kate took a deep breath. "I've entered the theatre corridors and I see there are many doors all leading to where the audience is sitting. It doesn't matter which door I take." Kate stood in the aisle between the seats and waited. "Oh, I see. I'm to go down through the seats and up onto the stage. On the stage there are little circles."

Kate moved swiftly and was soon on the stage. "I'm going to stand in one of them now. I wonder what I'm supposed to be doing. This is a real 'beam me up Scottie' thing Jamére. Standing on each of the other circles, human beings and ET forms are appearing. They've been beamed down. That's the only word I can give it." Kate looked all around her in wonder. "They're here on the stage with me. They're stepping out of the circles, so they are real, physical. We all stand together and without a sound look out over the astonished audience. The people are stunned into silence. They don't know what to do. I don't know what to do either."

"Keep talking," Jamére said.

"It appears to the audience that we are people simply arriving from other places. It's no trick, it happened. I'm as astounded as they are, even though I'm also on the stage with what I assume are space travellers.

"What do we do now Jamére? There are no words I can find to describe this more fully. We group together and hold hands and the energy that has beamed them down now includes me. It's a group beaming. I can hear a humming sound and a tingle runs through my body. Then suddenly we're all beamed up and are no longer seen. We're no longer there on the stage.

"Jamére, I can still see the stage and the audience, but we are not there. The audience has erupted. There's absolute confusion: pandemonium isn't quite the right word for what has happened. Some are just sitting and stunned; others are climbing over those sitting, scrambling to get out, presumably to report what they have seen."

"It's a demonstration," Jamére said.

"It's quite staggering, for I'm now with the same group elsewhere, on a star ship watching what's going on down below. I feel this is a genuine prevision of what will happen."

Suddenly Kate's awareness changed. She was no longer on a spaceship, but back in the garden with Jamére.

"You're quite right Kate. That was a prevision of the future for you. You may truly disappear right in front of others. You had to experience it, so that when it happens later it'll feel quite safe and unsurprising. We use many methods of travel through time and space. You're experiencing as many as we can safely give you." Jamére began to fade in and out of her sight. His colours stayed bright.

As if to explain he said, "We live in a multiverse, a multitude of time lines that are at the same time both highly similar and yet highly dissimilar to the one we are on. We are always on one time line or another. We sometimes move back and forth between this time line, and alternate adjacent ones. The energies that make you and everything else are constantly in flux. You'll never be here or there all the time. It's so rapid, so fast that you never realise that you've been elsewhere. You never realise that you'd moved into another dimension. Even when you are there you don't remember where you were when you started."

"Sounds very complicated," said Kate, still not understanding.

"We did slow it down a fraction for you this time, but for us to slow it down for you all the time would create confusion in you. This is what we're going to attempt to bring to your conscious mind, so that you can knowingly and comfortably experience both sides of this pulse. It's a very rapid pulse."

Jamére saw that Kate was beginning to feel really drowsy and had difficulty focussing on his words.

"Come inside now lassie. Time to get back to bed." He helped her back indoors and to her room. Both Jacob and Howie were still snoring, but more quietly now. Kate was soon asleep herself.

Next morning Jacob stayed in the chair he had collapsed into the night before, sleeping it off. Later he very sensibly made himself scarce and kept out of the way until Kate went to work.

CHAPTER TWENTY-ONE

UNCOMFORTABLE MEETING

Adam checked in to the Broomsquire Hotel very late the next day. His flight had been delayed and he had to wake up the night porter to let him in. He was recognised immediately and warmly greeted by the porter who'd seen him in full uniform more than once. Very impressive, was his comment later to Amanda and the rest of the staff.

"We have other guests in from America. But they're not American," he told Adam as he signed the register. Adam nodded. He wasn't in the mood for conversation and went up to his usual room overlooking the road at the front of the hotel. He'd visit Kate the next day. It was much too late to get in touch now and let her know he was in England, and close to her once more. He slept well, catching up after the long flight and drive from Heathrow.

Next morning, he entered the breakfast room refreshed and ready for a good meal. He helped himself to the buffet and looked around for a suitable place to sit. It was then he saw her. He gasped in surprise and halted in his tracks, and for one dreadful moment didn't know what to do. She had her back to him and hadn't yet noticed him. What should he do? At that precise second another person arrived in the room. It was Silas, who saw him immediately.

"My goodness! What brings you to this neck of the woods," Silas said in his clipped voice. "We haven't seen you for months and months. Business, is it?"

Adam had to think fast. "Yes. Yes, it is," he said.

"Come and join us. Helga is here and would love to see you again I'm sure." He drew Adam over to Helga's table. There was no hiding now. Adam decided to get his questions in first. Why were they here? This was too much of a coincidence for his peace of mind. How could he go to visit Kate now?

Helga beckoned for him to sit next to her. As usual Adam saw her try to control any emotion or surprise at seeing him. But she couldn't contain the brief surprise that flashed across her face by the turn of events. She looked him up and down with an icy stare. "Following us around, are you?" she said. "Taking your business elsewhere perhaps."

Adam frowned and didn't know what to make of that. "I'm here to close a deal," he lied. "Hush hush, you know." He tapped the side of his nose with a finger. That should be enough to stop them asking more questions. The gesture should be understood. Now it was his turn to ask questions.

"What brings you here? You're a long way from home in Dorset. I hear you're just in from America." Adam rightly guessed they were the ones the porter had referred to.

Helga glowered at him. "The old story. Satellites, you know. We have a branch of our firm near here and they've asked us to assist them. We attended a conference in The States about them." Adam knew it was a lie.

"How long have you been here?" Adam asked.

"Not long," was the vague answer.

Adam didn't believe her for a minute, but let it go. He wondered if Marco was here too. He'd have been put up in a bed and breakfast, not a hotel, if he was here at all. He could see the shock of seeing him was too much for them to engage in small talk. They finished their breakfasts and left the room, each one of them wary of the other. He had to get in touch with Kate and Jacob. He must warn them as soon as possible. Adam wondered if Silas and Helga had truly only just arrived, or they had been there for some time.

Back in his room Adam picked up the phone and called Jacob. He knew Kate would be at work. The phone rang and rang. Adam was just about to hang up when someone answered it, but it wasn't Jacob as he would have expected.

"Hello. Who is it? Kate isn't here." Adam recognised the voice immediately. It was that young man Howie. Adam's heart plummeted. What was he doing there so early in the morning?

"Where's Jacob?" he asked.

"Still sleeping. He had a big night last night. So did I."

Adam realised Howie knew it was Adam on the line.

"I - I thought you were in America," he stammered.

I'll bet you did, Adam thought. He didn't like the way things were turning out.

"I'm coming over. You'd better be gone when I get there. Wake Jacob up and tell him. *Now!*" He slammed the phone down.

Half an hour later it was Jacob who answered the door. "What's this all about Adam? I'm pleased to see you, but to give Howie the heave ho like that just isn't on. He told me how you ordered him out. He was most upset."

"I don't give a damn about him being upset. What was he doing here so early in the morning, and why was he here last night? He said you had a big night. What does *that* mean?"

Jacob sighed. "Calm down. I'll get you some tea. Or would you prefer coffee?"

Adam sat heavily in the nearest chair, all energy spent.

"I've some bad news. But first tell me what's been going on while I've been away."

"Do you think the world has to stop when you're not here, Adam? Of course things have been going on." He brought the drinks in and told Adam all about the previous night's events.

Adam listened in silence broken only by an occasional, oh no! until Jacob finished. Why did Jacob have to go into such detail with Howie about their Space connection with ET's? He'd gone too far.

"Why, Jacob? Why did you say so much?" He put his head in his hands in despair.

"He'd had a bad dream and I tried to explain we weren't spies. Then we both drank too much, and my tongue ran away with me," Jacob said looking down at his feet, "- and we passed out." Jacob looked shamefaced.

"And Kate didn't try to stop you?"

"She tried, but I didn't listen to her. I was on a roll." There was silence for a while. "What was it you had to tell me?"

Adam didn't know where to begin. What he'd heard was bad enough.

"Where's your car?" Jacob asked, trying to change the subject. "I didn't see it when you came."

"I parked it some distance away," Adam said.

"Why is that?"

"That's what I came to tell you. But we'd better wait until Kate comes home. She at least seems to have her head screwed on."

Jacob watched with a puzzled look as Adam began to pace up and down the room. It was clear something was seriously wrong. They ate some lunch in silence after which Adam went into the garden to think. Some hours later Kate arrived home. Jacob met her at the door with a worried expression.

"I have a surprise darling. Adam is here." Kate's face lit up straight away.

"Where is he? I didn't see his car" She ran into the kitchen to see if he was there.

Jacob grabbed her arm and stopped her. "He's in the garden. He has something to tell us, and it's not good judging by the state he's in." Kate didn't wait to hear any more and dashed outside where Adam was sitting on the bench, shoulders hunched over, waiting. She stopped in dismay when she saw the set look on his face.

"Adam, whatever's the matter? How come you didn't let us know you were coming?" Adam took her into his arms. How was he to tell her that the ones she feared the most were nearby?

"I'll have to tell you and your father together. It involves both of you." He put his arm around her waist and walked her back indoors. "Let's have tea first. Like old times." He laughed in a feeble attempt to lighten his mood. He wanted to put off saying what he had to say for as long as possible. But he knew there was no way he could keep it from them indefinitely. Anxious looks passed between Kate and Jacob while they sipped their tea.

"For heaven's sake Adam, tell us what you clearly need to say." Jacob could stand the suspense no longer.

Adam took a deep breath and dived straight in. "I saw Helga and Silas this morning."

"Pardon me? You saw them this morning? What, at the airport, in DC?" Jacob asked in a shocked voice.

"No, here at my hotel. At breakfast." Adam waited while their stunned minds took this in.

"I don't believe you," said Kate at last.

"It's true. They were as surprised to see me as I was to see them. They said they were here on business."

Jacob frowned but maintained his cool. "Well, that could be true I suppose. There's a satellite firm not too far from here. It's a bit of a coincidence though; don't you think?" he rubbed his chin.

"Did they ask you what you were doing here?" Kate asked.

"I said I was here to close a deal. Hush hush stuff."

"Did they believe you?"

"I don't know, and it doesn't matter. The fact is they're too close for comfort. Damn it, damn it! I thought we were all safe and secure. What have they found out, and what if it's not true about them having business in the area?"

"Howie!" shouted Jacob and Kate together. "It has to be. He must have told them after all."

Adam banged his fist on the table. "Howie! Of course. He answered the phone this morning when I rang. Oh hells bells! He will know I was coming here and would have passed the word on." He turned on Jacob. "He has your address. And you had the stupidity to tell him all about our work!" Adam started to pace up and down the room again. He had to think.

He stopped pacing. "Now let's all calm down." Adam turned to Kate. "Kate you're not still giving talks, are you?"

"No, I stopped when we moved here."

"That's good. They've nothing to pin on you. You're leading normal lives."

Jacob broke in. "Thank goodness Kate you didn't go ahead with having groups here for training in mind travelling."

Adam spun around. "You wanted to do *what*? What were you thinking of? You must be out of your mind."

"Well I'm supposed to spread the word; so how else can I do it? You tell me." Kate's face told Adam she didn't like the way this was going. Both men fell silent. There was no answer to that question.

Kate suddenly brightened as a thought struck her. "If those two do really know where we are then there's no reason any more not to get in touch with Poppy and Francine and let them know too. They could visit, couldn't they?" Adam could see that she missed Poppy more than she cared to admit.

"Think about it. We've nothing to worry about. I'm not giving talks. I'm not doing anything out of the ordinary as far as they can see. What can they do? Nothing."

"You are forgetting one thing my darling. Howie. What are we going to do about Howie?"

CHAPTER TWENTY-TWO

HOLLOW MOON

How can I sleep when I know the world awaits?
How can I dream when I know the world expects?
What can I do to change the way?
What can I say to make an effect
on this Earth of ours on which we stay?

Dear child of Mine, you take your heart
and offer it to all who need.
Dear breath from God, you give your soul to love, in life.
Sweetness of Light, you sacrifice yourself to show you care.
In this you will show the way that all will see and share.

Kate had another vivid dream that night. In it she was looking down at the moon from a great height. She felt she was hanging in space, just as astronauts do when in zero gravity. It was inky black apart from stars shooting by all around her. Her eye was caught by a crater on the moon. At first she saw what appeared to be a mouth opening and shutting. But then she saw it was an entrance into a tunnel. The crater continued regularly opening and shutting.

She took herself in closer and closer until she was right up near the entrance. In order to go through she knew she would have to choose a moment when it was open. She must sprint through and not get caught as it was shutting. Kate didn't know what might be on the other side, and didn't care, so she watched and waited. As it opened she dashed through and it shut behind her as she got in, just in time. She looked back and saw it was still constantly opening and shutting rhythmically. What did that mean?

She clearly heard a voice, "Moons are hollow and inhabited by people like us."

Surprised to get e response from her thought, she called out. "Where are you? Show yourself." Kate reassured herself that she was only dreaming and had comfort and safety in the knowledge. Nothing in a dream state could hurt her here, lucid or otherwise.

"We aren't who you think we are," came the voice, which sounded mechanical and not unlike the voices used on Satnav's, or with those used by individuals such as Stephen Hawking. Artificial or otherwise it wasn't threatening, merely informative.

"Who are you then?" Kate felt brave enough to ask. If you don't ask you will not find out was her mantra. There was a prolonged silence for a while. Kate's nose wrinkled as she smelt something. She puzzled as to what it might be and searched for a memory. At once she remembered the smell of burnt charcoal, or of ashes in a fireplace. She sneezed. Suddenly there was a click and the voice returned.

"We're a collection of space voyagers, along with some of your Earth humans. We've been here for much longer than you can ever imagine. We don't wish to suffer your invasive moon landings and get caught up with your constant squabbles. We know all too well that you're interested in mining our surface metals of 80% titanium. That much titanium doesn't exist in the entire planet Earth, which is why of course you're so interested. We have our own mining operations here. We have silicon, magnesium, iron, calcium, aluminium, chromium, and manganese. But then you knew that, didn't you?"

Kate didn't like being classed as one of those who mined. "*I* did not know that," she said to the voice. "Show yourself."

She heard a few more loud clicks just behind her. She turned around quickly, and again reminded herself that she was in a dream and was safe.

Surrounding her now were groups of people. They were not wearing any kind of uniform which somehow she'd expected they would. Most of them were just like her, human. More surprising to see were family groups, complete with children and women.

"We're the welcoming party," said one woman in blue overalls, stepping forward. "We saw you coming and thought you'd be more comfortable with someone like yourself."

"You knew I was coming?" Kate felt shaky. "How do you survive on the moon?"

"We use the North and South poles where there are areas which store vast amounts of water-ice. We can enjoy low levels of light from the sun for several months at a time. Instead of the blazing heat of the lunar noon, there's a kind of consistent balmy sunset, with temperatures around a more or less comfortable degree, due to the low angle of the sun." A child pulled on her mother's coat, impatient to be elsewhere. She patted to child on the head. "We're inside now," she said.

"Tell me," Kate said, "Why is the voice accusing me of mining? I've nothing to do with mining."

"Oh that! It's an automated recording, warning visitors off, those we do not want to come plundering our home."

"But you said, you knew I was coming," Kate said. "and I still got the warning."

"As I said, it's automated, and is on regardless of who comes. But you asked questions and we were watching you before showing ourselves to you."

Suddenly the automated voice got louder. Kate put her hand over her ears.

"We tried to warn you off on your first visit, directly because of your desire to own anything where you place your flag. Then war starts with other nations also wishing to own a piece of the property, and what they can get out of it. If we allowed your presence here, the aggressive nature of your militarised nations would soon take war to space. We're also aware that it would be a lot easier for you to have the moon as a base, rather than a floating space station open to many." The voice clicked off.

Kate thought about that before replying to the woman in blue Jeans. "I've heard there are big bases on the dark side of the moon. Is this correct?"

"I will show you. Close your eyes."

"That's stupid. How can I see if I close my eyes?"

She heard the woman give a big sigh. The child at her side tut tutted. "Don't you know by now that inner sight is much stronger and truer than physical sight? Shut your eyes."

Obediently Kate shut her eyes. Soon she had pictures, clear pictures. She saw hundreds of deep pits on the lunar surface that could provide shelter to astronauts. She saw moon water held in deep underground reservoirs that would supply explorers who remain long-term on the moon.

"The pits are located inside many larger craters on the moon. Many are estimated to be nearly 3,000 feet (900 meters) wide," the woman said. "So you see we are secure since these provide a very safe location for us. There is no radiation, no micro-meteorites, very little dust, and no wild day and night temperature swings."

"I'd have thought you didn't need to worry about such things with your technology," Kate said smiling at her.

"You forget there are many diverse cosmic races here. We're like a huge space docking station. We keep our enormous mother ships docked here on the dark side, the side you can't see from Earth. Look again." Her voice was more forceful now.

Kate tried to see more. Soon into view came huge, massive space ships arriving and leaving. It reminded her of a busy airport with planes coming and going every minute, only these craft were much larger than anything she'd ever imagined or seen before.

The woman was speaking. "The moon has an atmosphere which is growing. The dust particles on the dark side are of a negative charge and on the sunlit side are of a positive charge. So, we try not to be on the surface for two reasons. We prefer not to be discovered, and since the moon is hollow we can manage extremely well inside, as you could. You yourself discovered a way in, did you not?"

"Yes, but I'm dreaming."

"Are you? Would you like to hear a recording of what we heard during the eleventh landing here by your astronauts?"

"Oh yes please. Yes of course I would." There were a few clicks and whirring noises before it began.

"This is an authentic recording and proves without any doubt at all that your governments know about our presence here," the artificial voice said.

Houston:	*What's there? Mission Control calling Apollo 11...*
Apollo:	*These "Babies" are huge, Sir! Enormous! OH MY GOD! You wouldn't believe it! I'm telling you there are other spacecraft out there, lined up on the far side of the crater edge! They're on the Moon watching us!*
Apollo	*Those are giant things. No, no, no - this is not an optical illusion. No one is going to believe this!*
Houston	*What ... what ... what ? What the h--- is happening? What's wrong with you?*
Apollo	*They're here under the surface.*
Houston	*What's there? (muffled noise) Emission interrupted; interference control calling 'Apollo 11'*
Apollo	*We saw some visitors. They were here for a while, observing the instruments*
Houston	*Repeat your last information!*
Apollo	*I say that there were other spaceships. They're lined up in the other side of the crater!*
Houston	*Repeat, repeat!*
Apollo	*Let us sound this orbita ... in 625 to 5 ... Automatic relay connected ... My hands are shaking so badly I can't do anything.*

	Film it? G--, if these d--ned cameras have picked up anything - what then?
Houston	*Have you picked up anything?*
Apollo	*I didn't have any film at hand. Three shots of the saucers or whatever they were that were ruining the film.*
Houston	*Control, control here. Are you on your way? What is the uproar with the UFOs over?*
Apollo	*They've landed here. There they are and they're watching us.*
Houston	*The mirrors, the mirrors - have you set them up?*
Apollo	*Yes, they're in the right place. But whoever made those spaceships surely can come tomorrow and remove them. Over and out.*

Kate was silent. She didn't know how to react to that recording.

"Did you enjoy that?" the woman asked. "We told NASA in no uncertain terms to get off and stay off the Moon!"

"But they sent Apollo 12 after that," Kate argued. "They didn't listen."

"We knew they'd go ahead, simply because they had it already planned, and to cancel could bring panic to their people. They panic so easily. It doesn't take much."

"I suppose that's why you don't show yourselves," Kate ventured.

"You are correct."

"So why are you here on the moon? Space should be free, shouldn't it?" Hilarious loud laughter broke out from the automated voice at that idea. Kate wondered how an artificial voice could laugh so hard or hear her. It was then she realised it was yet another disguised voice, or maybe it was because she couldn't understand their language. She also realised that if she had a question, or even had a query in the mind, only then the voice would speak. Otherwise it stayed quiet. Was it a robot?

Kate decided to check it out and see what would happen if she investigated the surroundings. She'd discovered one entry into the interior. There were more for sure. Best to ask permission.

She turned to the woman heading the family group. "May I go in and see more?" She asked.

"Go ahead. We're watching you. In any case, what can you do?

Kate felt her way along the smooth polished walkway that was close to the group. Lights illuminated the way and a breath of spring-like air brushed her face. Soon she found a large hangar type door. She pressed the button at the side and it opened easily. *Not much need for security here,* she thought. Her mouth fell open at what she saw as the door slid to one side. It astounded her.

Massive space craft were lined up. They were so large, from where she stood she couldn't see both ends of any one vehicle. What else she wondered?

The response came quickly. "Would you like to see further ?" the mechanical voice asked. It was clearly following her movements.

Kate hesitated. What more could she take in? "Yes please," she answered a little shakily after a moment of consideration.

At once she found herself above the moon, looking down from a small craft. She had to remind herself that this was only a dream and it would end. Or would it, or could she be stuck here?

"You'll be returned," reassured the voice. "Look down."

Kate clearly saw the craters that are often seen from Earth as eyes. As she looked the eyes opened like doorways, circular shuttered doorways with the shutters acting as eyelids. As they opened, one could go in to the interior. Is this what she'd already done earlier?

She watched in awe as she saw huge cities and tall crystalline structures with spherical domes over half a mile in diameter. She saw towers inside the domes, which covered vast areas. These were not just bases; they were huge cities.

"Wow!" was all she could come up with after such a sight. "And we can't see them from Earth with our cameras?"

"Oh, they're seen alright, and filmed too, even though these are on the dark side of the moon. Why do you think we've positioned the moon so that you may never be able to see this side from Earth, unless you travel to the moon and go around it?"

That last piece of information was too much for Kate. "You positioned our moon?" At that very moment Kate's alarm clock went off and she woke with it all as clear as it could be in her mind. If only she'd set the alarm for a later time.

CHAPTER TWENTY- THREE

DILEMMA OF HOWIE

Silas and Helga were huddled over photos strewn about on the table before them.

"Look at this one." She pushed a photo across to Silas. "He's blatantly dancing with her. And he states he didn't know who she was? And that he had lost her photo? I don't believe that for a minute. We'd better get him in. It's time he knows whose side he's on."

Silas sighed. "He knows it's court-martial for him if he doesn't comply with our instructions. What are you so het up about?"

"We don't want him to discover more than we want him to know. If he stays friendly with Kate Greene and her father, they may tell him more than he needs to understand. Can we risk that?

"What do you suggest?"

"We put him to the test and get him to plant bugs. If he doesn't, then we will know for sure where he stands." At last and unusually, they both agreed on a plan.

***

Howie was also on Jacob and Adam's minds. They'd tussled with the problem for hours.

"You'd better invite him round again, Kate. I'll be with you this time. And we have to trust him now. He knows too much, thanks to you." Adam looked severely at Jacob. "Someone needs to make sure you don't both get drunk again."

Kate made the call. "Howie how would you like to come and meet Adam, and get to know him better?" There was a distinct lengthy pause on the other end of the line. "Howie? Are you there?"

She heard a short uneasy cough. "Each time I visit you I fall asleep, or get drunk and don't remember anything," Howie said, not unreasonably. "How do I know I won't have a repeat performance?"

"Adam will be there this time to make sure it doesn't happen again," she reassured him. She couldn't blame him for his reluctance. "Do come. We are still friends, aren't we?"

"OK!" Kate sensed his nod and breathed a sigh of relief. They arranged a date.

***

A few days later Howie sat twiddling his thumbs, looking extremely uncomfortable, with all three of them around the coffee table sipping tea and coffee. Kate passed sandwiches around. They didn't say anything for a while, each going over in their minds the events of the past few days. It was Kate who broke the uneasy silence.

"I had a dream last week that can do better than yours, Howie. Want to hear it?" Howie thought it was better than the silence and nodded.

"Yes, let's hear it," chimed in Adam and Jacob. "At least dreams can't be listened in on. Better check the room for bugs though." Howie thought that statement was a bit odd. He'd not yet placed bugs there, as instructed by Silas. Were they really psychic after all, and did they know what had been discussed in the meeting he'd had with those other two? He squirmed uneasily in his seat.

Kate began telling them all about the time she dreamt she was on the moon and what happened there. They listened attentively.

Howie was awestruck. "It sounds more real than a dream. Are you sure it was a dream?"

Kate turned to Adam. "Adam, is any of what I saw, and was told, true? You of all people are in a position to know." She leaned towards him, grabbed his hand and made sure Howie saw.

"Yes, it is. I can verify most of what passed between Houston and the astronauts. I have heard the same recording. I don't know about that mechanical voice though. We haven't experienced that. But then we're not you, are we sweetheart?" He leant over and gave Kate a kiss. Howie looked down at his feet, averting his eyes in embarrassment.

"Did you know that the energy that Earth loses is picked up by the moon, increasing its distance from the Earth, which means the moon gets farther away by 3.8 centimetres annually? That's about the time it takes fingernails to grow, or so I'm told. Howie, listen to this, if you doubt what I'm saying." Howie was pleased to be addressed directly and smiled to encourage more from Adam.

"Maurice Chatelain, a reputable space engineer has confirmed that those Apollo 11's radio transmissions were interrupted on several occasions, in order to hide the news from the public. Chatelain claimed that all Apollo and Gemini flights were followed, both at a distance and sometimes also quite closely, by space vehicles of extra-terrestrial origin flying saucers. Every time it occurred, the astronauts informed Mission Control, who then ordered absolute silence."

At this Howie did a 'zip it' motion across his mouth, showing he understood.

Adam saw this, smiled, and continued: "Chatelain said: 'I think Walter Schirra aboard Mercury 8 was the first of the astronauts to use the code name 'Santa Claus' to indicate the presence of flying saucers next to space capsules.' However, this announcement was barely noticed by the public. So, to us all it was a little startling when James Lovell on board the Apollo 8 command module when it came out from behind the moon, said for everybody to clearly hear on Christmas Day 1968:

PLEASE BE INFORMED THAT THERE IS A SANTA CLAUS."

Howie frowned and scratched his head. "So, what's the truth? Who can we believe, if not the government? Did Neil Armstrong really see extra-terrestrial vehicles on the moon?"

Kate looked at them all, her face creased in a frown. "What if what I dreamt isn't fantasy after all? Perhaps this is a safer way for me to get information? They can't bug a dream, can they?"

"What you may not have realised my darling daughter is that you're having these journeys alone, without the safeguard of Jamére of Sechem, or me looking out from here."

Howie became alert at the mention of bugs again. They must know what he was told to do, but how? He got hot under the collar and began to sweat a little.

It was time for him to speak up. "So, you *are* trying to get information. What for? And who are Jamére and Sechem?" Howie even now, still hadn't made his mind up about his part in this. He stood up feeling awkward, and made for the door, ready to leave.

Kate thought quickly. The men looked from one to the other, their faces showed concern. Howie didn't miss the anxious glances.

"Oh, they're the angels who look after me. We've given them names. You believe in angels, don't you?"

Howie wasn't convinced, but let it go and stayed put by the door. He felt guilty remembering how he was meant to spy on them. The mention of bugging and what he had to do gave him the shivers. He liked these people. What would happen to them if he followed orders? The face of Silas haunted him. At that moment he made his mind up and came fully back into the room

"Look, I don't know much, but I don't believe you mean any harm. However, it's not by chance that I am here in Tadley. It's not as you think. Yes, I know Kate invited me over, but I would have had to come anyway, but not necessarily on invite." He swallowed hard.

Jacob looked at his red face and downcast eyes. "What are you trying to tell us lad?"

Howie gulped and daren't look up. "I've been asked to bug your house." There he'd said it. To his surprise he saw they were smiling at his words.

"Sit down and relax, my boy." Jacob patted the chair nearest to him and Howie sat. Jacob put his arm around Howie's shoulder. "We knew all about you. We guessed you'd informed your superiors as to our whereabouts."

Howie jumped to his feet at once, angry, defensive and relieved all at the same time.

"It wasn't me. I didn't tell them. They discovered you through their own psychics' remote viewing. They wanted to know why I hadn't reported you when it was clear that I knew you. They'd taken photos of me and Kate together." Howie's voice broke. "They'll court martial me, or worse if I don't spy on you for them."

It was Adam who then leapt to his feet in alarm. "Oh my stars! You've been tracked once again, Kate. It must be when you do your journeys, through your energy signature."

Howie's brow furrowed in confusion. "Energy signature? What's that?"

Jacob explained. "Each person has an energy signature, in the same way that each person has a fingerprint unique to them."

"Kate, this may be why The Galactic Command Council is switching you to dream states now." Jacob said. "Their spies have your energy signature now, which is strongest when you set your intention to go through time. I don't think it is your signature when you dream, because it is the Command's intention, not yours. I am not sure of that though."

Adam closely watched Kate's face for her reaction. "What do you think we should do, Kate? You've been very quiet in all this."

"I think we should all calm down. It's a relief to know we don't have to pussyfoot around Howie anymore. He's a good person and will not do us harm." At this Howie blushed deep red and looked down at his feet, embarrassed. "It's no good checking for bugs, because if we find them, take them out and nothing comes through to them, they'll blame Howie for not doing his job and he'd get into trouble. Agreed?" Reluctantly everyone nodded.

"We can put false, nonsense information over the bugs till they give up listening." Jacob said.

"Howie, you can go ahead and put the bugs in place. Not in our bedrooms though." Kate put her hand on Howie's arm to reassure him, at which he turned an even deeper red. None of them knew how this was going to work out, but at least they all knew where they stood and could be prepared. Howie nodded to show he understood and left soon after. He'd a lot of thinking to do, and thinking wasn't his strong point. Obeying orders was, and it appeared that he had two entirely diverse parties giving him orders.

CHAPTER TWENTY-FOUR

GALACTIC MEETING

We of this evolutionary planet seek out the energy givers,
those who can supply the needs of others without hesitation or self-doubting.
Here and now we are speaking to you directly, if *you* feel yourself to be such
a one.

We seek selfless dedication to the task of raising mankind above its
previous level of existence. When this has been successfully accomplished,
man will have escaped the endless cycle of war, hate, greed, and all those
things which degrade the soul.

To be elevated is to experience joy, love and such harmony in the soul
as to be beyond expression in mere words. The value of this opportunity
to raise your own soul is immeasurable. Count on us for full support. God
bless you.

Ascended Masters

A serious conference was taking place in a celestial mother ship far above Earth's orbit, resting quietly in a Node. Many were seated but others had to stand since the Great Hall was packed. Everybody invited to attend had a vested concern over what was happening on Planet Earth far below. The call had gone out to interested parties, of which there were many. The Glorious Lords of the Universe were present. That knowledge alone was enough to bring in a huge variety of Space and Time Travellers, the Galactic Command Council, and Space Command.

A bell rang like a huge gong and the whole area lit up with stunning colours of many hues. An expectant hush fell over the assembly and all eyes turned in one direction. The one they were waiting for had arrived but could hardly be clearly seen through the blazing light that surrounded him. A host of magnificent angels accompanied him as he entered. As he moved closer to his position at the table eyes became adjusted to the brilliance and he was seen more easily without damage to the retina.

None would be turned away from this gathering since all were considered equal. One section of those attending stayed clumped together and continued to shade their eyes against the light due to the discomfort it caused them. There was much subdued muttering and grumbling among this dark group, as if they knew their plans might have to be redrawn.

Jamére, Sechem and Master M had been summoned to attend along with other time travellers. It was a humbling experience for all three, despite their own high level of spiritual enlightenment and endeavour. To be in the company of these great angels was something they'd never forget. They sat close together in respectful silence and waited with bowed heads.

The Great One stood and slowly looked over the large assembly, taking them all in his gaze. He smiled gently.

"Thank you all for coming," he said. His voice was soft and tender and many there recognised his enormous love for them and were unashamedly moved to tears. "We, all of us have a lot to be grateful for. I'm not unmindful of the astounding work you are doing around this universe. In particular most welcomed is the attention you are giving to the solar system in which is situated that beautiful planet Earth. As you know this has a special relevance to me. The future of the human race on planet Earth is the reason you've been called here. It's in some doubt as to whether it is viable for a future ongoing spiritual journey."

This alarming statement caused a stir and a great deal of muttering in the audience.

"We know that many of you do what you can out of pure love. Real love can bring even the strongest to tears. For it can be a release from all pent-up emotions that have been held in control for so long. Real love is felt and is effective in bringing about a change for the betterment of all.

"However, that's not true for some of those present here who are quite unable to feel love. We're aware that some here have agendas of power and greed, not love. We have seen how brother is fighting against brother with bad feeling created as a result of their presence. We have seen slavery directed by them. We have seen cruelty at an unimaginable level, as a result of mind control directed by these inferior creatures. Do I need to go on?"

In saying this, he looked at the collection of entities that stayed in the shadows It was obvious he was addressing them directly.

"Those despicable actions on Earth are having an effect. You're quite probably congratulating yourselves on this." This brought a clear but muted cheer from those hidden in the darkest place. The loudest cheer for a possible victory came from Gork, the dark one. From their attitude everyone else could see that this group were certain their interaction and their controlling power down on Earth was taking root, and they would be able to take over for sure.

The Glorious One continued, raising his voice above their cheers. "We stand and watch presidents, other high profile political leaders and awakened ones who've repeatedly issued warnings over the last 220 years, that some countries are under the control of a global invisible government that is incredibly evil in intent, owing no allegiance and acknowledging no responsibility to their own kind. People are handicapped when coming face-to-face with a conspiracy so monstrous they cannot believe in its existence."

The dark group appeared to swell in pride. Then the Glorious One outstretched an arm. Everyone went quiet, waiting.

"It is still possible for humans to make their choices, and still they may yet travel either a downward slide, or joyfully travel an upward climb on their soul journey. In order to give everybody a chance in 2012 we diverted a catastrophic timeline over to a more positive timeline. While we cannot interfere with the choices that humans make, we can monitor, and we do so. It's for this reason that we've called this meeting." He turned to one side and appeared to consult with the angels around him. They nodded agreement to him.

"We've decided to extend the previous period allowed to give time for the Human Race to move into a more loving timeline. Please note this extension isn't for an indefinite period. If the goal is not accomplished, there *will be* a two-way timeline division in the evolution of the Human Race. It'll be the choice of each soul to work against the love we give, or to embrace it."

The Glorious One continued. It was obvious that he'd registered the thoughts and jubilation coming from the shadowy area and wasn't pleased. Again, he addressed that area directly.

"Do not be so sure of your success. There's an upwelling of care, love and positive action from those who are awakening. They are trying to stimulate those others who haven't used their brains for so long that the poor things are huddled in a corner waiting to be fed. It's becoming abundantly clear that this upwelling of care for others is indicating that they'll no longer accept injustice, greed, and all those things that degrade the soul."

He turned his attention towards Master M, the Birdman from Sirius, who was sitting with the time travellers, Jamére and Sechem.

"You and your kind are going to inhabit the Earth *alongside* humans, when humans have raised their vibrations enough. First, they'll need to live in harmony and peace with themselves and other nations, because if they can't do that how can they do it with you?"

All three bowed their heads in humility as he spoke.

"Your role is to prepare Earth people to be comfortable with benevolent off world races, not to fear them. The fact that the human race is still breathing the free air of Earth is abundant testimony to the fact that cosmic civilizations aren't all hostile. All creatures on Earth will benefit by you being there. There's no difference in soul content among the creatures of Earth or of those from other planetary systems. It is a matter of physical form only. You are preparing the way."

The Glorious One then turned his attention to the great audience assembled in the Grand Hall.

"You must reinforce the energy grid, the auric shell that keeps Earth's energy field intact. Humans who are weakening the Earth through poisoning the soil, the waters and the air must try to realise what they're doing to their home, and do what they can, before there is irreversible damage. Changes in the vast cosmos are to happen soon. Earth needs to be strengthened to meet this change. If it's weakened, it'll take longer to recover."

The Glorious One bowed deeply. It was clear that the meeting was over when he turned and walked out of the Grand Hall. The Great Angels followed.

Such a hubbub ensued after the departure that it was difficult to make sense of how the information was accepted. Jamére, Master M and Sechem moved out into a quieter area. A division of the human race? It was unthinkable!

Once they were alone Master M was the first to speak. "Timeline division it may be but remember humans have always had divisions according to creed, colour and race. This is very different. This is a spiritual and timeline division that would be difficult, if not impossible to be undone. One would go on a downward slide into an unthinkable and terrible future, and the other could rise to a more loving world. Some would call this ascension. We cannot take his words lightly. If we allow the degradation of the planet that's now happening to continue then much of the human race on Earth will be lost."

Sechem spoke up. "Isn't this why we're asking Kate and her father to help? We need them to pass information around and change energies where it's damaging the planet and the souls of men."

"Yes of course. No question about it. This is why we cannot hang around chatting like this."

Jamére laughed out loud. "I never hang around just chatting. I am all for action." He did a little jig and dance, twirling and spreading his many colours all across the area.

"Stop showing off," said Sechem. Master M smiled indulgently at his two charges. They'd do fine. He'd chosen them well for the tasks ahead.

CHAPTER TWENTY-FIVE

THE KEEPERS OF THE GARDEN

Oh how the souls cry in their sleep
for peace, love and happiness.
Dear God, grant them what they seek.
Your name forever they will bless.
How can this be, our God replies,
for man himself creates his world.
Do they not know that all their sighs
result from actions now unfurled?
Dear children, listen to me.
If you would have a perfect life,
cease your endless strife and enmity.

From Spirit

Adam realised that Kate felt calmer now that the situation with Howie was out in the open. But he was anything but easy in his mind. He knew all too well the workings of those in power and his darling Kate was still naïve, despite her many journeys. He also knew that Helga and Silas wouldn't be appeased or put off so easily. Helga would have it in for Kate and Jacob no matter what they did or didn't do. Her history with them both wouldn't be erased from that dark mind. Her interaction with them had turned into a vendetta, nothing less.

Adam knew his role was to protect Kate, but he also knew he couldn't over-stay if questions were not to be asked by his bosses, and most certainly by the old general. Then there was the problem of lodging at the same hotel as Helga and Silas. They'd know of his movements. What should he do?

He was munching his toast in the breakfast room next morning mulling over the problem when a brilliant idea came. "That's it!" he shouted causing diners in the room to turn and look at him in surprise. Some of them smiled, amused. He finished his breakfast and hurried around to Kate's house. He had to get to her before she left for work.

He didn't bother to hide the car this time and rang the doorbell again and again. It was quite a few moments before Jacob, still in his pyjamas, came to open the door.

"My goodness you're an early bird, Adam," he exclaimed rubbing his eyes and yawning. "What's the panic? Come in; come in before you wake the neighbours." He looked up and down the street and pulled him inside.

"Has Kate gone to work yet?" Adam asked. "I need to see her."

"Yes, she left early so she could walk to the office. You can catch her if you hurry. By the way she takes a short cut so it's no good taking your car. You'd miss her."

"Bless you," said Adam as he planted a kiss on Jacob's head. He dashed out of the house and set off at a run. He hoped he'd see the short cuts as he went. He'd never been to her office but had a vague idea where it was. It wasn't long before he realised he may have missed some of the alley ways that she might have taken. He looked up and down the road. There was no sign of her, and he was definitely lost. It was still too early and there was nobody about to ask where the Estate Agency was. He turned around and went back to see Jacob. He rang the bell again.

"What is it this time?" said Jacob as he opened the door.

"I missed her and got lost. Do you have her office address or telephone number?"

"Of course I do. If you hadn't been in such a hurry, I'd have given it to you." Jacob tut tutted, went back inside and grabbed a piece of paper and pen. "Here you are. There's a map. Why don't you phone her?"

"I have to speak to her face to face. I have to see her reaction. I'll take the car this time." He left clutching the map and got into his car, leaving Jacob on the doorstep with a puzzled expression on his face. After making a few wrong turns in spite of the Satnav Adam parked the car and walked to the Estate Agency where Kate worked. He could see her though the window, busy on the telephone. He rapped on the glass, forgetting it was triple glazed to keep out the traffic noise. He waved his arms at her through the window to no avail. Clearly, he'd have to go in and risk getting her into trouble with her employer who he knew didn't encourage personal business to encroach on the work of the day. As soon as he opened the door all female eyes turned towards him. It wasn't often they had such a good-looking young man come their way.

"Can I help you?" A plump girl was up on her feet before any of the others could get to him. She blocked his way to Kate who'd watched with amusement the attention he'd drawn. Adam had to think on his feet.

"Um! I think I need to see that lady over there," he said indicating Kate, "She's the one I need to speak to since she has details of my needs already. I spoke to her on the phone earlier."

Not to be outdone the plump girl replied. "How do you know it's that person, if you only spoke on the phone?"

"She gave me her name and there it is on her name plate," he lied. Adam brushed past the girl, moved across to Kate's desk and sat down. Kate looked entertained by the interplay.

"Would you like to write down what you are looking for, sir? she asked, and tried to keep a straight face. She passed a notepad and pen towards him, aware that the other girls were watching and envious.

Adam was grateful for her sharp mind. He wrote quickly, *'I have a solution to the Howie problem. Can you arrange to have your holidays soon? Like now? Meet me for lunch at the cafe down the road.'*

Kate said loudly enough for everyone to hear. "No problem, sir. If you can come back here after lunch, I'll have a few places for you to go over. Can you do that?" Adam nodded and got up to leave. He gave a friendly wave to the rest of the staff and winked at the plump girl as he left. All eyes watched him go.

***

Adam hung around Mulfords Hill high street and passed the time looking into shop windows. Getting tired of that he decided it was time for a coffee and went into Café Retreat as it was the nearest to the Estate Agents where Kate worked. He reasoned she would most likely pass this way to lunch. Adam chose a table by the large clear window so he could keep a look out for her. He could hardly wait to tell her what he proposed. At last she arrived. She'd been hurrying and was a little out of breath.

She gave him a kiss on the cheek and sat opposite. "Well what's so important you have to risk the wrath of my boss," she asked laughing. Adam grabbed her hand and held it tight.

"You know you said how you missed Poppy, and even Francine, despite how she is towards you? I know how we can all escape for a while from Helga, Silas and Howie." Adam waited for her reaction.

"Oh, no. Not again. You don't mean another escape to a new start as before. Running away again?" Kate started to get upset and was ready to leave.

"Calm down. I'm only suggesting we go to *visit* Poppy and your mother.

Helga will not in a million years think we dare to go back. Going there will give us all a respite from their attention and time to think of something, and anyway Poppy isn't exactly in the middle of town, is she? They'll draw blanks on their bugs, and Howie could even be called back to America. I can come with you, my darling. What do you think?"

Kate stared at him. "You'll come too? Do you really think we can go? Really?"

"Yes, really. What can they do to you now? You're not doing anything wrong, and you'll be far from Helga's psychic snooping. She won't be able to track your energy signature from there if she's staying here."

Kate wasn't convinced. "Well, they did try to kill me when I was there," she said.

Adam patted her on the hand to comfort her. He got up and ordered coffee from the girl at the counter and went back to the table.

He squeezed her hand and tried to reassure her. "No darling. They tried to frighten you into stopping your journeys and talks." Adam knew full well that if he hadn't got them both away the outcome would have been different. He loved her too much to tell her that.

Kate beamed. "Alright. I'll get some time off arranged today. I'm due holiday, so they can't refuse. It'll be wonderful to see Poppy again."

Adam thought, *and maybe they would at long last have some alone time together.*

"It's settled then," he said. "And you, darling can go to bed tonight happier than you've been for many weeks. You and I will be away from them. Your dad can come too of course."

The coffee arrived and as they sipped it Adam hoped Jacob wouldn't be in their way when they wanted some time alone. He grinned as he saw the joy on Kate's face at the prospect of seeing Poppy.

***

That night Kate slept as soon as her head hit the pillow. She was in dreamland, but it wasn't the dream she'd wished for. In it she wore a green gown and her thoughts were of the rainforest and pure nature, where there was no interference by man. She took her time to actually look closely at the tiny creatures scuttling away from her feet, and to look at the trees and bushes as she walked along.

She passed through tall trees which had been there for ages, or so it seemed to her and reflected that impenetrable nature always has its own way. She breathed in the scent of pine and moss as she walked. She felt human beings weren't as important as they thought they were, nature was. Nature would survive no matter what humans did, no matter how hard they tried to destroy it, nature would always be the winner. Kate passed out of the trees onto a nice and easy sandy shore. The sand was soft and loose, and her bare feet sank in at every step. Near to the water's edge she heard the rattle of small pebbles as the waves drew them back and fore. A few sandpipers probed and prodded the wet sand hoping to find a treat. Further back from the sea were small dunes covered here and there with tufts of grass. It was easy walking in the bright sunlight and a soft breeze lifted her hair.

As she walked Kate saw an old man clothed in green sitting on the sand just in front of the dunes. Kate immediately knew he was a Shaman, a man of nature waiting for her. He held out a weathered bony hand.

"You've come at last," he said.

Kate's eyes widened in surprise, then took his hand and helped him to his feet. She knew he didn't need help, but she offered it anyway. He kept tight hold of her hand and led her away from the beach, back into the trees, along a very narrow trail that she wouldn't have noticed without him. It led to a clearing, as somehow she knew it would. There were a lot of families in the clearing with children running happily around, all living their lives amongst natural surroundings. They'd had no outside influence and were at one with nature.

Kate asked the Shaman at her side. "I want to know what this dream is trying to tell me."

The Shaman said, "Everything has its place, everything's in order. There's no need to strive. Life happens naturally. Nature being the key word. Whether you enjoy it or not is entirely up to you. There's no need to stress over anything."

Kate nodded. The children she saw playing were certainly not stressing.

"You might say, these people here still have to catch their food, eat the right things, they have to prepare meals, give birth, clean themselves and do all the things that you all do in your culture. Even they need to pay attention to all of that. They too have their rules and regulations and they too have their emotions, hurts and the aggressive nature of man that upsets things."

"I can see that," Kate said. "It's the same for everybody, everywhere."

The Shaman's steely blue eyes looked into Kate's face. "All do this, but everything that is here is natural. It's not changed by outside forces that mean them harm. It's not interfered with by forces stronger than themselves, by other power hungry and greedy humans. They alone are responsible for themselves and do not try to control those they have no contact with."

"I still don't know what this is telling me. What's the point of this?"

"You have been stressing about the future of Earth, haven't you? What we're trying to put over to you is that nature will take its course, whether it's interfered with or not. The natural cycle of events will continue as before, irrespective of damage done by others from outside." He waved his arm in a circle indicating the family groups. "The souls in this environment will live and die in the same way that you do. Their souls will have to account for the way they've behaved during their lifespan, in the same way that you will."

Kate frowned. "I still don't get the point of your story."

"It's exactly the same for those others who do not mean well, who harm others by their deeds. They too will have to account for their actions. So you see, nothing's really changed. Focus on the life that you've decided to live. Don't be so concerned that the human race will not survive, for it will. All souls will reap their rewards, or account for their doings. Nothing's changed in that respect. Be more at peace. Everything is in order." He spread his arms wide as if to indicate the Universe.

Kate's thoughts strayed, then turned to him and said, "What about the activities of those who would damage Earth itself, through nuclear weaponry, and the use of nuclear energy. That would certainly have a bad effect on the natural world and all who lived in it."

The Shaman had still more to say. "We have witnessed elsewhere on other planets, destruction of habitation and the inability to exist, as a result of nuclear activity and gross mismanagement of the environment. We've learnt from this and won't allow the planet Earth to go the same way that others have in the past. Much damage has already been done, but it can be reversed. This may take time. The planet Earth will continue."

"But why are you giving me this information. I already know much of this."

"You may know, but we've seen you and others worry just the same, because you feel you are helpless to make changes in the way people think. Is that not so?"

Kate nodded and tried not to cry as his words struck home. "Who are you and how do you know so much about me?"

"We're The Keepers of the Garden. How do we know about you? Are you ready for another journey to allow me to explain?"

Kate took a hasty step back and nearly fell over. "In my dream? Am I safe?" Kate looked at his bony frame and wondered how he could possibly be a Keeper of the Garden.

"As we said, you worry too much. Are you ready?"

"Yes." Kate took a deep breath and waited for the change she knew would come.

Suddenly everything was yellow. The colour always reminded her of using the mind. She saw a large office, similar to a library with lots of books lining the walls. There was a solid door leading out. She realised she was in a building, office, or college. She went through the door into a corridor dotted with doors on both sides. Soon she found the one she somehow knew was hers. It was just a green painted, ordinary office door. There was nothing special about it, but Kate hesitated, although she knew she had to go in at some point. She couldn't remain standing outside in the corridor. She turned the brass doorknob and went in. Inside there were many desks, but nobody was sitting at them.

"Show me what I need to see," she called out to the empty room. It was then that she saw that one wall was like a giant screen. It lit up suddenly and startled her, as if someone had pressed a button, like putting the TV on. It covered the entire wall. It was so bright it took a while for her eyes to adjust. The screen showed moving pictures big enough for her to walk into. Kate looked in horror at scenes of warfare, men with guns and exploding bombs at every corner. It was a battle scene. Smoke filled the streets and Kate watched as women and children ran here and there trying to escape. So much noise, it was deafening. This could be anywhere on the planet and she remembered the children waiting to be born.

"What am I supposed to do with this?" she asked out loud.

To her surprise the Shaman appeared beside her. "Walk into it. Be there on the ground, in the middle of all the noise. You know you're alright because you're not physically there."

"But what am I doing here? I can't be everywhere, and this scene is almost over all the planet these days."

"Yes, you can be everywhere. You know that. We told you that. Your consciousness is everywhere at all times and your presence here will change the energies. It will make a difference. Walk through into this."

Kate wondered if this is what she was supposed to teach others to do. Consciousness is everywhere, he said. If her conscious decision to change things made a difference she would give it her best. So Kate walked quite openly into the screen on the wall and into the mayhem. All around her men were dropping as shots rang out. She watched as a wounded man lying in a pool of blood struggled to get up. The stench of burnt flesh and sweat stung her eyes and invaded her nostrils. A little child no more than three sat down near the lifeless body of his mother, pushing at her trying to wake her up. She heard screams from women and children as they ran away from men bent on murder and worse. Buildings collapsed as mortar shells exploded.

She stood quite still in the midst of all the destruction, shut her eyes and visualised peace, calm and happy children playing. In her mind she saw the opposing forces were now laying down their arms and hugging each other. Buildings were being constructed and lorries containing food supplies and water drove along the streets. Women waved cheerily to each other from doorways of rebuilt houses. There was a knowing that the other consciousnesses of her were enacting the same change in other areas. Kate didn't need to see the results, because as she stood and created a better scene she was certain the effect was taking place elsewhere too. She didn't need to see it. It was happening.

"Just keep walking through it all and know that the essence of your consciousnesses has an effect on each scenario," the Shaman said.

At last she left the screen wall behind. "Well that was good, but walking in seemed a bit weird," she said to the Shaman.

It dawned on Kate that anybody could do the same and make a difference. They didn't have to dream but could do it in meditation and with intention. Was this what the Shaman was trying to teach her, so that she could teach others?

She looked at him in wonder and said. "Multiples of me and we are all connected. My word!"

Next moment Kate realised with a shock that she was back in her own bed. She couldn't move, no matter how hard she tried. Moments passed - and she tried again. This time she was able to turn over. Was it all a dream or something else?

CHAPTER TWENTY-SIX

VISIT TO POPPY

Sechem took a chance and decided it was time to visit Helga. Adam had told him where to find her and about the bad luck that she was in the same hotel as himself. The time traveller hoped that at night Helga's psychic senses would be deadened while she slept so she wouldn't know he was there in her bedroom.

Both Jamére and Sechem were standing outside in the darkness of the hotel car park.

"Wait for me here. If I don't come back quickly- - -," Sechem dimmed the light of his energy field. "if I'm away too long come and get me out of there." It wasn't that he was afraid, but he knew that the dark shadow energies that surrounded her could alert her, and then she'd know all about him. She'd know that Kate was receiving his help.

"Are you sure you want to get involved with her? You know she's mind controlled, don't you?" Jamére cautioned. "What if the shadow government catch on to what you intend to do?"

Sechem shushed him.

"I'm not sure visiting her is a good idea. This isn't our brief," Jamére said.

"I have to try and see if I can disconnect her from the control. At least Kate would have a chance then." Sechem whispered.

"I don't know how you can do that. See inside her mind?"

"Exactly!" Sechem felt it was worth the risk. "Keep a watch. I'm going in."

He looked around the heavily patterned wallpaper and grunted in dislike. He detested the energy around her so much he almost changed his mind and left. He wandered around the bedroom until he was close to Helga's head. She was asleep all right, judging by the loud snores coming from her. He focused on seeing the neural networks inside her brain hoping to see some kind of device. He saw nothing pleasant! He knew he could enter her sleeping body if he wished. He did not wish. Their energies wouldn't be compatible, and it would be too dangerous to try.

Just as he turned he imagined he saw a shadow flitting across the room from the window. Then some more shapes flashed by. He felt tentacles reaching for him and as one coiled itself around his neck he grabbed it and shook it violently till it fell to the floor. Sechem gagged as a disgusting smell pervaded the room and he saw more dark shapes gathering. Each time he spun around to see, they vanished. Helga slept on totally unaware. It was enough for him to leave, and he knew it wasn't too soon.

Sechem re-joined Jamére outside and told him about the shapes. "What do you think they were?" he asked.

"At a guess I'd say they were the shadow people. They haven't decided on which side of the fence they wish to be. Let's all hope it's on the loving side and not a controlling one."

"Well if they're getting involved we need to know. Let's get back to Kate and Jacob. They may need our help." Sechem was disappointed he hadn't been able to locate Helga's implant.

***

Kate's boss was busy on the phone when she walked into the office next day. Kate waited until she put the phone down and launched straight in with her request.

"Is it possible to have my holiday entitlement, now that there is not much going on?" she asked.

Her boss looked up in surprise. "Well, we are in a very quiet period, so I think it would be good to go now before we get busy again."

Kate beamed. "Thank you so much. Can I start today?" Her boss nodded agreement and got back to her paperwork. "Two weeks," she said.

Kate went home excited at the prospect of two weeks with Adam and a visit to her friend and mother. She could hardly contain herself. Over dinner at home that evening they discussed the trip. They decided that they would travel together in Adam's car as it was the largest.

"Are you sure it's not bugged?" Kate joked, laughing at the idea.

Adam cleared his plate and finished off a glass of wine. "I'm picking up a new one on my way to collect you, so there's no opportunity for Howie or anyone else to do that," Adam reassured her. "I'll be here early tomorrow morning. Be ready." He kissed her on the cheek, got up from the table and left.

None of them had told Poppy or Francine that they were coming. It was to be a surprise. They'd arrive at Poppy's house first. They knew she wouldn't be away since she rarely left home. She had her dogs and a variety of animals to care for and that kept her close to her land. Kate could hardly contain herself, anticipating the look on Poppy's face when they turned up on her doorstep.

"Get to bed early, Kate," her father advised. "It'll be an early start." Kate was all too happy to comply and was tucked up in bed by 9.30 pm. What she didn't expect was yet another dream and in the company of both Jamére and Sechem. If she was truthful, since Adam had arrived she hadn't given either of them much thought, so she was more than surprised when they turned up in her dream.

As she drifted off she saw them both standing in front of her. "What are you doing here?" she asked.

"We don't like leaving you alone," they said together. "We're a bit worried about the shadow people. Whose side are they on? We've decided we would shadow the shadows."

Kate frowned. What were they talking about? Shadows? She dropped deeper into the dream.

She soon heard, "Go for it Kate," Sechem encouraged. There wasn't much Kate could do but agree.

"It's a funny sort of a dream with you here with me," she said. "I'll tell you what's happening, shall I? But then you already know, don't you?" They both nodded together and waited for her to begin. She slipped deeper and deeper in to the dream journey.

"My stairs are very steep so I have to go down backwards, like on a ladder. It's like a gangway on a ship. I see I'm on a vessel or ship of some kind. Whether this is an airship or sea ship I don't know. There's still movement, even though I've reached the bottom. This means I'm not on solid ground. Movement has to mean on something that is moving, doesn't it?" She turned to look for their approval. They nodded again but seemed to be preoccupied in looking all around them.

"It's a confined space, not wide. The walls are metallic. There's not a lot going on here. I'm looking for an exit from this place. There's not much space, but I'm sure I'm on a ship. I've found the door out of here now. I step over a door sill and go out down a lit corridor. It's a narrow one, nothing ornate, very basic and functional. This isn't a luxury ship, not a cruise liner. I walk past several doors. Finally, there's one that says *'come in'* to my mind. So in I go, over another sill into yet another small space. I don't know what kind of ship this is, a submarine perhaps."

Both Sechem and Jamére followed her and kept close.

Kate continued to speak to them. "It's odd because *I* am not quite steady. This is a cabin alright, and there are charts, so I must be on a ship, but *I* am the one that's not steady, not the ship. My head is rocking. I feel as if my body is waving to and fro, as if I'm not really here. I'm not solid. I think I'm experiencing being an energy form again. I'm not third dimensional here so I can't keep my shape steady. Help me Sechem."

Kate felt for his hand and grabbed hold. "Where am I?"

Some voice she didn't recognise answered. "You are beneath the waves." Kate looked to see where the voice was coming from and saw a tall, slim, blue, jump-suited man standing in the doorway. He looked quite young, but Kate felt he was old and experienced enough to be in charge. He didn't look at all surprised to see her, but seemed unaware of Sechem and Jamére, or he was ignoring them. The cabin was getting rather crowded.

Kate recovered her own surprise at seeing him and said, "I figured that much out. That's not telling me where I am."

"You're in a restricted space."

"I figured that out as well."

"We mean, restricted in the sense of not known, not acknowledged, even by the usual military forces. This one is secret."

"OK. Whose secret?"

"It's not one of your government's official endeavours. This is from space. It's occupied and directed by human beings from space."

"Human beings from space? Incredible!" Kate studied him, thinking he looked so normal, so human. "What are they doing here? What's their purpose?"

"This is an inter-dimensional scientific research vessel. We're testing the condition of your seas. We're testing Earth's ability to maintain a balance with the creatures and the system that uses the oceans, for the health of your planet. If this system fails, then your planet is in a dangerous situation. So we're here, testing."

Kate frowned. "Why if I'm not in a solid, third dimensional form down here you can clearly see me?"

"You can't enter here while in a physical third dimensional form, so we arranged a dimensional shift to enable your entry."

"Is this why I went all rocky? I still don't get it. Never mind. Is this the only vessel?"

The slim man moved in from the doorway further into the cabin and sat down.

"Please take a seat," he said, and pulled another chair over to her. She sat.

"Let me explain. There are other vessels like this one in all the major seas and all the major lakes on your planet. There are many like us monitoring the condition of your waters. This is vital work for the benefit of your planet."

Kate was thinking hard. "What about those forces from space that are not well intentioned towards Earth?"

"We're aware of them. They have their agenda, but we're operating separately from them and don't interact with them."

"Why are you a human? I'm puzzled."

"We're not all human, but we're all humanoid. The human race on the planet originated from us. So we are the originals, as you would call us."

"Is this a small vessel? Everything seems very confined." Kate waved her arm indicating the small space in the cabin. As she did she saw Sechem and Jamére in one corner, watching her.

"It's a large vessel with many compartments, rather than open plan, such as you might have in your houses. The reason for the small compartments is that each wall is like the wall of a cell and provides greater strength throughout."

"Who are you?"

"My my! You do have a lot of questions," he said. "But then I suppose that's why you're here. We're a mix of races, as you well know. Andromeda is our main base."

Kate wanted to know more, much more, but at that point he began to fade in and out of her vision. He was breaking up, as were the surroundings. Kate looked around for Jamére and Sechem but couldn't see them at all.

"Wake up Kate. Wake up." It was Sechem. "Have you had a good time?" he asked. She noticed Jamére standing by the window.

"Is there to be no privacy?" Kate asked as she rubbed her eyes. "Why are you now following me in my dreams?" He looked heavenward and ignored her question.

"Kate, remember you're a time traveller, and you can travel anywhere and into the future and bring back what you learn to your current time and pass this along. In future before you go to sleep direct your mind to gather information and bring it back to consciousness and combine it with the knowledge of your present day. This is what you must do from now on."

Kate thought quickly. "Jamére, but we, all of us, are leaving tomorrow to go and visit Poppy and Francine. I won't be able to do my work while I'm there. They wouldn't be able to understand."

"You will do even more." It was a swift reply. "We'll be with you." So saying they both disappeared. Bang went her chance to be alone with Adam, was Kate's immediate reaction.

***

The message came through on Howie's mobile as he was shaving that morning.

"You're to report to us straight away." He recognised Helga's voice of authority. He was to do whatever was asked of him. He quickly wiped his face, got dressed and left his lodgings. Minutes later he knocked on the door of their hotel room at The Broomsquire and waited. After a mumbled 'come in' he entered to see them poring over maps and papers. Howie stood stiffly to attention in the doorway and saw Silas and Helga huddled together. They ignored him. He waited for them to speak, but they seemed to think it was alright to keep him in suspense. He coughed politely.

It was Silas who looked up first. He wasted no time. "Have you planted the tracking devices in their cars?"

"Yes sir. I did it when I visited, last time I was there." Howie squirmed. It hadn't been easy, but it was made easier now that Adam was parking his car further away and out of sight of the house. He felt most uncomfortable about his earlier deception to Kate, but now she knew about his part he felt better. If he hadn't done what Helga and Silas asked they would know immediately each time the cars were driven. He was in an impossible situation.

"Excuse me sir," Howie just had to question. "May I ask why you want to track them both? Isn't it Kate Greene you're trying to follow?"

"We too have our orders young man." Helga scowled. "It's not your business to know any more." It was clear to him she was certainly not going to tell him who'd given the order. They both turned back to the papers and maps. Howie waited, uncertain what additional task was expected of him. Then Howie's need to know more overcame his fear of Silas and Helga.

"I don't understand what it is she's doing wrong." he stuttered. Silence followed. Had they heard him? He tried again. "She doesn't appear to be doing anything wrong. What has she to do with the country's security, and why are you following her and her father? I don't understand what this is all about."

Helga turned around. Howie reeled at the hatred showing on her face. He flinched and stepped back. Silas put a restraining hand on her arm.

He turned to Howie. "Young man, you don't understand. Appearances are deceptive. This young woman talks to extra-terrestrials."

Howie laughed nervously. "Lots of people say they do that. Nobody takes them seriously. Do they? I can hardly believe she is being chased for that alone."

Silas frowned at his disbelief. "She does more than that. She uses her mind to travel where she's not wanted and can see what she's not supposed to see. We're worried that she will disclose what she learns to the public. That's the security risk."

"You mean she deliberately goes where she's not allowed to go?" Howie asked.

Helga snorted in disgust and started to gather up the papers on the table.

"She's a loose cannon. I - we do not like that," she said, recovering from the slip of her tongue. "We cannot control her. She must be stopped."

Howie thought this over and remembered what Kate had told him about the moon and astronauts and her dreams. He was lost in confusion.

"What about her father then? He doesn't do anything like that. Why go after him?"

Helga almost spat at him. "He supports her actions. He helps her. Without him she'd be nothing." Howie recognised hate when he saw it and backed away. He forgot to ask about Adam.

"Thank you," he said lamely. "Is there anything else?" They waved him away. He was dismissed. He'd obeyed orders.

CHAPTER TWENTY-SEVEN

THE EVENTS TO COME

Adam was up early and packed his few things. He signed out and left the Broomsquire Hotel well before breakfast knowing that Silas and Helga would still be in dreamland and wouldn't see him go. He'd arranged to pick up his new BMW 518D as soon as the garage opened. He would leave his previously rented vehicle with them. The BMW was roomy and comfortable and had enough space for them all and their luggage. He didn't really know how long they'd be away but he hoped it would be for a considerable period, but two weeks annual leave was all Kate could get.

Both Kate and Jacob had been ready for ages and were on tenterhooks when he drew up, although it was still early with the dawn light just appearing over the rooftops. Dew was on the ground and a light mist rose from the street. Jamére and Sechem were nowhere to be seen but Adam knew they'd never be far away. They loaded the car in silence so as not to wake the neighbours and sped off full of joyful expectation.

"Isn't it great, Dad? We're going to see Poppy again, and Francine." She added as an afterthought. "Won't they be surprised!"

They drove nonstop and just over two hours later they pulled up in Poppy's long drive. Kate leapt out of the car and rushed to the front door. She knocked, heart hammering with excitement. Poppy, with her mouth full of toast opened the door. Adam was filled with emotion when he saw the obvious joy that spread over Poppy's face as she saw her friend.

Adam stayed by the car, keeping a respectable distance. He wasn't sure how he'd be received. He knew Poppy always saw him as someone who'd taken Kate's friendship away from her. She saw him as the cause of Kate's disappearance and wouldn't forgive him for that easily. To his delight Poppy released Kate and waved to him to come over.

"Ooh! Posh car! she said. "I hope you've been looking after my friend and have kept her out of trouble." She gave him a hefty but playful shove. "She can get into the most awful scrapes."

Poppy turned to Jacob. "Mr Greene, I know we haven't met many times before, but I'd heard a great deal about you from Kate. I assume you knew where she went when she disappeared so quickly."

Jacob was immediately charmed by Poppy and smiled his best smile. He shook her hand vigorously. "Not Mr Greene please. Do call me Jacob. It's a very long story and I'll be more than happy to tell you all about it."

"What a ninny I am," Poppy exclaimed in a fluster. "Keeping you all standing on the doorstep. Come inside but mind the dogs."

She led them into the stone flagged hall. Adam felt he'd stepped into a world from the past. Old country farmhouse was an understatement. It was more like an old baronial hall.

Poppy saw Adam looking and noticed his evident admiration for what he saw. "It's been in our family for generations," she said. She also noted with satisfaction the warm attention the dogs were giving him.

"I see you like dogs. They certainly seem to like you."

Adam breathed a sigh of relief. At least he seemed to have passed the acceptance test. He patted the large German Shepherd who was by his side the moment they'd come into the house. Boris, the grey wolfhound who was Poppy's favourite, stayed close to her.

"Everyone come into the kitchen while I make you all a drink. You must be tired. Or are you? I've no idea how far you've travelled."

Adam smiled to himself. If only Poppy knew.

They followed her into an enormous country style kitchen which impressed Adam even more. A grand old cooking range looked as if it could roast a hog. Gleaming copper pans hung from hooks near it and a solid wood table took centre pride of place. Adam could envisage hard working farm men eating their meals there. An old oak dresser stood against one wall with plates lined up along the back. There was even a rocking chair in one corner.

Jacob was the first to get there and sit. Adam saw it was his kind of home. Poppy was so happy to see her friend that she frequently stopped what she was doing and hugged her over and over. At last she had the refreshments on the table and sat down with them.

Her mouth full of food Poppy said, "I must tell you who I've had visiting and asking questions about you. Not your mum though. I was surprised at that, but I suppose you'd told her where you were, hadn't you?"

Kate shook her head but said nothing.

Poppy gave detailed accounts of the men in black and their reaction to the dog, which made them all laugh, and of Helga's visit. Adam could just imagine her seeing off such people and looked at her with new respect.

Her runaway tongue eventually slowed down. Her eyes burning with curiosity she asked, "What have you been up to Kate? It must be serious if those kinds of men are looking for you. The three of them looked at each other. Who'd go first? There was silence for a brief moment, then Jacob began talking.

The next few hours were spent giving Poppy limited information about what had happened since they left Dorset in such a hurry. Poppy was dead quiet as they finished. She got up from the table and fussed around clearing the dishes. It was a lot to digest.

"We're on holiday now," said Jacob. "We all needed to get away for a bit."

Poppy turned away from the sink and stared at them as they sat waiting for her reaction. After a few uncomfortable moments she said, "Well you must stay with me. No arguments as I have plenty of room here."

Big grins and relieved sighs greeted this. "We were hoping you'd say that my darling friend," said Kate. They hugged each other again.

"Let's leave the girls to it, shall we?" Adam said, and the two men took themselves off for an exploratory walk around the extensive grounds of Poppy's home. The dogs happily followed them, except for Boris, the wolfhound. It was all going well. They could feel safe once more.

***

That night Poppy excused herself and retired early as was her habit and left her three visitors to chat in front of the fire. They knew she had to be up at dawn to see to her animals. They were a necessary part of her life. Adam, Kate and Jacob relaxed in the sitting room. It felt really good to get away from Tadley.

"When are you going to see your mother?" Adam asked Kate.

"No hurry. She can wait." was her abrupt reply. He wisely left it at that. Both of them were disappointed to find they'd been allocated separate rooms. Poppy could be a bit prim in that respect, so they said nothing. Kate looked meaningfully at her father.

"Aren't you tired, Dad? It has been a long day." It took him a few minutes for her meaning to sink in.

He exaggerated a yawn and stretched his arms. "I am a bit weary my sweet. If you don't mind, I'll go to bed." He kissed Kate on the head and left the room.

"Alone at last," said Adam. "I've been waiting for this so long my darling. Come closer." Kate snuggled into his arms. She could forget all the journeys, all the stress and all that was expected of her. Adam reached out an arm to switch off the light.

It was then they heard, "Ahem!"

"What was that? Did you hear that?" Adam drew back from Kate.

"It was nothing," said Kate who was enjoying the warmth of Adam's arms around her. "Come here you!" She pulled him close again.

"Ahem!" it was louder this time. They both sat up straight. "We don't want to disturb you but there's work to be done." They looked around but saw nobody.

"Over here." They scanned the room until they could dimly see both Sechem and Jamére leaning against a bookcase.

"We had to stop you before you - - -, well you know."

"Why now? What's so important it couldn't wait?" Kate cried.

"There's work to be done," repeated Sechem. "Important work."

"Why can't it wait?" It was Adam who was objecting now. His first chance to be alone with Kate was taken from him.

Jamére moved up close to him, so close that Adam backed away. "Tomorrow Poppy will be awake and we need Kate to do this now, not later. Do you understand? She needs to be contacting those who use energy to manifest. This is for the events to come. There's no time to waste. We can either put her to sleep or we can use you to assist. What is it to be?"

Adam knew when he was beaten. "I have to remember the bigger picture I suppose," he said. "Let's get started."

"Does anybody care what I think?" Kate asked. But inside she felt growing excitement at the prospect of another journey.

Sechem stepped forward and held her hands tight. "Focus on cosmic energy and relax."

Kate heard his voice as if in a dream as she sank lower and lower. She was starting her journey into unknown realms once more.

Jamére turned to Adam. "You, sir, you will be the one she talks to. You are so close and so in harmony with her it'll be easier for her. Ready?"

Without waiting for an answer Sechem continued to instruct Kate: "Use cosmic energy Kate. Manifesting what you want is part of your learning. Use your desire to start the active process. Formulate the desire, then set about working at how it may be realised. Manifestation is more than simply visualising as you did before. It is work, thinking, feeling, and perseverance to bring about in practical reality that which you manifest in your mind. Go to it. As usual tell Adam what's happening to you."

Kate was already well on her way. As her vibration rose she began to disappear from their sight.

"I'm on a floating platform in free space. The steps down are like stepping stones, also floating. I step from one to the other. No rail, there's nothing to hold onto. Although they're floating they're actually quite solid. I'm going down to Earth, travelling down through the cosmos. Floating platforms! Amazing! I must keep going. I can't see the bottom; it's a long way down. I'll skip ahead to the bottom to save time." Kate giggled. "Save time! That's a laugh!" She giggled again.

"I'm down on the Earth now, on solid ground, literally on gravel, soil, dirt, grass. There's a path, being formed by whatever creatures have been this way before. It's a well-trodden path bordered by lush green grass and bushes. It continues under a canopy of trees, dappled with light streaming through the foliage. I just have to follow it. If I don't I'll get lost.

"The path is leading me to an entrance to a dark cave. I hope there's somebody or something inside it to meet me. I'm walking inside it now. There's a nice, damp, warm feeling. I sense there's something in here but it's too dark to see what. The path is well marked all through the cave, so someone's been here before. I'm wandering around, hoping to see some sign."

Kate called out. "Show me something; show me where to go, where I'm meant to go,"

"Right at the back of the cave I can see a sheer wall. It looks natural but it isn't. It looks impenetrable, but it isn't. I know I can see myself on the other side." Kate paused.

"Adam, are you listening to me?"

"Focus on being on the other side," Adam said.

"I'm doing that now." *pause*. "I'm through. It's getting interesting because the other side is completely different. It's a hive of activity. There's so much going on here. It's alive with bustle, and I can hear soft music playing in the background. There are many humans, and there are extra-terrestrials, if one can call them that, for I feel they are now terrestrials. They've been here so long. They all have jobs to do."

"Show me what they're doing." Adam said.

"Adam, I can hear a voice, close by me. What do I do?" There was no answer.

Kate looked to see where the voice was coming from. She made out the shape of a tall figure, glowing in a golden aura. His eyes were of the bluest blue

Kate had ever seen. He was clearly a spaceman for he wasn't quite human. His skin was glistening white and had hair like white flax. His smile was broad and genuine. He was an impressive figure dressed in white robes. He stepped forward and stood in front of her. He looked her over with gleaming respect in his eyes and Kate immediately forgot about reporting to Adam.

"My name is Draylan, the space man said. "It's good to see you here. It's been a very long time." He put his hand on her shoulder and steered her to where a mixed group of extra-terrestrials were busy using their hands. Kate looked at her companion for an explanation.

"They're manufacturing things by using energy that they draw from the great energy that's available to everybody. It's energy that can penetrate rock, the energy that's all around. They convert this energy into denser matter, they condense it."

"I don't understand," Kate said.

"Imagine smashing a cup and it flies into bits. Then bring the bits back, like when you rewind the picture, it comes back to being a cup," he said. "This is similar, correcting random free energy and bringing it back into a solid state. They can do this. This is all we're using, condensed energy. They're condensing energy, using their minds to produce physical objects."

Kate was impressed. "What are they making? I can't see what they're making."

"What they're doing is providing survival equipment and nourishment, and anything that a human being might need in the event of an emergency." Draylan said.

"I'm not sure what you're trying to say here. Emergency? There's that scary word again."

"They can produce whatever's required at any given time by this technique. We don't need equipment or machinery, and we don't even need to mine for metals. We simply use our collective minds to condense the energy that's around, using focussed intent to produce what's needed. This is why we're doing this, ready for the events to come."

"Why are you showing me this? The events to come?"

"Because with intent you too can do this. Start practising now. Start practising imaging what you desire and call on the energy that surrounds you, all of which has consciousness. Bring it into being. This is your next learning step. You will teach others to do this. Remember the cup that was broken and then remade? This will be important."

"My Goodness! All right, I'll try."

All of a sudden the energy dropped drastically. Kate began to reappear in the room at the exact moment the dog that had been lying at Adam's feet leapt up. It started scratching frantically at the door. Adam reached over to Kate and massaged her icy cold hands.

"Are you alright Kate?"

She stirred and rubbed her eyes. "What do they mean, for the events to come? What's going to happen?"

"There are a lot of hidden meanings in that experience my darling, but I really think you need to rest now. Time to call it a day." He looked around for Sechem and Jamére but they were nowhere to be seen, at least not by him. Tomorrow was another day.

CHAPTER TWENTY-EIGHT

HOWIE

Back in Tadley, Howie nervously watched Helga as she strode up and down her hotel room. He saw that things weren't going as they'd planned.

"Are you certain you placed the tracking equipment where it couldn't fall off?" she demanded. "The signals from the colonel's car are bizarre. Not once has the car gone to where you say Kate and Jacob live."

She rounded on Silas who was occupied with looking at himself in the mirror over the dressing table. He smoothed down his hair and sighed.

"Perhaps he was telling the truth and he was only in the area for a business deal after all. But then the tracking devices on the other two cars are also static and silent. Why aren't they using their vehicles?"

Howie was puzzled. "I'm certain I fixed all the devices firmly." he said. "They were secure."

"In that case I want you to visit the last place the cars were tracked to. Go now!" Helga said.

Howie looked over to where Silas was watching him. Those cold eyes gave him the shudders. Silas nodded agreement and Howie was glad to leave. At least he'd been given permission to visit Kate's home again. He hadn't broken any rules and had obeyed.

Howie arrived at Kate's house at the time he expected her to be home from work. He knew from what Adam said that she often walked to work, so he wasn't surprised to see her car parked on the drive. But it had been raining hard that day so surely she would have used it. It should still be warm. He put his hand on the bonnet. It was stone cold. Clearly it hadn't been used. Jacob's car was also there. The thought crossed Howie's mind that perhaps Jacob was ill and Kate was at home looking after him. It was time to pay them a call.

He walked up the path and rang the bell and waited, and waited, and waited. There were no lights on and papers were sticking out of the letterbox.

It was clear they hadn't been home for several days. Thoughts raced through his head. Where could they be? He was supposed to be monitoring their movements. He'd be in trouble for sure. Quick thinking wasn't Howie's strength. He realised he had been recruited for his knowledge of nuclear work which enabled him to be in the right position to find Kate.

It eventually dawned on him to check out the colonel's car as well. Thankful that he had a record of the car's movements, he checked the latest co-ordinate on the tracker. To his surprise it led to a garage not too far away. He leapt into his borrowed car, followed the co-ordinates and located the garage. It stood almost hidden in Greenham Road and Howie remembered what he'd read of the Greenham Common demonstrations by women against nuclear weapons at Aldermaston. It'd lasted for a very long time. The area didn't look so impressive now and there in full view was Adam's car. He hesitated and got out of his car. He'd have to do something to explain his interest if asked. It was obvious to anyone with half an eye that he wasn't in the bracket to rent or buy such an expensive vehicle. But he had to know. Maybe it was in for repair?

He stood in front of the car scratching his head wondering what to do. The garage owner came out from his office. He was a burly man in grubby green overalls. He eyed Howie up and started walking towards him. Howie hesitated, unsure what to say or do.

"Dreaming of owning a car like this are you? You won't get a better bargain." Howie stopped trembling.

"I was just imagining what it would be like to drive one of these," he said and ran his hand lovingly over the bonnet, "How many owners has it had?"

"It's only been rented so far. Posh guy in uniform had it! He exchanged it for another a day or so ago. Wanted more room he said."

Howie decided it was unwise to ask for a name. He patted the car and left. At least it explained why they weren't getting tracking reports. All he had to do now was pass on his findings.

Helga wasn't pleased. "You didn't think to ask for the make or details of the fresh car he rented? Unbelievable!"

"I never thought!" Howie replied.

"That's the trouble. You never think. Get out of here." Howie left in a hurry.

***

Silas and Helga eyed each other up as they sipped coffee in the hotel lounge. Seeing they were alone Silas decided it was time to say what was on his mind.

He gave her a withering look which she ignored. He was getting fed up with Helga taking the decisions all the time.

He sneered. "Doesn't look as if your carefully laid plans are working out, are they, Helga? You would insist on taking the lead. Look where it hasn't got you."

A line appeared between her brows. She glared at him.

"I'm right, but you just don't want to admit it." Silas said and puffed up like a peacock about to spread his brilliance and take charge. He smoothed down his sleek dark hair with long bony fingers. "What you ought to do is call on your famous team of men, those you didn't want me to join. After all they're the ones who sent us down here, aren't they? Maybe they've some idea what to do next." Silas gloated as he imagined what the Gork, the top man there would say to her when he found out she'd failed.

"I'll think of something," she said curtly. She went to the phone at the side of the room and called reception. Silas could see as she put the phone down she wasn't reassured by what she'd heard.

"Colonel Fenshawe has booked out of the hotel and isn't expected back," she said. "I'm calling in my remote viewers."

"Oh, and they'll soon pick up on their energies, will they?" Silas said with sarcasm, but with less confidence. He smirked. "If you ask me I think the birds have flown the coop."

Helga scowled and got up to leave the room.

As she reached the door Silas called after her, "There's no point in hanging around here. Don't you have work to do? You'll lose your job if you stay away too long. You know I'm right. You may be a manager, but your boss Mr P isn't in the big picture and will ask questions about your prolonged absence. Best to get back, eh?"

***

A few days later Silas and Helga stood side by side in a tight narrow room lit only by a strip light on the ceiling. The room was small with plain unadorned walls painted in an off white, almost battleship grey colour. A large round clock was fixed to one wall. Silas's mouth set in a hard line as he watched the men through the mirrored wall. The strip light flickered erratically casting a reflection on the glass.

"Damn light!" he exclaimed. "Can't they get anything right?"

His tall, immaculately dressed figure hid the anger building inside him. He could see by Helga's expression that her patience was fast running out too. A little vein on her forehead twitched uncontrollably. They'd been standing there for almost one hour. Silas kept looking at his watch and then swivelled his eyes back to the men seated at a table on the other side of the mirror. They fiddled with sheets of paper and seemed to be drawing on them.

"Why are they taking so long?" he snarled at the man standing behind them in the room.

The uniformed man shifted his feet. Silas noted the bead of sweat on his brow and sneered at his discomfort.

"You cannot hurry our remote viewers," the man said. "They need to take their time and cross check their findings with each other."

Silas tapped his foot, irritated beyond words. He lifted his hand and snapped his fingers.

"Enough!" he said. "If they haven't traced these people in all this time we'd better find another way."

Just as he uttered these words one of the men in the closed room looked up and raised his hand. He stood up, scraping his chair away from the table.

"They've found them," the man behind Silas said with obvious relief. "Let's go and see what they've got." He opened the door into the empty passage and led them a few feet along to a door painted a muddy green. The remote viewer was already there waiting for them.

He scratched his head and said, "We think they're in Dorset, outside a main town in the countryside. We saw green fields and one large building. Could be a sizeable house."

Silas banged his fist on the table where the papers covered with drawings were spread. "You think! You think!" he shouted. "Can't you be more precise than that?"

The uniformed man stepped forward quickly. "Sir, we explained the procedure . . ." He saw that the remote viewer was becoming more than irritated by Silas's attitude.

"Sir, you haven't let me finish. Do you want the information or not?" he pointed to the spread of drawings. "There are other buildings. We found these on our first sweep. Look!" He thrust the papers under Silas's nose.

Both he and Helga bent over the table. "Doesn't make much sense to me," Helga said as she looked at the lines and squiggles. Suddenly she let out a holler. "Look, can't you see? This is our own firm building. There's the car park. There's the long drive. "Silas, they've gone back." Silas saw the look of triumph on her face.

"They'd hardly go back to the office," he said damping her spirits. "Don't be so stupid. Let's look at the second attempt." He thrust the papers to one side almost causing them to fall to the floor.

The remote viewer leapt forward to catch them. "Be careful. There are hours of work here."

Silas ignored him. "Fools!" he muttered. "Look here. It's clear. They're not going to the office. They're visiting that ridiculous woman with the dogs. She's the one with the large house well out of town. She has a long drive too."

Helga stared at him. "They wouldn't dare. They wouldn't be so stupid."

"It's obvious," Silas said. "They intend to visit that vain mother of hers." Silas could hardly contain himself with excitement. "We've got them." He turned on Helga. "So much for your psychic abilities," he smirked. "Your own team of men did nothing. Let's get down there before they move again."

CHAPTER TWENTY-NINE

POPPY GETS INVOLVED

As usual Poppy was up early long before her guests had surfaced. An early mist rose from the fields and the birds were in full song in the nearby woods. The sun was just rising, the weather perfect for her early morning walk with the dogs and the skies were clear. As she walked she went over in her mind the information that Kate had given during her earlier talks. She'd spoken of the extra-terrestrial's warning about the dangers we ourselves imposed on the planet through our misuse of Earth's resources. It must be serious she mused, if so many channellers were bringing through the same messages from guides, angelic beings and angelic masters. As a self-confessed sceptic she now admitted to herself that there must be something to it.

Poppy gave a quiet groan causing her dogs to turn and look at her. She began to worry about her world and realised these messengers were talking to anyone who would listen. They seemed to be extremely concerned about nuclear devices which are threatening, not only Earth, but parallel worlds; many other worlds, which in periphery could still be perceived at the edge of the universe.

To her great surprise Poppy heard, as if she was receiving directly, as if a voice in her head was speaking to her. *'You must understand that the universe is an immense living organism. For as with you, a toe injury is felt all the way up to the brain in a fraction of a second and the whole body becomes aware of the injury. It's no longer important to know WHO is sending WHAT. Messages of awakening, severe warnings, waves of growth, frightful images of disaster, all are necessary to wake everyone up. Man is now both a threatening and a threatened species'.*

Poppy was shaken, but was it all true? Was she going mad? She'd been enjoying the long walk with her dogs but it was now time to go back and join her friends. She couldn't put her finger on it but something else was bothering her.

It was still very early so she was surprised to hear the sound of helicopters filling the air over the countryside, disturbing the peace. An early mist still clung to the land, creating a magical feel over the fields. The birds sang in full song which was now drowned out by the harsh clatter of the rotors overhead. Becoming alarmed Poppy quickened her pace and almost set out at a run as she neared her home and wondered if they, in their machines could see the little figure below them and would ask themselves why there was such urgency in her walk.

In her haste to get home Poppy didn't notice the tree root crossing her path until it was too late. She fell heavily and landed facedown. The breath was knocked out of her and for a terrifying moment she thought she'd passed out. Her dogs were all over her, licking her face. She grabbed the collar of Boris, her favourite and tried to get up. The sound of helicopters got even louder, deafening her. The trees and grass blew wildly. Surely they couldn't be landing? Then Poppy remembered the men in black who'd visited her and went pale. She felt a thud as something slammed into her leg. It was the last thing she remembered as she lost consciousness.

***

Kate overslept and chided herself for letting precious time with Poppy pass by. This morning she'd go and visit her mother and take Poppy with her for moral support. Surely she'd be delighted to see her? Or would she? She turned over in bed, wanting to stay there in the comfort it gave her. She sighed, it was time to get up. Adam and Jacob would already be eating breakfast. They were always hungry. She heard the faint mumble of male voices coming from downstairs and was comforted. After washing she hastily pulled on jeans and a blue checked shirt and took a quick look out of the window over the countryside and made her way down the stairs.

Both men looked up as she entered the kitchen. Jacob brushed the crumbs from his mouth and kissed her on the cheek as she passed. "Good morning, late bird."

Adam smiled broadly. "Had a good sleep? We thought you'd never surface." He patted the chair beside him.

Kate filled her plate from the dishes laid out for them by Poppy. "Anyone seen Poppy?" she asked. "It's getting quite late and she should be back from her walk by now."

Jacob scraped his chair back from the table. "I'll go and look," he said and left the room. A few minutes later he returned, his face sombre. "I can't find her anywhere. Most odd!" he said. "Only one little dog has come back without her and she'd told me they always stayed together."

Both Adam and Kate got to their feet. "She'd never stay out so long, especially with us here," Kate said, alarmed now. "Get the dog."

Jacob went out and brought the little white terrier in to the kitchen. They could all see the note tightly fixed to its collar.

"Let me," Adam said. His fingers trembled as he took the note and read, *"If you want to see your friend returned, present yourselves at the front of the house."*

The kitchen was at the back and no-one had ventured to the front that morning. They hadn't heard a thing through the thick walls of the old farmhouse. As one, they rushed to the front room and looked out. Lined up on the drive were military jeeps and cars with blacked out windows.

"What do we do?" whispered Kate. "What have they done with Poppy?" Her voice caught in a half sob. "It's all my fault. We should never have come here."

Adam put his hand on her arm, comforting her. "I'll think of something," he said and pulled out his mobile.

Suddenly Kate knew what she had to do to save her friend. She turned away from the window and quietly left the room. Adam focussed on his call and Jacob continued to stare out of the window, one hand placed on the little dog at his side. Neither of them noticed her leaving.

Kate went to her room, closed the curtains and sat still in an upright chair. If she could mind travel at home she could do it here, or anywhere. Intention was the key. It had to work for Poppy's sake. It took her a little while to go into trance, but she had clear purpose now. This journey was no longer to be a random thing. She focussed on the face of her friend until she could clearly see her in her mind.

A few moments passed when Kate realised she was truly alongside Poppy, but that she was unaware of Kate's presence. Was this what her training had been about all along? To be invisible? Kate's mind flashed back to when she'd been told, and she heard again the words:

'In your altered higher state of vibration you can move and change third dimensional things.'

Kate realised that this was why she'd been able to de-activate nuclear devices, change unsuitable futures and move objects. Another realisation hit her hard. Anybody could do it, anybody, and it was up to her to show how. They didn't need the implant she had within her brain.

But right now Poppy was her concern. Her friend couldn't see her, although

Kate was right there beside her. From the look on her friend's face Kate saw how frightened Poppy was. Yet another memory surfaced. '*Remember*,' the voice in her head said. *'Remember rescuing those captive extra-terrestrials.'* Kate remembered quite well. It had taken a lot of energy, but she'd done it.

Kate looked around her for ideas. Poppy was sitting on a cheap, white plastic chair at a white plastic table. It was obviously a temporary arrangement. Kate moved herself straight through the door to outside the room. A blue uniformed man stood guard. How was she to keep Poppy quiet while she moved her? She had to think quickly before anyone arrived. Poppy didn't have a psychic bone in her body, but perhaps the close bond that they had between them would be enough. Kate moved back into the room. She saw that Poppy's hands had been tied behind her. That would be a start. Kate mentally saw the bonds loosen until at last they fell to the floor.

Poppy started up in surprise and almost let out a yell. She rubbed her wrists and Kate leaned in close and whispered in her ear. "Poppy, stay still and don't utter a sound."

Poppy opened her mouth, then shut it again. She looked around, but it was clear to Kate that she saw nothing.

"Poppy, it's me, Kate." Poppy shook her head as if realising it wasn't her imagination.

"Is it really you?" her voice hardly a whisper. She began to cry.

"Shush! They'll hear you," breathed Kate. "Whatever happens, don't make a sound." Kate hoped her friend could hear her. "Nod, if you can hear me," she said.

Poppy nodded. Relieved, Kate could see by the expression on her face that Poppy still wasn't sure if what was happening was real or her imagination. It was then that Kate noticed Boris sitting at Poppy's feet. He clearly saw her and snarled quietly and yet wagged his tail at the same time. Kate almost laughed at his confusion. She'd have to take them both and it had to be soon before the remote viewer psychics picked up on her energy signature.

She listened to the voice in her head. *'Extend your energy field just as you did with the little guys.'* Kate almost laughed again at the expression.

Suddenly the door burst open and a dark suited man entered, followed by the guard. Poppy jumped up. Kate didn't know what to do next. Could they see her? There was no way now that she could remove Poppy and the dog. It would require her absolute focus, something she'd lost the instant the men entered the room. She left.

***

Jacob grabbed Adam's arm. "Never mind the phone. You must get out of here quickly. If they find you here it's curtains for all of us."

"I don't want to leave you or Kate, but you're right. I mustn't be seen with you."

"The cellar Adam. You can get to it through the kitchen. Poppy told me last night about the cellar where she keeps fine wines. There's an exit from there to the old barn out back. It's your only chance. Go now!" Jacob pushed Adam so hard he almost fell over.

"I'll catch up with you both later," he called out as he ran from the room.

Alone now, Jacob took a quick look out of the front window. The cars and jeeps were still there. What were they waiting for? Where was Kate? Why wasn't she here with him?

As if in response to his question Kate appeared behind him and tapped him on the shoulder.

"Where have you been?" he asked, his voice a little high.

"I'll tell you later," she said. "I've seen Poppy. She's alright."

Jacob hugged her. "Adam got away. He had to go, but don't worry he'll get us out of this." At that moment there was loud hammering on the front door.

***

Sechem felt he could take it easy now that Kate had found her feet and was managing journeys on her own. It had turned out much better than expected. But he was in for a rude awakening. The call came from Master M. It was like a telephone had been planted in his head, ringing loudly. It was something he couldn't ignore.

"Get in touch with me immediately." There was no explanation. It was a summons to attend that Sechem didn't dare ignore. In any case he particularly liked visiting the Mother Ship, and to go into Master M's quarters was an honour. He went at once.

The entrance to Master M's chambers glowed in many colours as it always did. Sechem walked through the shimmering wall. To his surprise Jamére, looking rather subdued was already there seated on a low stool before Master M.

"Take a seat, Sechem." Master M's face was stern as he indicated that he should sit alongside Jamére. They both waited in silence. Although only a few seconds passed it felt to be much longer. Jamére began to whistle which drew a sharp look from Master M. At last the master stood. He looked at them both with the air of a headmaster gently rebuking his pupils.

"You've neglected your duties towards Kate and her father," he said in a quiet voice.

Jamére looked up sharply at this. "But I was with them only a short while ago. Everything was going along fine."

Sechem got to his feet. "But you sent Adam to take care of them. Anyway they're on holiday."

"Adam can only do so much." Master M snorted. "They're all in deep trouble at this very moment. You haven't been keeping an eye on things, have you?"

They both hung their heads low and said nothing.

"I don't know how you are going to handle the situation that's going on RIGHT NOW in Dorset," Master M said. "But you must think of something. You, Jamére follow Adam, and you, Sechem get yourself down there. As you are well aware, Kate is your charge." Master M rose from his chair. The meeting was over.

***

Adam worked his way along the dark passage from the cellar, brushing off cobwebs as he went. He hoped it would come out far enough from the house for him to be undetected. He flicked open his mobile and punched the numbers. Unsurprisingly, there was no reception this deep down. He could do nothing from this position. Would Kate and her father be safe? And Poppy, what would happen to her? He'd grown very fond of Kate's bubbly friend. As he passed rack after rack of wine bottles stored in the cellar he was amazed at the vintage and obvious age. How long they'd been there he could only guess. Did Poppy know she was sitting on a fortune?

At last he came to a door which didn't look as if it had been opened in many long years. He breathed a sigh of relief when he discovered it was unlocked. He pulled hard on the iron ring fixed to the door until it gave way. He saw it opened onto a long flight of stone steps which led up to a metal grating. Light filtered through the vegetation that had grown over it. Adam pushed and pushed, using his shoulders, until at last it moved and he broke through into fresh air. It had started to drizzle. It was time to call in for support. He flicked open his phone and tried again, this time with success.

***

Two men in dark glasses sat in silence in the back of the first car as they watched the front door of Poppy's house for any sign of movement. Silas nervously lightly tapped the dark suited companion on the arm.

"What do you think?" he said. "Will they come out?" He sniffed, as one used to taking snuff. Cautious in his dealings with this team he knew they could be ruthless. He knew all about being ruthless, having operated this way himself.

The man said nothing, put a gloved hand to his earpiece and raised his binoculars. He ignored Silas.

"What are we waiting for?" Silas asked again.

"He'll be arriving soon," was the curt reply.

"He?"

"You'll soon see."

As if on cue a black helicopter clattered its way over the trees and landed a little way off. A large, heavy man got out and made his way to their car. Silas got out with the driver to meet him and quickly lowered his eyes when he saw it was Gork. He didn't dare meet those dreadful eyes and stayed close to the car. The creature looked both men up and down with scorn.

"Take me to them," he commanded. His voice boomed across the land.

"They haven't opened the door," the man stuttered. "We waited for you."

"Incompetents!" the creature snorted. "I'll deal with this." He strode towards the house and left them standing with their mouths open. Silas watched him go and sighed with relief. At least he wasn't expected to go along.

***

Kate and Jacob couldn't ignore the urgent heavy banging on Poppy's front door any longer. Whatever or whoever those outside had been waiting for had clearly arrived. They watched through the window as a giant figure approached the front door. Jacob drew back in shock and alarm.

"We'd better open it," Jacob said in a quiet voice. "I feel he could break it down with one blow of his hand, and it is after all Poppy's beautiful door."

He saw on Kate's face the look of concern over her friend's fate. He put his arm around her.

"Don't worry, my darling. Don't forget Adam will be doing something." What Jacob hadn't said was that he recognised the man, if he was a man at all. He was to be feared. He prayed Sechem would be able to do something, and quickly, anything against such an evil force. He'd met it only once before.

It seemed a lifetime ago now, before Kate was born. There'd been immense opposition from Gork to the union with Joslene, his love.

"No good will come of it," the Giant had warned, snarling and growling like some wild beast.

Jacob knew this creature didn't want any strengthening of the bonds between humans and beings from Sirius, for it meant more strength to those who wished for an elevation of the human soul. The creature had frightened him then and frightened him now all these years later.

"We'd better open the door," he repeated. "Get away, get well back, Kate." He pushed her away from the door and reached for the handle, but as he did so another long-fingered hand grasped his.

"Sechem!" Jacob almost sobbed with relief as he turned and saw his friend. "Get Kate out of here," he pleaded. "Do not let her meet that creature. She's not strong enough to withstand such a malevolent force."

Jacob knew the power of such evil and any not strong enough to endure it would be sullied by the contact.

Sechem turned to Kate. "We'll all go together," he said as calmly as he could. "Kate, use your powers, now."

They all held hands and focused on bringing the energy of the cosmos down into the crown of their heads and coursing through their bodies. Their combined energy increased and slowly all three began to disappear. They'd done it! There'd be no one in the house for the creature to find.

***

Having felt Kate nearby had given Poppy strength. She got up from her chair quickly regaining her usual force of character as the two men came into the makeshift interview room.

"Sit, please," one said. Poppy obediently sat. The dark suited man sat down opposite her and removed his dark glasses. The other stayed by the door.

"Would you like a coffee?" he asked politely. "We have some explaining to do." He coughed into his hand and looked embarrassed.

"Too right, you do." Poppy said with force. "Who do you think you are, kidnapping law-abiding citizens in that manner?"

"We thought you were a terrorist," he explained, getting red in the face.

"We? Who are 'we'?"

"I had my orders," he said. "We thought you were someone else. It was a case of mistaken identity." His expression hardened. It was clear he had no intention of saying more. "We have a few formalities to go through and then we'll make sure you are returned home." He snapped his fingers and the man at the door stepped forward with some papers.

She signed the papers and a few moments later she was escorted, holding tightly to Boris's collar, out of the room and into a waiting car,

"You'll be hearing from my lawyers," Poppy said, knowing full well she still didn't know who 'we' were.

***

Arriving at the airport Adam breathed a sigh of relief. Things had moved fast and his phone calls had brought results. The helicopter pilot had been told of their mistake in picking Poppy up from her land. He checked in and while having a coffee made arrangements for the garage to collect their rented car after a decent interval. All was in order and he thanked the universe for mobile phones. Poppy would require some sort of explanation, so he sent a long ambiguous mesage into her voice mail. He knew she was bright enough to understand his cryptic message. He'd got rather fond of Poppy, and like it or not she was now involved.

Howie was not so easily dealt with and Adam experienced a little guilt over that. He was an innocent party in the whole thing. He'd probably be sent to some obscure post, or even could be made to disappear. Adam decided there and then that the young man would come to no harm and he would make sure he was well looked after. But for the moment he had to focus on Kate and Jacob. He thanked his stars that nobody had made contact with Kate's surrogate mother and that she would have been unaware of the whole episode.

He wondered what Jamére was doing all this while? As if in answer to his thought, Jamére, the impudent time traveller suddenly appeared by his side. Adam was sitting in the VIP departure lounge at Heathrow waiting for his flight to Washington DC. Fortunately, the lounge was empty. Although Adam knew nobody could see the glorious flamboyant figure they would have been able to hear his part of any conversation between them. He hadn't yet perfected the art of two way telepathy.

Jamére walked up and down pulling at this or that and inspecting it all with great interest. "All this just to move people around?" he said.

"Jamére, for heaven's sake. Have you never been in a lounge before?"

"Not like this," Jamére said and waved his arms wide. "Oh, by the way, Jacob and Kate are alright. Sechem has whisked them home to Tadley."

Adam choked. "The fool. They'll be caught there."

"No they won't. They all think they are still holed up at Poppy's."

"And how long do you think that will last when they find them gone?"

Jamére looked offended. "No need to take on so," he said. "I'll be doing one of my tricks."

Adam groaned. Whatever Jamére did it would still only be a temporary respite. He'd have to move the two of them on again. He needed to have a word with The Master, and soon.

His flight was called over the tannoy. Adam turned to Jamére. "I have to go. See what you can do." He got up and quickly made his way to the gate.

***

Silas watched from the safety of the car as the giant Creature approached the front door of Poppy's house.

"What do you think he'll do?" he asked the man standing beside him.

The man looked at Silas with scorn in his eyes. "He'll sort them out. If he can't do it, nobody can."

Silas looked up at the sky and frowned. "It's going to rain. Look how dark it's getting."

It was indeed growing dark. The skies turned black and there was a flash of lightning. A loud clap of thunder shook the ground. Then came the rain. Such a downpour as had never before been seen in Dorset. The driveway quickly became a torrent. Every man who could scrambled to get into their cars, but the flow was so strong the vehicles started to float and bobbed about like toys.

"The Creature," Silas yelled. "What about him?"

"He can look after himself," his companion said. "Let's get out of here."

Gork clearly thought the same. They watched him as he turned away from the door and waded away from the house, creating a bow wave as he went. Only a few heard the laughter that seemed to come from nowhere.

***

Arriving at Dulles airport Adam caught a taxi and went directly to his lodgings. As he opened the door to his apartment he saw the blinking light on his answering machine linked to his office. He pressed the button and heard the unwelcome gruff voice of the old general urging him to get in touch.

Checking up on me, are you? thought Adam. He sent a brief text reply, so the old man would know he was back within his reach and able to attend the next meeting. Next on his 'to do' list were arrangements to meet Master M.

That night he meditated and requested immediate contact. If Kate can do it so can I, he reasoned. She made it look so easy and he envied her the implant she'd had since before her birth. There were many things he still didn't know about Master M and it wasn't really his business to find out. He did know of the special interest he had in both Kate and her father and he often wondered about that. After all there were many others on Earth and elsewhere who required Master M's attention.

He didn't find it easy to make a connection that night. Maybe it was because of the long flight that he soon drifted off into dreamland. He was in a deep sleep when he felt a tug on his arm.

"Adam! Adam! Wake up." It was Master M. "You wished to see me?"

Adam struggled to clear his mind and looked all around him. To his surprise he was back home on the Mother Ship. The familiar coloured lights and gentle music were a balm to his troubled thoughts. He shook himself fully awake.

"Master M, I'm so glad to see you. We have a problem". Irreverently the old hackneyed phrase from the film came to his mind. 'Houston, we have a problem'." Adam smiled.

"I'm glad to see you smiling," said Master M. "Tell me about it, son."

Adam related the whole story. "That devil Gork has set his mind on getting Kate," he said. "It's not only Silas and Helga we have to worry about now." He frowned.

Master M sighed. "Yes, I agree. We cannot let him get near her. One single contact could put her in jeopardy. What do you propose doing?

"We have to relocate her and her father once again. Will you help?"

***

Sechem looked around with satisfaction as all three of them arrived together at their home in Tadley. They simply materialised in the kitchen. He saw from the look on Jacob's face that he was badly shaken and knew that this was quite a new experience for him. Kate's eyes gleamed with pride at what their combined energy had achieved. Sechem grabbed her hand as she stood stock still while trying to pull her thoughts together.

With the gait of sleepwalkers, they moved into the front room of their little house which looked just as they had left it days before. Sechem saw Jacob hadn't stopped trembling, so he took his arm and gently guided him to a chair and made him comfortable. The dear man had gone through a lot of surprises over the weeks. Sechem realised being transported in this way must have unnerved them all.

"Kate," he said. "don't you think your father would like a cup of tea?"

Jacob heard him and vigorously banged the arm of his chair. "Something stronger would be more in order."

Kate, now fully composed, laughed out loud. "Now, Dad. You know what happens when you have a drink. Anyway, you and Howie finished off the last bottle. It'll have to be tea."

"Ah yes. Howie." Sechem said, for a moment sadness clouded his features. "Poor lad. I'm sure he'll be alright. After all he did carry out his orders and they can't blame him for that."

Sechem could see doubt written all over Kate's face. "I wish we could be sure of that," she said. "He's an innocent in all this."

The ancient time traveller frowned. "Well, he is single and as far as we know he has no really close relatives. We could move him ahead in time and wipe his memory."

He saw Kate's eyes widen. "You could do what?"

"Or we could take him back in time and wipe his memory of now. It never happened kind of thing. They do this all the time with the people they send to Mars, sometimes for twenty years." He watched with some amusement as her face registered absolute disbelief. "Kate," he said. "There's still so much you do not know. But it's not my place to tell you."

Jacob stirred and appeared to have recovered at last from the teleportation. It was clear to Sechem that he'd been listening carefully to what Sechem was telling his daughter.

"Drat!" Sechem muttered. "I've said too much." There were times when he wished he could obliterate his words. But it was too late now and obviously what he'd said could stimulate more questions. He would no doubt be reprimanded by Master M for his indiscretion. He looked around the little front room, but everything appeared to be normal. There were no ghostly figures or Shadow People to be seen. That was a relief.

"Let's get down to practical matters," he said. "Kate, tea first, as always."

Kate bustled off into the kitchen and soon returned.

"There's no milk," she said. "You'll have to have green tea, black coffee or go without." All she got in return was a grunt from her father. A few minutes later they were settled and sitting comfortably, immersed in their thoughts sipping tea.

Sechem broke the silence. "You're still on holiday from your job so nobody will worry if you don't turn up there." He paused. "That's right isn't it, Kate?"

Kate nodded vigorously.

"What happened today is just a temporary respite. They still don't know Adam's part in all this, which is just as well. But they'll be scratching their heads as to why both of you are missing from Poppy's home when they had the house covered front and back. They'll come looking for you, you can be sure of that." As he said this Sechem seemed to rise to an even greater height. The constant field of colour around him appeared to brighten and strengthen in brilliance. He knew he'd need his full energy for the next phase, whatever that might be. He sighed when he saw Jacob burying his head in his hands.

***

On board the Mother Ship Adam sat patiently waiting for Master M to consider his request for help. The great birdman lowered his shining head and Adam could see he was thinking deeply. After what seemed to be far too long he looked up at Adam with enormous, penetrating eyes.

"We'll fetch them to us here on the Mother Ship. They'll stay until we decide what to do next."

Adam was surprised. He jerked his head up in astonishment. "But that would be more dangerous for them. They might not withstand the change in vibration if they stay too long. They are in human bodies after all."

Adam didn't like questioning the Master, but he wasn't happy. "And what if they bump into Gork? He visits the Mother Ship too. It's open to all."

Master M blinked his great eyes several times. "He will not gain access here in my chamber. We won't keep them too long for their comfort. They've already withstood one visit with no ill effects."

"Yes, but it was for an extremely short time. They were returned almost immediately."

Master M was adamant. "We'll fetch them tomorrow. It's time they were given the full picture." He blinked again, and Adam watched as his form began to dissipate. Then he was gone. Adam realised he was back in his apartment in Bethesda.

***

Helga frowned. "I can't understand it. One minute the sun was shining and the next minute the skies opened. She rubbed her arm up and down on the glass to clear the car's fogged up windows. She peered out, worry etched all over her face.

"It's alright to get out now," reassured the driver. "We're back on dry land." He gave an uneasy laugh.

Silas opened the door of his car some few feet off from Helga's vehicle and stepped out nervously. They all looked anxiously at the sky. Occupants of the other vehicles were also emerging with caution.

"What happened?" one man asked. "Let's get out of here." He waved his arm signalling the other vehicles and one by one they left.

Helga saw that they'd all floated out onto the main road. Not a drop of water could be seen on the tarmac there. It was then that Helga remembered the tornado event at her home and the voice that came from nowhere warning them about messing with the weather. She shivered and felt panic rising in her.

"Let's go, *now*," she told the driver. She was terrified at what might happen next?

"What about him?" Silas indicated the huge form wading out towards them from the drive which was still under water.

Helga sniffed. "He has his own transport." She got into her car again and pulled Silas in after her. She shouted to the driver. "Go, Go. There's nothing more we can do here."

***

Later that day everybody had left the drive. The water had drained quickly and a few moments later a black helicopter hovered looking for a dry patch behind the house on which to land. It settled down with care. Steps were lowered and two men gently assisted Poppy to the ground.

"The ground is too soft to land nearer your house," explained the man in dark glasses. The wolfhound Boris was lifted down and he immediately rushed around in frantic circles.

"Can you find your way back, Ma-am?"

"It's my land, you fool." Poppy glared at him. "You're trespassing so you'd better get out of here. Now!"

She moved away and watched as the helicopter lifted off. Secretly she'd rather enjoyed the whole experience now that she'd seen what Kate could do. So this is what her friend's life was all about. She made her way to the back of the house and let herself in through the kitchen door. The dogs scampered up to her in a frenzy of delight.

Poppy called out. "Kate, Jacob, Adam?" Boris jumped in alarm at her raised voice and ran to the safety of his favourite bed.

She called again. "Where are you?" Silence followed. Poppy ran from room to room searching, but all rooms were empty. She felt the stillness and hush and was unnerved by it. What should she do now?

***

In Tadley, Jacob watched Kate with half closed eyes as she poured the tea and smiled to himself. The little room in Pinks Lane felt comfortable and normal to him.

"I hope we don't have to move again," he murmured, more to himself that to anyone in particular.

"What was that, Dad?"

"Nothing." He reached for his cup. "What no biscuits?" He longed for things to be normal again but knew it could never be. "What about Poppy and Howie?" he asked.

Kate looked up sharply. "We can phone her and explain it all to her."

"That'll be a good trick," Jacob said drily. "She's a sweet woman but she'll never understand. I don't want her harmed in any way."

"That's understood, Dad. She's my best friend and I don't want her hurt either."

Jacob realised that Sechem was listening hard. "She'll be alright," The Time Traveller turned to him and said. "She's tougher than she looks and can hold her own."

"I'll keep you to that, Sechem," Jacob said shaking his finger at him. "It's all been too much for me and I'm used to all this shenanigan. Can you imagine what it's been like for her?" He wiped his brow.

"I think you both need to catch up on your sleep," Sechem said. "I'll keep watch."

Both his charges took advantage of his suggestion and gratefully retired to their rooms.

CHAPTER THIRTY

GORK

The Plough Inn village pub on the Silchester Road was surrounded by quiet fields and trees but today it was buzzing. Little groups of concerned people had gathered there to find out if what they'd heard was true or not. Word was that the authorities had requisitioned not only their favourite watering place but also the village memorial hall on the green in Tadley. Both were to be used for a special exercise by the Americans at the nearby military base. A grizzled old man perched on a stool at the pub counter and held out his glass for a refill. A hand grabbed it and quickly ordered another round. Old George was well recognised for gossip and his knowledge of any kind and he enjoyed the attention it gave him, to say nothing of free beer.

"Well," he paused for effect and took a deep draught of beer. "I heard the men talking as I walked by them outside the base this morning. It's an exercise against terrorists they said."

A bright, much younger man in a blue overall stopped him mid flow. "We ain't never going to have any terrorists here in this village," he said and thumped his fist on the bar causing the glasses to jump.

"No, you're right there, Fred," the old man said and took another gulp of beer. "but they have to do their practice and exercises somewhere, don't they?" A murmur of agreement rippled through the little crowd.

"They even have helicopters," added another. Nobody paid him any attention. Eventually there was nothing more to say and each drifted away leaving George to his drink.

***

Inside the village memorial hall Silas was arguing with the village councillor.

"Sir, we thought you'd left," he said, his voice sounded weak even to himself.

"I've done what you should have done yourself," the Creature said.

Silas could feel the glare from behind the dark glasses and shuddered.

"I sent a couple of men back to the house and found nobody there except that crazy woman."

Gork moved closer to Silas who took a hasty step back, almost falling over in the process. "They've slipped away yet again. How is that possible?"

Silas had no answer. He wondered, not for the first time why Gork was so interested in Kate and her father. Would he ever find out the real reason?

The Creature placed a heavy gloved hand on Silas's shoulder. Silas felt a shaft of fear course through him at the touch. "I'm leaving you now. I can't keep running around this country doing your job." Gork turned and left the hall escorted by two men in combat gear. Silas heard the rotor of the helicopter and breathed a sigh of relief. It was then he noticed Helga standing way back in the shadows. Silas was mortified to realise she'd witnessed the whole exchange. She moved towards him and it seemed to him in a 'let me take charge' manner. For some obscure reason he was irritated by the sharp clip clop of her shoes as she walked across the wooden floor.

"We'd better find them and quickly," she said. "Let's go back to Pinks Lane and search their house. We might find something there that will give us a clue."

Silas nodded. He didn't have a better solution and watched tight lipped as she issued orders over her mobile.

***

Kate was awakened by the sound of urgent knocking on the front door. She hurried to the window and saw Howie panting on the doorstep as if he'd been running. Hearing the commotion Jacob came out of his room and together they rushed downstairs to let him in. Where was Sechem, she wondered? Kate opened the door and Howie almost fell inside.

"They're on their way here," he shouted. "They're going to search your house."

"How do you know this, Howie?" Kate saw how distressed the young man was. Agitated, he began to stride up and down the room and Kate could see he'd no idea what to do next. She pushed him towards the door.

"Howie, you'd better leave quickly," she said. "You'll be in trouble if they find you here."

Howie ran down the path. He'd done what he could.

Kate called out. "Sechem!"

Then she saw him calmly walking out of the kitchen as if he hadn't a care in the world. "What can we do?" she wailed.

"Don't take on so. *We* have a plan." He waved his arms in a wide circle.

"A plan, what plan?" Jacob said. Kate saw worry etched all over his face. Sechem pulled them close together.

"Get your things," he said. "We're leaving. Hurry."

"Dad, I hope this isn't a repeat of when we had to flee before. I don't like it."

However, they grabbed what they could and headed for Kate's car.

"Go where you were dropped off before in the woods," Sechem called out and then disappeared.

Kate knew exactly where he meant. She drove as fast as she could to the clearing in the woods where she'd picked up her father after his trip to space. As she turned left from her lane onto the main road she saw a small convoy of cars coming up fast behind them.

"They've got us," Jacob yelled. "We'll never make it to the woods before they catch up with us."

Kate took a quick look in the rear-view mirror. He was right, they'd never make it. She put her foot down hard. She took another look and was puzzled when she saw the cars were left behind.

"What's happened, Dad?"

Jacob laughed. "Can't you see, darling? Jamére has been up to his tricks again. A tree has come down just in front of them and they can't get around it." He laughed again. "It couldn't have happened at a better time."

Kate wasn't laughing. "Can't you hear that chopper?" she said. "We're done for."

"We're almost there, Kate." It was true. The now familiar patch of cleared ground was in front of them. They'd arrived. They gathered their few belongings and got out of the car. Sitting prettily in the clearing was a shiny silver space craft, humming gently.

"Now, Dad. This *is* one of mine." She rushed towards it and together they climbed the ramp. "Just like old times," she said happily.

As the ramp closed seamlessly into the ship they saw Sechem sitting inside, grinning like an idiot. "Off to see the wizard," he joked and helped them into their seats.

Better still, thought Kate, that those after them still had no idea of their connection with Adam. Was he safe too, and what was coming next?

CHAPTER THIRTY-ONE

ARRIVAL

Master M looked up at Adam from his console. "So, they left safely." It was a statement not a question. "Bring them to me as soon as they've docked. I don't want them wandering around." Adam, now dressed in a tight-fitting silver suit, bowed his head and hurried off.

Master M sat with one hand holding his shining head in just the manner of Auguste Rodin's 'The Thinker'. Like the sculpture he too had a lot to think about. On his desk was another little sculpted figure. It was a gift to him by a much-loved soul to remind him of a time that could be no more. He'd got into the habit of tapping the head of the dancing figurine and talking to her.

"My darling, should I tell Kate and her father who she really is? That's a big question, and am I prepared to do that at this early stage of her life? Will she be able to cope with the responsibility? I realise that they might both be wondering why there's such a big effort by Gork to get hold of her. What can Kate do to him when he is such a powerful entity himself? She can hardly be a threat. Or can she? Gork must have discovered who she is, even if she has no idea of the truth." He patted the figurine fondly on the head and sighed.

Master M fought back tears and made an effort to smile as he looked up as the four people he loved so much were ushered in. Jamére and Sechem stood to one side of his private chamber and Kate and Jacob moved forward to stand in front of him.

"We are so pleased to meet you again, Sir," Kate said. Master M noted with pleasure how she resisted the urge to hug him.

"Please sit," he said. They sat. "You won't be staying long but arrangements have to be made before you can return."

Jacob groaned. "Oh please, not another move, Sir. With respect we're getting fed up with being moved around the country and having to start all over."

"Hold your tongue." Master M spoke sharply and with authority. "When you hear what I have to say you'll understand more clearly."

Jacob shut up fast and looked down at his feet.

"We're waiting for the arrival of Adam. He has to be present to hear what I have to say."

Kate's face lit up at this news. "He's coming here?"

Master M gave a brief nod. "He's already on board making arrangements. Would you like a drink while we wait?"

Jacob was the first to put his hand up. The others simply nodded. Master M pressed a button and almost immediately two small greys brought a trolley of drinks and nibbles of all kinds. They helped themselves and sat and waited, all the while conscious that Master M was studying them closely with his large, dark eyes. Sechem and Jamére remained impassive as they stood together on the side. The waiting stretched on and on until Kate's head drooped with fatigue. She shook herself, trying to stay awake.

They became alert when a musical chime was heard from outside the chamber. They turned their heads expectantly towards the entrance. Adam strode in, fully dressed in a silver suit. He bowed respectfully to Master M and grinned at Kate. She gaped in astonishment at Adam's attire

"Sorry I took so long," he said. "It's not easy to get everything in place."

Master M clapped his hands together. "Well now you're here we can begin." He looked around at them all. "Jamére, Sechem, sit down do. You look like sentries standing there. You also need to hear what I have to say."

Jacob whispered to Kate through a mouthful of food. "This looks serious."

"Be quiet, Dad. This *is* serious. Can't you tell?"

"This will take some time." Master M began. "You'd better make yourselves comfortable.

***

Kate's jaw dropped and watched in awe as Master M's energy field began to expand until it filled the entire chamber with colours she'd never seen before. The colours whirled and spun around them. She remembered how the unseen teacher voices had showed her how to expand in the same way when she had energy work to do. She wondered if she'd appeared in similar manner to Master M's glorious energy as it expanded.

Sechem and Jamére's energy and colours were bright but were nothing compared to what she was witnessing in the chamber. *I love it, she breathed to herself.*

Master M was speaking. "You've probably been asking yourselves, all of you," he looked directly at his two space travellers as he said this, "many questions," he added.

"Why is Gork so intent on getting Kate in his clutches? And why are the military so keen to get hold of her? After all, she's just another psychic who can do things the majority of people can't. There are many like her. So why her?"

"I've often wondered that too," Jacob said.

This comment brought a sharp *'don't interrupt me'* look from Master M. "As you already realise, their official line is that she may stumble upon a secret project in her journeying, and that's a threat to them all. She may make it known to the general public what is really going on in the world. She's already done that to some degree. That's the official line and this allows the military and the CIA to use preventive measures against her.

"Jacob raised his hand. "But if that's the case, they could take her out any time they wished to. Couldn't they? They've done this to others."

"Good point." This time Master M smiled at him. "I'm so glad you're paying attention. Your role as a father has been important. We chose you wisely."

Jacob turned red and looked embarrassed. "So, why haven't they taken her out?"

"You're forgetting that creature Gork, who they're all so frightened of. He has his own agenda for Kate."

Kate remembered the shudder that came over her when she'd seen him, even at some distance from Poppy's house. The mere sight of him had brought terror to her heart. She realised with a start that Master M was clicking his fingers at her to bring her thoughts back to him and away from her fearful memories.

"The creature known as Gork is all powerful and is at the head of the Shadow Government on Earth. Many rightfully fear him. He's taken the mantle of a human being, but it's not enough to hide what is beneath." Master M paused and studied the little group. They were all silent. "Even Silas and Helga are scared of him. They'll do whatever he asks." He paused again and rubbed the head of the figurine at his side. It gave him comfort.

Kate drew closer to her father and held his hand tight. She looked over at Adam who'd taken a seat facing her but to the side of Master M. It seemed to her that it was his official position. Master M looked around at the worried faces before continuing.

"I tell you this now. Gork is able and free to visit this Mother Ship whenever he wishes. We do not prevent any from using it since it is an intergalactic way station, used by all races."

Adam frowned. "Unbelievable!"

Master M turned his head to Adam and gave him a sharp look. He held up his hand for silence. "It's a bit similar to you having neutral countries on your world when there is war."

Kate felt a wave of fear wash over her again at the thought of Gork being so near to them.

Master M glanced at her and felt her fear. "We take care not to intermingle of course. That's pure common sense. But Gork is desperate to get hold of Kate."

"But I just don't understand why," Kate said. "What's so special about me? It can't just be the implant. There must be more to it than that."

Master M sighed heavily. "This is the reason for this meeting." He looked around at them and Kate saw absolute love in his expression. "Gork and I hold equal power, but we have opposite agendas. I wish for the human race to continue in a better way. His agenda is to destroy you all and fill your planet with his kind. As I've already said, we are equal in power and strength.

At that crucial moment they were interrupted by one of the guards outside. In spite of his size and strength he seemed to be very agitated.

"Master, Master, Gork is on board. He's heard of your meeting and who you have here with you. You're all in danger."

Master M waved a hand. "Calm yourself. He's not allowed access to my chamber or this section of the ship."

"But, but," the guard stammered. "He *has* got in. He's in our part of the Mothership. What shall we do?"

Adam gasped. "How can that be? You said he couldn't get in." He leapt to his feet.

Sechem and Jamére rushed to Kate's side. "We'll protect her," they said together. Kate waved them away, slightly embarrassed. She noticed how only Master M had stayed calm, but she also noticed how he'd blanched at the news.

He put his hand out to her and drew her close to his side. "Don't worry my child. His vibration is too low for him to break through into the energy field that exists here in my chamber."

At this point they all heard a loud banging and commotion coming from outside the entrance.

Sechem wasn't so sure of their safety. "He's very close, Master M. I'm afraid." A roar of pure rage was heard by all and the walls of flowing colour shuddered as if they too were afraid.

Adam looked around at the flimsy walls that surrounded them and for the first time Kate saw fear on his face. He turned to Master M. "You said Gork was equal to you in strength and power. How can you keep him out? Why don't you? We're lost."

Before Master M had a chance to reply a rush of freezing cold air swept into the chamber. They watched in horror as the icy blast caused the flowing walls to freeze and remain still. The furnishings began to develop into ice and the very air turned into crystals. Something or someone had entered, but they couldn't see through the haze of frozen air. Utter silence followed, and time passed.

CHAPTER THIRTY-TWO

THE GOLDEN ONE

How long they remained in this state was unclear. At last the outer guards realised they had lost their connection with the inner guards and investigated. Horrified they saw the frozen figures of the inner guards but were afraid to touch them in case they harmed them. There was only one thing to do - summon The Golden One from the Galactic Spiritual Council. Never before had this section of the Mother Ship been breached by an unauthorised traveller. It was not to be allowed and questions would be asked.

The Great Golden One arrived surrounded by a host of angelic souls and was swiftly escorted to Master M's private chamber. He waved his escorts away and entered the outer reception area alone. He tut tutted when he saw the guards standing stiffly in frozen postures and released them by his touch as he passed. The golden glow of his passing remained with them for hours. He met the wall of ice that now surrounded the inner sanctum and walked straight through as if it didn't exist.

The frozen air crackled as it disintegrated with his presence, revealing the six frozen forms lying immobile. His golden eyes surveyed the scene with displeasure. How was it that even the famed Master M had not been able to prevent this abomination of trust? Gork had broken the rules of the Motherships and this could not and would not be tolerated.

Right now there was work to be done. The Golden One closed his eyes and focussed strongly on the task ahead. His Divine energy expanded until it filled the chamber with golden light. The walls began to shimmer with coloured bands as before and he knew all would be well. He quietly left the Sanctum.

***

None of them knew how long they'd been in a state of nothingness. Kate was the first to surface. She felt as if she was emerging from a deep sleep of dreams. Master M's arms were wrapped around her and she shifted position until she could stand alone without disturbing him. She watched as one by one, first Adam, then Jacob, Jamére and Sechem regained their senses. They stretched their arms and rubbed their eyes but were too dazed to speak. Full colour began to return to the room and the shimmering walls of colour began flowing once more. At last Master M moved and Kate saw him shaking his beautiful head in disbelief.

"What happened? How did that creature get in?" he said.

He turned to Sechem. "Did she see him?" he nodded towards Kate.

Sechem blinked. "I don't think any of us here actually saw him. It happened so fast."

"I didn't see anyone or anything," she said. "I got so cold and fell asleep. What happened with the guards?"

"Don't worry about them for they'll be alright for sure," Master M said. "I am just so relieved you didn't see him, for if you had you might not have survived the full force of his eyes."

Jacob gathered Kate in his arms and held her tight. He turned his attention on Master M and scowled. "I don't like this at all. You're frightening her."

Adam also looked at Master M. "I think it's about time you tell us what this meeting is all about and why we're here. It's not just about getting away from Silas and Helga, is it?"

Kate saw hesitation written all over Master M's face and wondered at it. "Please do tell us," she pleaded as softly as she could. Adam shook his head, cautioning her.

"I suppose it has to be said, sooner rather than later." Master M sighed heavily. "Please all of you sit down and relax. I daresay we can still have refreshments?" He pressed a button and once more the same little greys as before brought in a fresh trolley of food. Kate remembered that these little ones were there to do what they were told and not to think or have emotions. They were the ones often seen collecting samples and carrying out other tasks on Earth.

The experience of being frozen hadn't diminished her father's appetite one little bit and she put her hand on his arm to stop him filling his plate too much. "It's enough, Dad."

She realised that Master M was putting off the time of disclosing what he had to say and felt his obvious distress. Whatever could it be that had such importance?

As the visitors ate their faces showed they still had questions and were trying to understand everything that had happened.

Master M cleared his throat loudly and they all looked up, waiting.

"Have you done eating?" he asked. "I can tell you now why this meeting has been called. What I have to say may explain a lot to you." He looked at Kate and drew her to him. "Kate is a key player in the battle between good and evil."

"What?" Kate exclaimed, her cheeks turning pink. "How can that be?"

"Calm down and I will tell you. I haven't wanted to disclose this but now I have no option, as Gork was so close to destroying you, and will not give up until he does."

They all waited. Sechem rolled his eyes heavenward.

Kate watched Master M take a deep breath. He grasped both her hands in his long bony fingers and held them to his face. "My dear child, my real identity and name is Osishoo, even Gork does not know that and it must be kept secret."

"Your bloodline mother is Joslene, who is my beloved daughter, and we chose Jacob as a kind and honest man to be your father." It took them all a moment or two for this news to sink in.

Kate gasped. "But, but that means . . ."

"Yes, dear one. You are my granddaughter. You are my representative on Earth."

Kate watched as tears ran down his face.

"We cannot, must not, let anything happen to you. Remember Gork is powerful and he knows your identity. If he gets hold of you . . . well, it doesn't bear thinking about."

Adam muttered to himself, *'Evil versus love. Just as it is in the world.'*

Master M turned to Sechem and Jamére. "I give her into your charge. She has much more work to do. Adam you are to make sure she does not come to any harm."

Kate reached out and kissed her grandfather for the first time. Looking around she saw from the faces of her friends and her father how stunned they were. Adam took her hand and drew her close.

"Did you know this all along?" she asked.

"I had a suspicion, but I wasn't sure my darling. Now I know. Don't let this go to your head," he said laughing. "You'll be returning to Earth soon enough."

TO BE CONTINUED

APPENDIX

QUOTES:

Dr Brian O'Leary, Former NASA Astronaut and Princeton Physics Professor.

There is abundant evidence that we are being contacted, that civilizations have been visiting us for a very long time. That their appearance is bizarre from any type of traditional materialistic western point of view. That these visitors use the technologies of consciousness.

Paul Hellyer, Former Canadian Defence Minister

Decades ago, visitors from other planets warned us about the direction we were heading and offered to help. Instead, some of us interpreted their visits as a threat, and decided to shoot first and ask questions after. It is ironic that the US should be fighting monstrously expensive wars, allegedly to bring democracy to those countries, when it itself can no longer claim to be called a democracy when trillions, and I mean thousands of billions of dollars have been spent on black projects which both congress and the commander in chief have been kept deliberately in the dark." –

Recommended reading

Calling Earth volume one	by S M Battie
Being Human	by Shirley Battie
Spirit Speaks	by Shirley Battie
Beyond the Stairs	by Shirley Battie
The Source Field	by David Wilcock
The Missing Times	by Terry Hanson –Xlibris Press
HAARP	by Jerry E Smith- Adventures Unlimited Press
Awakening	by Mary Rodwell
The New Human	by Mary Rodwell
Millennial Hospitality	by Charles James Hall (all volumes)

Recommended web sites:

www.littleowlonline.co.uk
www.jaimemaussan.com
www.exopolitics.org
www.spiritbeingalliance.com
http://walkinevolution.com/
http://www.bibliotecapleyades.net/montauk/rainbow/phoenix_2.htm
ForbiddenKnowledgeTV.com Alexandra Bruce, Publisher
http://www.bibliotecapleyades.net/montauk/rainbow/phoenix_2.htm
http://www.projectpegasus.net
http://www.projectmars.net
WWW.GALACTICCONNECTION.COM
The Secret Mars Colony
https://www.acern.com.au

Presidential Warnings About the Invisible Government Running the U.S.

According to six US former presidents, one vice-president, and a myriad of other high profile political leaders, an invisible government that is "incredibly evil in intent" has been in control of the U.S. government "ever since the days of Andrew Jackson" (since at least 1836). They "virtually run the United States government for their own selfish purposes. All of the quotes have been verified as authentic and have associated links to the source materials. Also included below are statements made by David Rockefeller, Sr, former director of the Council on Foreign Relations (CFR), and Federal Reserve Chairman's Alan Greenspan and Ben Bernanke that appear to confirm some of the warnings. The warnings listed below, began with the first president – George Washington. The last president to speak out was JFK, who was assassinated. Read what they and other political leaders have said about the invisible government. George Washington wrote that the Illuminati want to separate the People from their Government

"I sincerely believe, with you, that banking establishments are more dangerous than standing armies." —Thomas Jefferson, President of the United States (1801–1809) and principal author of the United States Declaration of Independence (1776), in a letter written to John Taylor on May 28, 1816.

"Behind the ostensible government sits enthroned an invisible government owing no allegiance and acknowledging no responsibility to the people. To destroy this invisible government, to befoul the unholy alliance between corrupt business and corrupt politics is the first task of the statesmanship of the day."— Theodore Roosevelt, 26th President of the United States, Theodore Roosevelt, An Autobiography, 1913

"Since I entered politics, I have chiefly had men's views confided to me privately. Some of the biggest men in the United States, in the field of commerce and manufacture, are afraid of something. They know that there is a power somewhere so organized, so subtle, so watchful, so interlocked, so complete, so pervasive, that they had better not speak above their breath when they speak in condemnation of it." – Woodrow Wilson, 28th President of the United States, *The New Freedom*, 1913

"The real menace of our Republic is the invisible government, which like a giant octopus sprawls its slimy legs over our cities, states and nation New York City Mayor John F. Hylan, New York Times, March 26. 1922

It operates secretly, silently, continuously to transform our Government... This ruthless power-seeking elite is a disease of our century... This group... is answerable neither to the President, the Congress, nor the courts. It is practically irremovable." – Senator William Jenner, 1954 speech

"The individual is handicapped by coming face-to-face with a **conspiracy so monstrous** he cannot believe it exists. The American mind simply has not come to a realization of the evil which has been introduced into our midst. It rejects even the assumption that human creatures could espouse a philosophy which must ultimately destroy all that is good and decent." – J. Edgar Hoover, The Elks Magazine, 1956

Our way of life is under attack. Those who make themselves our enemy are advancing around the globe... no war ever posed a greater threat to our security. For we are opposed around the world by a monolithic and ruthless conspiracy that relies primarily on covert means for expanding its sphere of influence–on infiltration instead of invasion, on subversion instead of elections, on intimidation instead of free choice, Its preparations are concealed, not published. Its mistakes are buried, not headlined. Its dissenters are silenced, not praised. — John F Kennedy, 35th President of the United States, from a speech delivered to the American Newspaper Publishers Association on April 27, 1961 and known as the "Secret Society" speech.

"There exists a shadowy government with its own Air Force, its own Navy, its own fundraising mechanism, and the ability to pursue its own ideas of national interest, free from all checks and balances, and free from the law itself." – Daniel K. Inouye, US Senator from Hawaii, testimony at the Iran Contra Hearings, 1986

"A power has risen up in the government greater than the people themselves..."
– John C. Calhoun

Because of a deep-rooted belief that the U.S. government is "for the people" and the protector of the free world, many will reject the notion of an evil shadow government. When our beliefs are challenged or when two beliefs are inconsistent, cognitive dissonance is created. It's human nature to try to hold our beliefs in harmony with our world view and avoid disharmony (or dissonance).

If you have enjoyed this work please let the author know.
www.littleowlonline.co.uk